PRAISE FOR QU

M000028745

"The New York artist Quintan Ana Wikswo
accentuated by simulations of the hypersens
—The Guardian UK

"Author and visual artist Wikswo's juxtaposes dreamy, surreal prose with shadowed, ambiguous,
occluded dreamscapes to haunting effect—heady, euphoric, and full with loss. Wikswo's singular
lines strike like the tone of a bell while her beautifully composed images echo the surprising twists
of language. [Her work] defies genre or distillation and instead takes the reader/viewer on a journey
where myth, mystery, and the impossible have never seemed more real."
—*Publisher's Weekly*

"These stunning, solitary and cinematic letters to the self (think of the Quays and Béla Tarr speaking
together in dreamtime) bear witness to a world beloved and betrayed, the spent and brutal collisions
of irretrievable loss with what might have been possible."
—Rikki Ducornet

"Desire bends the world with transmogrifying persistence in Wikswo's debut collection, *The Hope of
Floating Has Carried Us This Far*, until the reality we thought we knew erodes into the background
of a whorling landscape rife with longing. The tragedy of embodiment, of our inherent separation
from one another, permeates a text whose protagonists strive to rewrite the rules of creation, that it
might contain a space where they can love. It is no wonder, then, that the text obliterates boundaries
of form, structure, genre, and medium like a typhoon."
—*The Rumpus*

"Quintan Ana Wikswo's trenchant interdisciplinary investigation into the sites of massacres and other
atrocities is a vivid reminder that art no longer serves religion, but is progressively supplanting it
in terms of ritual and sanctity."
—Thomas Micchelli, *Hyperallergic*

"Quintan Ana Wikswo's debut book of stories and images, *The Hope of Floating Has Carried Us This
Far*, is an intoxicating read that feels at once universal and personal, comforting and jarring, ethereal
and earthy, and after reading it once I read it immediately again. And then I read it again. And then
I couldn't stop recommending it to everyone I know."
—*Electric Lit*

"A seduction and an insurrection: a paean to lovers, explorers, resisters, and those without borders."
—Sarah Shun-lien Bynum

"It's more than the way W.G. Sebald, Jesse Ball and Teju Cole have used photographs to punctuate
and accentuate the narratives they write; there's a sense of collage here, of the images being used to
state things where words no longer suffice."
—*Chicago Star Tribune*

A LONG CURVING SCAR WHERE THE HEART SHOULD BE
Copyright © 2017 by Quintan Ana Wikswo
ISBN: 978-0-9984339-8-1
Library of Congress Data available on request.

First paperback edition published by Stalking Horse Press, October 2017

www.stalkinghorsepress.com

Photography by Quintan Ana Wikswo
Design by James Reich

Stalking Horse Press
Santa Fe, New Mexico

Stalking Horse Press requests that authors designate a nonprofit, charitable, or humanitarian organization to receive a portion of revenue from the sales of each title.

A LONG CURVING SCAR
WHERE THE HEART SHOULD BE

DEAR READER:

Please refer to the endnotes for methodology on the sites, my photographic process, and the specific contexts that inform the book. While this novel is a work of fiction, the photographs and text draw from particularly powerful obscured sites and contexts with significant impact in the lives of marginalized and persecuted inhabitants of Virginia, South Carolina, and Tennessee, including my family and ancestors.

DEDICATION:

For Julia Wikswo
and my African, African-American, and Indigenous ancestors and relatives whose family histories were almost—but not entirely—silenced.

TO THE SPIRITS, RELATIVES AND ANCESTORS:

Oh flesh of my flesh, my family line—a thread of different weight. Rough, strange. Twisted in spirals, in curls. Our blood confined, concealed, and bursting. The bodies of my people dwell in the quiet, in the dark. Underground. There are night colors inside us. Violet. Indigo. Blue. Black. Brown. Yellow. Night secrets. Our wounds as invisible as ourselves – instructed to be silence in the night.

Oh bone of my bone, these rosy-fingered institutions—their pink fingers inside our skin render us limb from limb.

Oh soul of my soul, where could they bury us, that we might not rise again? No ditch knows deep enough for that. Some root or fern may pin our secrets safe til we uncut our tongues and speak.

Oh mind of my mind, untie our binds and say: no one shall be master of us here.

DESPITE...

...MY ENEMIES WHO WENT TO GREAT EFFORT TO SILENCE THIS project, including the Sons and Daughters of the Confederacy, white nationalist hate groups and the KKK of Virginia and South Carolina, the Virginia State Police, and the Central Virginia Training Center (formerly Virginia State Colony for Epileptics and Feebleminded), and my ancestors and relatives who committed trespasses against humanity.

SUPPORT PROVIDED BY:

Creative Capital; The Corporation of Yaddo – Pollock Krasner Fellowship; The National Endowment for the Arts; The Virginia Center for the Creative Arts; Dorland Mountain Center for the Arts; Lynchburg Legacy Museum – Preserving African American History; The Theo Westenberger Foundation; Montalvo Arts Center; Lynchburg Old City Cemetery; Lynchburg Museum; African American, Gullah, and Gullah Geeche folks of Edisto Island, South Carolina; Djerassi, the Millay Colony, UCross, Ragdale Artist Residencies; San Francisco State University Creative Writing Department; University of Texas at Austin Gender Studies and African American Studies Departments.

SELECTIONS OF THE MANUSCRIPT AND PHOTOGRAPHS HAVE BEEN PUBLISHED, EXHIBITED, OR PERFORMED THROUGH:

Tin House, Conjunctions, Gulf Coast, Alaska Quarterly Review, Folio, Denver Quarterly, Anomolous Press (formerly Drunken Boat), and Memorious, St. Marks in the Bowery, The Poetry Project, Bowery Poetry Club, F.A.C.T. (Foundation for Art and Creative Technology, UK), Irish American Historical Society, Beyond Baroque, Museum of Jurassic Technology, and 610 Isis (Los Angeles).

ACCOMPLICES

Eternal gratitude to my publisher and editor, James Reich;
and Anitra Budd

&

Stacy D. Flood
Dr. Robin Kilson
Robert Willis
Maxine Chernoff
Richard Corral
Cabaret Q and its Comrades
Matthew Contos
Sarah Clark
Dominique "Nicky" Giesler
Arthur Kell
Catawba Indian Nation
Eastern Cherokee Nation
Fort Sill Apache Tribe of Oklahoma
Mescalero Apache Tribe of the Mescalero Reservation
Agua Caliente Band of Cahuilla Indians
All the Southern Queers Who Loved Me

&

Spyder, Rü, Mukanday if by Sea, Avishai the Sublime, Onophria
Ixtlán, Antares, Nora Maynard, Mona Washington, Megan Camille
Roy, Paetrick Schmidt, Richard Horiuchi, Daniel Levinstein, Jo
Ellen Arntz, John Wikswo, Veronika Krausas, Samantha Stiers, Risa
Mickenberg, Marya Errin Jones, Matthew Wikswo, Fontaine Rodgers,
Rodgers DePue, Kent Wolf, and Niklas DeRouche.

ALSO BY QUINTAN ANA WIKSWO

The Hope of Floating
Has Carried Us This Far

QUINTAN ANA WIKSWO

A LONG CURVING SCAR WHERE THE HEART SHOULD BE

STALKING HORSE PRESS
SANTA FE, NEW MEXICO

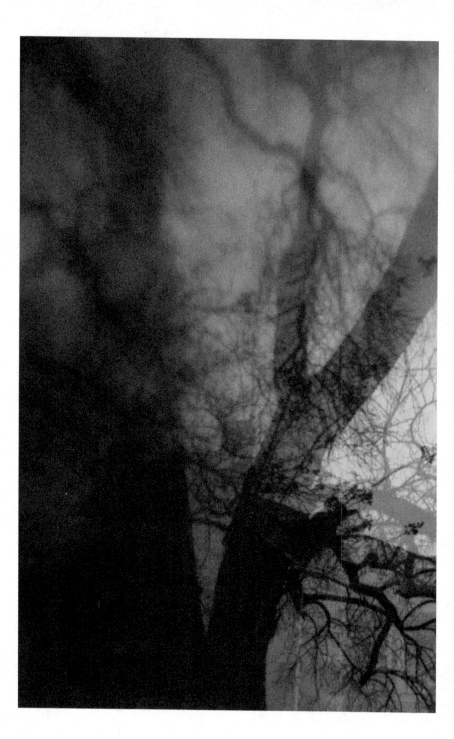

PROLOGUE

ALL WINTER LONG THE GIRLS SMOKED TOBACCO LEAVES

Up in the hills the talk was of the men all disappeared and presumed dead. The women didn't like the talk up in the hills: it was all about the men who used to be there but weren't any more. It was talk about how maybe they fell down into the bottom of the valley, or how maybe it was that the valley rose up into the hills at night and swallowed them whole. Just the men. Gone in the cold damp of night, warm wedge of empty stink in their beds. Up in the hills the talk was never about how it was before, the way it was when Maw was a child, before Sweet Marie and Whitey were old enough to remember, but Maw said there were gumdrop trees and lemonade rains and all the children were fat and tasty and made of gingerbread and oh how they lined up to climb onto the cookie sheets at lunchtime. But up in the hills the talk now was of the three hundred men all disappeared and presumed dead.

❦

Up in the hills after the men disappeared there was nothing but rocks and sticks, a slate-gray iron nothing. They ate even their very own fingernails, with salt, and the clipped nails of their babies. The nails were very soft. The dirt under their baby nails was milk chocolate. Their teeth were always clean from eating rocks and sticks and nails but there was never anything to smoke. Sweet Marie let Whitey smoke manure. It made her stomach feel more full, but there was no rush of wildfire—dung won't smoke the same, even after it's spread out flat to dry in a stiff paste on the dog's house. Whitey and Sweet Marie didn't like the talk up in the hills: it was all about the sick, the mad, and the left- behind women, and the why-hows and the what-fors of it all. *First the valley took our loam, our dirt, our mud, our soil, our seeds, our weeds—now the valley take our men too, and leave us nothing but rocks and sticks, a slate-gray iron nothing.* That's what the sick, the mad, and the left-behind women would say. *We must eat our very own fingernails, and the fingernails of our very own little babies.*

❦

LAFAYETTE WAS A MAN WHO LIVED IN A DOG'S HOUSE, A MAN with four legs, all crooked, who barked at raccoons and gnawed bones. He licked his own asshole to get it clean, but left his hair hanging in muddy clots. Lafayette was the only man still up on the slate-gray iron hills, the only man to come down off our hills to the muck of valley and go back up again after. The only man to go down and back up. Sweet Marie asked him what he saw down below but he just licked his asshole, and barked at the raccoons. Sweet Marie asked him where the three hundred more men gone but Lafayette just laid down, he'd lay down on his own ticks and they would burst in little sacks of blood. Lafayette was this man—their father—who lived in a dog's house.

❦

IT WAS LAFAYETTE BROUGHT THEM DOWN FROM THE HILLS TO the valley. Lafayette brought Whitey and Sweet Marie down on his back, he plunged them down the mountains using his crooked legs and the fuel of his own funk. He used his funk for gasoline. They rode him to the bottom, Whitey hanging on to Sweet Marie, Sweet Marie hanging on to the ticks, the ticks gripping on to Lafayette's syrupy old veins. Nobody could have fallen off; it would have been impossible. The haze of flies and polly-poddies held them on. Though it was the afternoon they suffered from night-blindness. They were riding him as though blindfolded—their eyelids blinked blindly on some vicious nettled whiteness. Sometimes it seemed like they were riding bad road, other times a high bridge, or some terrible hard sulphurous riverbed strewn with rocks. Their bottoms hurt from riding the ridge of his spine and there was nothing to do but talk so Whitey asked Sweet Marie if they could eat and drink and smoke

when they got down to the valley. She said, *Whit*
Whitey asked Lafayette, *Could we eat and drink an*
just barked at her to lick his asshole. So it was La
them down from the hills to the valley.

❦

DOWN IN THE VALLEY EVERYTHING WAS VERY DIFFERENT. THEY
saw that when Sweet Marie let go of the ticks and Whitey let go of
Sweet Marie. At first they saw nobody in the valley. From up in the hills
they could have looked down in the valley and seen the black devil's
birds winging through empty winter branches, foxes and bears and
big cats and monkeys swiping at the devil blackbirds from branches,
hoping to catch a bird to make a bird pie. Whitey knew she wanted
one of those pies. But at first they saw nobody when they came down
into the valley from the hills. In the valley all their dirt from up on
the hills had run away from its cold high rocks and came laid down
to rest in the valley. Now down in the valley they sunk in mud up
to their knees. In the valley there was lots of tobacco: giant tobacco
plants so huge that the big cats used the plants for hiding. In the valley
was all their dirt from up on the hills. In the valley Sweet Marie and
Whitey saw no man hats above the tobacco plants, nor heads of men
with guns in the woods, but they saw the big boot prints of their men,
following one the next all in a line. In the valley the boot prints sank
into the mud. There in the boot prints the men had left behind their
copper pennies, photographs, wedding rings and hatbands. A deep
trough of our men's boot prints filled with false teeth and pocket
watches, potato eyes and matches, patches and pouches and shirt-
buttons. Down in the valley everything was very different. The girls
could see that when Sweet Marie let go of the ticks and Whitey let
go of Sweet Marie. In the valley all their dirt from up on the hills had
run away from its cold high rocks and now they sunk down in the
treasure of it, all the way up to their knees.

❦

THEY FOLLOWED THE BOOT PRINTS THROUGH THE DIRT. THE
prints led to an enormous house, bigger than a tobacco plant. The
girls' pockets were filled with the men's gold teeth and silver dollars,

ser zippers, whittle knives and banjo picks, heel taps and spurs and spit-curls. The house was made of dull white wooden boards and broken windows. In the windows were hanging curtains with a pattern of red roses with no thorns. From the house came the smell of sassafras and tobacco smoke. The house was slanted, so big that it was built too big for the valley at the bottom of their hill so everything was in danger of running out the front door, which we saw was swinging open. Whitey and Sweet Marie followed the boot prints through the stolen dirt. The prints led into the enormous whiteboard house and through the front door, which they saw was swinging open.

♥

WHITEY AND SWEET MARIE HAD NEVER BEEN INSIDE THE HOUSE before but the house was filled with beautiful girls who fucked for free. Some girls were rich and plummy, and some were stringy and taut, beautiful violins. Some were tawny or milky, the colors of ink or of tea, limestone or onyx, parsnip or blackberry or chestnuts in October. The beautiful pussies smelled like sassafras.

They couldn't sing, not a one of them, but they knew how to dance. The beautiful girls took their clothes off and danced, and when they began to sing their dogs went to hide in the smokehouse. In the smokehouse the dogs took off their fur and danced naked, and when they began to sing the rats and mice would crawl out of the hams hanging there in the smokehouse and the rats and mice would run hide in the outhouse and take off their hides and dance, and when they began to sing their fleas would crawl out of the bellies and ears and run hide in the house, where they would jump out of their shells and commence to dance and sing in the hairs between the legs of the beautiful fat naked dancing girls who fucked for free.

♥

WATCHING THEM DANCE MADE WHITEY HUNGRY TO EAT AND drink and smoke. After the rich and plummy, stringy taut girls finished dancing they gave Whitey and Sweet Marie eleven blackbird pies. The beautiful naked dancing girls were not good cooks. The birds still had their feet and wings, their oily feathers filled with tiny mites that ran under the crust making little creeks and roads among the rotten birds. The beaks had fallen off into the pokeberries, looking like the ends of some evil pairs of scissors. The pokeberries were not pokeberries, they were buckshot. The beautiful naked dancing girls made pies of dead birds, mites, and buckshot. It tasted like tar. Graveyard tar. Like the sludge that drains out of a coffin. Watching them dance made Whitey hungry to eat and drink and smoke.

♥

WHITEY FOUND SOME TOBACCO HANGING DRYING IN THE RAFTERS good for smoking. *I don't think that's for smoking, I think that's meant to wrap the bodies of the dead,* Sweet Marie said, looking at the giant bundles of tobacco leaves tied up and hanging heavy, trussed like country hams, swaying from giant meat hooks, dangling from the rafters of the porch, swinging from the ceiling of the parlor of the house. Whitey and Sweet Marie were hungry to eat and drink and smoke and fuck. They unwrapped one of the bundles on the porch and inside it was a tremendous nugget of ham, but yellow and stiff, with dull brackish orange patches from the nicotine on the dried, hairy skin. It looked to be their neighbor, Old Charlie. Twenty-six yellow teeth rattled out onto the floor. The eyes had dehydrated and rolled out of the sockets, little raisins held on only by a thread of wasted tendon. Whitey reached for them; she thought of eating them with milk. *I don't think that's for eating, I think those were his eyes,* Sweet Marie said, looking at the mummified body in its tobacco-leaf shroud, which had crumbled to reveal the fat tobacco bugs who had dug little canals through the beef-jerky musculature of the old man. Whitey wanted to eat the tobacco bugs. *I don't think you should eat them,* Sweet Marie said, *I think those tobacco bugs are fat because they've been eating the bodies of our boys, wrapped in tobacco leaves.* Sweet Marie is the voice of reason. The fat tobacco bugs lifted up their blind heads from the yellow mucus when they heard Sweet Marie speak with her voice of reason. They paused and would have blinked at her, if they could have blinked at her, but the fat tobacco bugs instead lifted up their heads and licked their slimy feet out of respect. Sweet Marie brings that out. It always pays to listen to Sweet Marie and her voice of reason. *I don't think that's for eating. I think that's our dead.*

We watched the three hundred giant bundles of tobacco leaves tied up and gently hanging, slowly swaying from giant heavy thick steel meat hooks, the three hundred tobacco bundles suspended from the rafters of the porch and the trusses of the smokehouse and from the ceiling of the parlor of the house, swaying, hanging at a slant with the slope of the hills.

♥

THE GIRLS PLACED THE BODIES OF THE MEN IN STACKS ON THE back porch to drain before they wrapped them in the giant leaves of the tobacco trees and hung them on iron hooks in the smokehouse. The girls' pussies tasted of sassafras. They were beautiful fat naked dancing girls who fucked each other for free. The house was slanted, it was built on the hill so everything would run out the front door, which was propped closed with the bodies of our men from the hills. The beautiful naked dancing girls who fucked for free placed the bodies of the men in stacks on the back porch to drain before they wrapped them in leaves from the tobacco trees and hung them in the smokehouse. The slope of the porch bothered them, the way it poured downhill a little more each year as the front yard sank.

PART ONE:
THE LEFT ATRIUM

WHAT LIES IN A TIME OF NEED

MAW WAS THE FIRST TEACHER. FOR THE TWINS, SHE WAS THE GOD of all things above and below. Tied to a string around her waist Maw kept a heavy black ring of keys to all the doors: to the springhouse, the red clay dirt-floored kitchens with their shallow canyons of footpaths worn between pantry and sink, to the porch doors and the bedrooms, the hallways and closets and cabinets, to the abandoned slaves' and overseer's quarters and the master's rooms and the mistress' and the secret paths they trod to other rooms, the whispering-softly places that Maw said were old and holding sorrow still. In the mornings Maw would get up and unlock these places and the twins would go through them. In the late dark of evening Maw would take these places away again and the girls would wait until it was light again and the entrances would be reopened to them again. Maw kept the keys to more places, more doors that nobody had even found yet.

♥

MAW WAS THE FIRST TEACHER. TO HER GIRLS, SHE WAS THE GOD of growing things. Of the trees, Maw was the god of the tulip poplar, the sumac, the sugar maple and the oak, the cedar trees in particular with their painful sacred quills. Of the flowers, she was first to teach the twins the stories of the dog-toothed violet, the ladyslipper, pitcher plant and honeysuckle, and of the preacher-in-the-pulpit: she was the god of all their names and places. How the pulpit stays wet and arches over the sun-shied preacher, a fleshy deliberate thing whose feet reach deep into the stem.
Also the god of burning things: the fireplaces, the lanterns, stoves and

ovens, skin salves and bandages and painful urinations and the sun at noon; she was the keeper of kindling and matches, glass lenses and mirrors, chimney pots and cigarettes, pipecleaners and corn cobs. Maw had ten scepters in her fingertips and crowns of gold hanging heavy in her ears. Every chair ached to be her throne.

Their Maw was the god of all that took water, from the scarlet tanninger to the bedpan.

All that bled.

All that lived on paper and within pens.

The god of thread and string: doll clothes and curtains and pigtails and ribbons, things that had broken and things recently fixed, hearts embroidered on tablecloths and dishtowels, menstrual rags and wool stockings and tourniquets.

The god of the contents of bottles and jars.

The god of emissions and tears and discharges.

The god of sopping up.

Maw, the god of ringworm and lice.

Of the clean slice through the core of an apple.

She was the god of lice on the scalp. Quick braids and cow mange. Of the vinegar-and- lye rinse.

The rag curl.

The snarl.

❥

MAW TAUGHT HER GIRLS THROUGH THE RIP AND TEAR OF her losses. Always the absence of her husband, a cut that ran her through.

Hers was an empty cleaving, hands grasping at his phantom. Yet she loved her girls in a way that sharpened her teeth to razors, a brutal love of ages.

Maw was the god of all things of the above and the below.

Their Maw was a rock forever crumbling off the cliff-side of love, a limestone love in sheets that cracked to cysts of geode with their secret crystal flames—her girls hid themselves in this cleft in her rock.

Her girls felt the stone boulder of their Maw's love and the cracks running through it and they held up the stone as Maw scraped at the shards, planted lichens on its surface, shredded hatchets into slivers, left seeds to sprout within its fissures.

What weight they lifted up, what a high cairn to her passion and sadness they carried on their backs.

They crawled through their world collecting gravel from her love.

♥

WHEN LAFAYETTE LEFT HER, MAW AT FIRST TURNED THE DECAYING whiteboard mansion into a tomb. The baby girls she wrapped in black, but sewed their clothes with embroidery of red roses with no thorns. She sang dark songs to her baby girls and smelled the tops of their heads, wiped their skin with frankincense and myrrh and smelled them again and coiled her face into a love-knot. She agreed with Lafayette—the girls weren't entirely of this world. To her they were creatures come to life with their perfect shining white eyes that blinked and their tiny sharp fingernails that left scratches on her breasts when they fed, one on each teat; the heat they left on her sheets when she picked them up in the morning: that wasn't like a thing of this earth - there was no cruelty to it - and she loved it. They would stay with her forever—she knew this—they would remain in their tiny clothes with the tiny pearl buttons and their amazingly tiny socks and the soles of their tiny feet would never walk the ground without the guide of her hallowed hand.

She would stare at their open mollusk mouths through the bars of their cradles and know they belonged fully to her, for she had made them.

♥

SHE HAD NEVER BEEN A YOUNG MOTHER, NEVER, NOT EVEN AT the beginning, when she was only twenty. Her carefree weeks with Lafayette had been an ill-considered sojourn into an unknown womanhood; she had plunged her curious pain into a calm sweet pool of hope and thought it would sink to the bottom instead of swim. By the time she found that her ravenous pain thrived on hope, gulped it down and guzzled hope, filled up its mouth and gut with the stuff and still took more—by the time she found that out it was too late, and Lafayette was gone. And so Maw returned to being early-aged and wearied by her losses, which she counted every night before she went to bed, and counted again upon waking. At noon she took their weight and measure, just to see always where she stood. She had one necklace strung with beads of pain, and one necklace strung with beads of hope and she wore them entwined around her heart, the muscle feeling the constant bruising pressure of the beads. Her pulse pressed through this close-strung web of pain and hope and she knew every one of the beads, their smoothness and roughness within her flesh.

She was only twenty when she bore the twins, but all who looked into her white-blue eyes knew that the very same eyes that gazed out from her face had hung there in her skull for as long as the sun had scorched the skies.

♥

WHEN LAFAYETTE LEFT HER, THE MONEY REMAINING WAS NOT enough. The estate was small and old, and its prideful history of slaves and servants, new white paint every spring, all the grass in the fields scythed each fall—all that a distant memory of days before Lafayette had chosen to walk away from her down that most terrible well-trod path. And Lafayette's family long departed from the murkish whirlpool of his world when he married dubious. *Passing*, they whispered behind her. *Passing.* The ladies in Lynchburg whispered *passing.* She turned and it seemed that there was no one uttering those words, and then she turned again and they were all licking the taste of the word off their lips. *Never you mind,* said Lafayette, *for I love you so. I want you to have the best home. The best things. The best people.*

And so she chose to believe him, that love was enough. And she muffled the whispers in her burgundy velveteen curtains. And after he left her, disappeared, she didn't know where to contact his family, somewhere farther to the west or south. She could ask. But no one would tell. No one would allow the line was going to trash: they had contested the will that left Lafayette with the property. No more profit to be made. No more free labor. No more black and brown and bare bronze feet making paths from field to grave. Used as a hospital during the battle, too much blood in the floor boards. Amputations of all kinds. None of them the right kind, not for Lafayette's family, soft and pliant as a whipstick soaked in water before a lashing. *Passing,* she heard the lawyer say. *Better off without it,* and *let her have it,* she heard the wives say. Or did they say *better off without her,* and *let it have her.* His eleven brothers, all of them angry, all with angry wives, and angry children, all of them with bitter faces, closed against the clever innocence of Maw, her innocent cleverness, her newfound property, her rising station, her new dresses, her dissipated husband and her roots that went down into the hardscrabble hollows, her lack of schooling, the preposterous lusciousness of her once-delicious curves that took their heir and wasted him. Everything she held fed their bitterness, including how she held the estate, tightly to her chest, hand in hand with its demented dead, with its disguised atrocities, and one by one the relatives melted away pale into the fog of white that blocked her every window and every door.

None of them had attended the wedding, nor had anyone from town. It had been a small one, in the whiteboard and brick house in Lynchburg. *The Plantation,* some still called it, though fewer than before the war. Maw and Lafayette had stood nearly alone at the fireplace with flowers on the mantle, she in a white lace dress she'd made from tablecloths and doilies, and he in his gray Sunday suit and the photographer had taken the picture—the flash seemed more to make them married than the words from the preacher who wedded them; the photographic plate—proof that she was a bride, the first picture she had ever seen of herself—taken at the apex of her hope.

After Lafayette left her, Maw examined his face in this portrait for signs of panic or imminent departure and found none. The shy and innocent smiles spread sweetly across their faces, their white teeth and clean skin; didn't that point to future happiness? He had seemed to love her so much—not even looking at her but looking at the photographer, Lafayette seemed to be saying, *I love this girl, my bride.*

And then sometimes in the photograph she tried to see no love in his eyes, and to turn his sweetness into fear, and the tenderness into a desire to run away from her.

Maybe he didn't feel anything. Maybe the adoration in his gaze was emptiness of spirit.

He had been just a boy. His shoulders at that time were muscular but still soft, rounded under his shirt. His belly was firm and bowed out slightly from within, as if it contained some soft plump loving creature warmed with down. He would press against the hollow of her lower spine and warm her back with his heat, his cock nestled into the cleft of her ass, rocking and crooning to her. His hands were delicate, mica thin flat nails with shallow pocks upon their surface, the nails seemed soft too, like his skin, and the fragile red hairs that split his chest from sternum to hip. She had planned upon him hardening with her, callusing somewhat, their worn places, achieved together, would yield great strength. How was she so wrong? He had been new, so new, and she had imagined a great new strength growing in him, a strength fed by his desire for family, for wife, home: their home. She had imagined he'd known it would require a fortitude of will. She had been too ready to be his kingdom and have him watch over her and keep her. She had envisioned him gradually cleaving to her, building around her a kind of fortress, a castle of love mortared with honey and gunpowder.

He had been just a boy. At nineteen he had been eight. The egg of his head was unformed. How had he been grown but not cooked—

And when the birth of his girls cracked him open, she herself had watched, horrified, as his yellow curd ran out of him in a sick stream of raw bilious liquid—

How had he made children with her when he was still a child?

Had he looked in his daughters' eyes and been jealous of their position at the teat?

Was that it?

Was that why he left her there, barely off the birthing bed, her gown still stained red with the uterine inks—

It was no use. He had been in her and he had made babies in her and it wasn't her fault, none of it was her fault, not the raw egg in his head. What was her fault were her dreams of honey and gunpowder. No one but her would build such a fortress for her or for her babies.

But no, on that day they were happy. She knows it. Wild roses were everywhere, they sprang up in their footsteps. The sky had been the blue of saints. The air was holy— grains of gold scattered in the wind and caught in their clean shining hair. The world had opened like a blossom at their touch. On that wedding day she had said goodbye to everything she hated, everything she railed against, all the shame and self-pity and guilt and obsequiousness that had always boiled up when she thought of what a worthless person she was to the world's estimation. She had said goodbye to the outside of things. She had stood in the parlor in front of the mirror with the flowers on the mantle and thought, *this is now my home.* How in her old home everyone had died—first her mother, then her father, then new people had come and later gone, and all of it reeked of something not fair, not right, everyone cheated by life—*life*, they called it, but it was the town that did it, the breaking, the disrespect, and the brutal reminders—the ones who vanished north with visions of another way, and then how she herself had left as well, for love not freedom, though there was nothing much to leave: the river always threatening the bricks and roof, walls and windows stuffed with the rags of ancestors' clothes too precious to give away, too hard-won to bury, too mended by hands now dead but not forgotten, the smell of the place—bacon grease, lye, a quiet grinding grief of memory and loss that soaked the house in the scent of sour milk and kerosene, the outhouse built too close to the porch and never moved for what would they have done with its contents—and then the smell of this new place, her new white home where they would have their babies together and grow as old and sturdy as the ancient boards beneath their feet. How new to her that day was the smell of the lemon wax on the highboys, and the lavender soaps in the bathrooms, inside, the bathrooms were inside, and clean linens with expensive sachets of lily-of-the-valley, the flower of the eternal month of May, and the rich wooden goodness of the grand piano, whose dust smelled like the wings of angels to her. The house and all it contained and promised were a miracle, the golden air itself was cornmeal to the starvation in her soul. She had never been as hungry as she was on her wedding day. Devourous. Incredible, it had been to her, that she could step off the logical progression of her life: cigarettes smoked in an alley behind the grocery store—if she had kept her looks she would have grown old fitting gloves on the hands of ladies in the department store and had a counter meal once a week on pay days, a single room in some old woman's boarding house, with water-stained wallpaper and whiskey stains on the bureau and menstrual stains on the sheets and above it all one small mirror with cracks along the edges and mould beneath the silvering, and one day she would have died in that stained room with a cheap cigarette stubbed out in the cheap dimestore cold cream and her hair tied up in ancient oily rags, cheap houseslippers still on her dry bunioned feet, and without instruction they would have buried her cheaply in a lonely plot at Thorn Rose, with a cheap and simple headstone flush with the grass, and no one would have visited her grave because she would be all alone and no one would care or remember, especially not after she lost her looks, and her sagging empty childless breasts would slowly rot and no one would even give pause to think *what a shame.*

She was saying goodbye to all this when she said *I do.* She was imagining a manicure and getting her hair set every Friday for the rest of her life, and no more cigarettes and a ring, a shiny ring, maybe white gold, maybe a diamond with the light of the Star of Bethlehem rising from its cuts, and bright clean new blood in her children's veins, and a good row at the Church on the Rock with Lafayette admiring her hat and saying she was beautiful and the preacher turning his head to look at her but her holding the hand of her husband in the good row, where the all the very best people prayed.

❦

BUT IN THIS PHOTOGRAPH SHE IS ONLY NINETEEN. SOMETIMES she looks at the photograph and a sense of disgust spreads when she looks at herself—the changeling eyes glinting with a contented triumph, the defiant black hair carefully knotted and curled and clasped with fresh cut flowers, orange blossoms, how smooth and sweet they had smelled when she'd plunged her face into her bouquet before crossing the room to her new husband with her dumb rosebud mouth and the stupid creamy caramel-filled hollow of her collarbone—

Lafayette had reached for her body in his sleep on their wedding night. Eyes closed, the scent of sleep on him, he opened her nightgown to find what he was looking for, to take what was his. How he took her hand and placed it on top of his penis, took her wrist and moved it gently, slowly, up and down. How fortunate she felt in that, she felt fortunate. How he had leaned into her with his sleep heat, heavy and warm, the press of his flesh aligning to her curves. She had kept herself awake that night, resisting sleep to know some more of this perfect feeling. The way he stroked her hair away from her temples, tucked her rough smooth curls behind her ears. That was when she felt most loved. That one time he was unconscious of himself, and thought only of her, of his need for her, and the way in which only her presence could bring him the solace he was seeking.

She wants to burn herself with acid to remove the memory. She touches her face and its ridges and dimples now make her sick: this is the nose he kissed and then left; this is the chin he cupped with his hand; these are the eyebrows he smoothed with his fingertips when they were wet from the bath and she was laughing; the eyelashes he said he adored, his butterflies, how he would touch them while she slept. She wants no reminders of it.

❦

WHEN LAFAYETTE LEFT HER, THE GIRLS TOOK HIS PLACE. TWO babies with his narrow furrowed forehead and small flat ears and apricot lips growing on their faces, his delicate hands, crying in the night for her to come to them, curling around her breasts and shoulders for comfort. She transferred her love and pain into her girls. She deposited her longing for him into their bodies—they fed from her breast and she nourished them with a pure desire. They ate of her sorrow and memories.

She was fascinated by the cruelty and comfort of it.

❦

WHEN THE TWINS WEREN'T HUNGRY FOR HER ANY LONGER, DIDN'T cry for her in the night or tug hungrily at her chest, then she began to feel the old loss again, and their lack of need, and she couldn't see that a changed need was a need still because she wanted no more change in her life. When Sweet Marie walked across the room for the first time, Maw recognized the door as the mouth of some hideous grinning monster through whose jaws everyone she loved would always leave her. And she determined that her doors would keep her girls in and keep the world out, keep out its temptations and distractions, its petty desires for fuel and food, pennies and quarters and husbands. She would create a place for her girls from which no exit would be desired. The girls became her prisoners, and she loved them for it. She always feared their leaving. She was fascinated by the cruelty and comfort of it.

❦

THAT WAS HOW MAW CAME TO GIVE UP ON THE DISTANT RELATIONS, and upon passing, and upon her husband's eventual return, and upon any money in the bank or even hidden under the bed, where she kept the pink satin slippers from the years that came before.

When she realized she would allow no one ever to leave her again, she decided to open a home for the elderly, the veteran, the sick and the discarded. The unwanted. The unbelonged. Their warm needy dying bodies coming in and never going out except in death. Every room in the unwanted mansion with a bed. Each bed with a body. Each body crying out for her, each body seeing her as a saint, an angel, a minister of relief—

And so Maw taught the twins to be her guardians against loss. Her sorrowful healing watchdogs. Her girls her host of ministrators. From Maw, her twins learned a kind of courage: the relentless procession of motherings. Undue compassions. Sacrifices of and to the highest orders of pain. The succor of sad veterans. She showed them a wanton compassion: to weave a long plait of yes. She taught her girls to stitch and darn the raveled sleeve of life, to baste it to the vestments of all those lost and never found.

Their sharp young fingertips learned how to feel for tumors. In their newly adept hands they wielded needles for the lancing of boils on the palms and soles of the suffering. Maw taught her twins how to pull out their own ribs for use as splints and back-braces. She invited them closer—into the surgeries and doomed birthings, diagnoses at dawn, to bear exhausted candles at unanticipated wakes. They saw how they should thread crosses of absolution through the closures of a shroud. Never to avert their eyes from those of the misshapen and dehumanized, the cast off and secret people, tucked into invisibilities of all sorts by families of all kinds. Always to press clean handkerchiefs to the eyes, lips, and nostrils of the sobbing heavers. Always a cold glass of lemonade with ice chips. A square of dark chocolate or a sliver of peppermint, a leaf of feverfew placed on the tongue.

Maw was their teacher of loosening nooses, of dulling the knives, flushing pills, unloading the gun, of sucking out the poison—all the tricks to extending a life, to forestalling a leaving—of passing.

❦

MAW WAS THE FIRST TEACHER. FOR THE TWINS, SHE WAS THE GOD of all things above and below. Wild roses sprang up in her footsteps. The twins knew they belonged fully to her, for she had made them and made their sky that was the blue of saints and made their air from dust off the wings of angels.

Their Maw had existed for as long as the sun had scorched the skies. From her holy flesh they fed upon a gruel made of honey and gunpowder.

Tied to a string around her waist, their Maw kept a heavy black ring of keys to all the doors which she counted every night before she went to bed, and counted again upon waking. In the mornings Maw would get up and unlock these places and the twins would go through them. In the late dark of evening Maw would take these places away again and the girls would wait until it was light again and the entrances would be reopened to them. Maw kept the keys to more places, more doors that the girls had not yet even found.

QUICKSILVER COME TO CURE ME

THE SMALL TWIN GIRLS SQUAT ON THE FLOOR AND BETWEEN THEM they roll a silver ball of mercury. The syphilis ointment has dropped and broken, yielding slivers of thick pale glass and a fat and heavy load of mercury. Every few moments the sphere shatters into smaller balls and scatters, and the girls utter muffled shrieks and scuttle sideways on their heels, half attempting to avoid the mirrored balls but still not allowing them to disperse into the cracks of the floor.

The floor is hard wood, sanded yet still rough. The mercury leaves tiny beaded glittering tracks behind it which the girls try to gather up with scraps of paper. Whitey, the smaller of the sisters, pokes at the mercury with her fingernail and it pushes off from her almost before she's even touched it. It's cold and wet, alluring, and she tries to touch it with her tongue. *If it don't kill you it'll cure you,* says a patient from the bed, pressing a swatch of flannel nightgown to the rotten hollow in his face.

❦

TWO SMALL GIRLS SQUAT DOWN IN THE RAVINE AND LIFT UP THEIR thin, stained dresses. The larger one frowns, concentrating, her plump lips pinned under her teeth in focused effort. The smaller girl lays her head down on the ground, grinning, to watch as her sister pushes out a long thin satiny cord of dung. It lays itself down in a coil on the hillside and its maker, Whitey, christens it a snake. Carefully the girls align three stones to its tail.

A *rattler*, Sweet Marie says, and Whitey bravely inserts two twigs as fangs.

❦

WHEN HE FIRST SAW THE TWIN GIRLS EMERGE FROM HIS WIFE, the egg of Lafayette's mind rolled into a deadly fall from the nest and cracked open, hard, and his white parts and his yellow parts ran together on the ground. Before he saw his own girls, Lafayette had two halves distinct in every way: adult and child Lafayette, smart and dumb Lafayette, kind and cruel Lafayette, patriarch and rebel Lafayette. But then he saw—swimming in their own afterbirth—two creatures so immediately loathsome to him that he might have killed them in fear if he'd stumbled upon them after dark. If he'd seen them after dark, he thought to himself, then licked up the thought with a spoon and choked on it.

It wasn't the bloody fluid that threw him but their eyes, closed as if weapons sheathed and then suddenly open, the pupiled depths inside sucking him straight to God behind the sky, then drowning him down to hell. Their eyes were soft marbles, so milky they looked blind, a hallowed-be-thy-name kind of blindness like Saul's, or the violent powerful blindness of the unshorn Samson at the temple pillars.

Lafayette saw that they were some terrible angels—even the blood that rushed to the underneath of their newborn skin couldn't disguise their origins in some other world than this—they nearly glowed. Golden as spirit candles in the swamp. The unpaid reparations by ancestors, glimmering in the blood. And yet their heavy floating weightlessness, like huge hollow-boned sea birds stripped of their wings. Spirits, demons, annihilating angels, Lafayette knew the twins were kin to those bloated spectral bodies that seemed to hang in the upper branches of trees before morning, that seemed to call out things to him that made him shake. No, these babies of hers weren't his, these strange fleshy things mumbling eerie incantations and searching for a teat.

❦

THE TWO SMALL GIRLS ARE UNDER THE KITCHEN SINK COLLECTING jars. Three or four small jars with lids that screw tight. They have found razor blades and carefully scrape the glued labels away from the glass.

The razor blades make an unnatural sound against the glass and, so as to camouflage it, the girls run a thin stream of water from the faucet. Hidden back behind the cupboard doors they listen to the water gurgle down the pipes, and giggle.

The two small girls begin to fill the jars with poisons.

Whitey has taught herself to pass gas and she positions a jar against her small haunches and releases. Sweet Marie, poised with the lid, clamps it down. In the five other jars the girls deposit flypaper in rancid milk, the discarded claws of the rabies cat, skunkweed in vinegar, old man Sangster's bedpan piss, the corpse of a chicken embryo.

On the hillside, the two small girls set the jars in a circle around a cross of white rocks and birch bark.

❦

THE TWINS' BIG WHITE HOUSE IS AT THE TOP OF A TALL, STEEP hill. Lifted up and left there by the family who knew them and didn't want them. Behind the house and at the bottom of the hill lies the river. The drop down towards the river is so sharp it's almost a cliff; it's as though the river, or something that came from the river, took a vicious bite from the hill—as though if there had been a second chance, that something would have eaten the big white house as well.

Even without the gigantic mouthful, the girls are forbidden to play in the river. For Maw, it holds a host of ills that prey on children: the kind of mud that swallows, the cottonmouth snakes that lie on rocks, the snapping turtle lurking in the undertow hungry to remove a foot; or the black widows in the reeds, or bacteria, typhoid, or fevers; the broken glass and leeches in the shallows, or rusty tetanus metals deprived of oxygen, or the kind of people who roam riverbanks and prey on other folks.

The river took your father, Maw tells them, lying, but her words stop them cold, just so.

❦

MAW, HIS WIFE, THOUGHT THE BABIES WERE FINE BUT LAFAYETTE'S eyes were cooked, burnt so hard he could see nothing but a charred and blackened life ahead of him, the children augering some strange and awful omen, and so he ran, ran off the map of the town and clear onto another map that included another town, and then another, and finally reached its edge in a tattered crumpled whorehouse that gripped him, in a scared and sodden wonder, by the Gulf.

It was there in the house with the Gulf Girls that Lafayette folded himself in. His head was cracked but gentle. He was skittish, yes, but helpful with the wasp nests under the eaves or with a baseline at the guitar when Sikes, the seven-fingered drifter whose three phantom fingers reached too often for the bourbon.

Betrayed now by his eyes, bringers of visions, he ignored them and drove towards the pleasures of taste and touch and smell instead, stabler senses which didn't warp and bend into something horrible the way his sight might. He'd blow his breath out over his upper lip when he saw things he knew he shouldn't, mostly just vague and sinister shapes but sometimes fishes slithered up from the drain, climbed out, and put on dresses before walking upright to his bed. Or an ear of corn might swell larger and larger until it forced him from the kitchen, Lafayette running away with the quick but fragile steps of an old man. He would watch, stricken, as the afternoon light turned mean, making everything wan and ugly.

His worst would be when he angrily tugged and pummeled at his cock, looking to hitch a ride up out of his tormented visions, but instead seeing his own grown twins clinging naked to the ceiling, clutching with strong fists to the dried-out flypaper, their four critical dawny eye beams following the motions of his fist, up and down, up and down.

❦

DOWN IN THE TWINS' RAVINE THERE ARE CRABAPPLE TREES ALONG the river banks. The pocked and ugly fruits plummet into the river, sinking down a good two feet before rising again, drowned, to the surface. The river licks the peel, softens it, ducks into the white meat along alleyways left by worms. The river plucks up their seeds and eats them—cool, quick—and shits them out along the banks before returning for another taste. New trees are born from the bodies of their elders and the river will eat them, too. The river loves hard and well.

The river knows all there is of love. Among its loves are the four of them from the big white house above. They have been known by the river, who has waited for them each hour of each day for years. The father Lafayette once swam in the river long ago, a grown load of ripe fruit. When the river went into Lafayette's open mouth, filling it, the river got caught up in the gullies of his tongue, the pockets of his armpits; the river ran up his ass and floated his cheeks, raised them up to the current's surface like a gift to God. And the girls. The little daughters are the river's plumpest berries, superior even to the velvet skin of a raspberry dropped by a passing bird. Their tiny dry girl berry hairs rise up in static panic against the dampness of the river's liquid hands crawling quick along their fibers— the girls' delicious skin soaked through with dewy skank and slime of river muck.

❦

WHEN LAFAYETTE'S VISIONS GOT TOO BAD HE WOULD RUN UPSTAIRS to the Gulf Girls and they would press the soft pads of their fingertips down against his eyelids and push his head into the darkness between their legs. It was there in the feline hollows of the Gulf Girls that Lafayette began to worship the four inch slice of closed yet open flesh that runs between a woman's legs, worship the way the tissues themselves transmitted a highly compelling odor to anything that touched them: a fold of a nightgown caught up high and twisted around the hips in sleeping, or his fingers. The way the quarter- or half-inch growth of the knotted fur between their legs was saturated with the stench, each hair laden with sweet ointment. Sometimes there was a canker-pus or some mites—that didn't warn him off, nothing could. If he came upon a fruit in the forest, he reasoned, he would eat it no matter the ants or flies, or tiny bud of worm, it was all natural, all to be expected, everything was simple and lovely, and if he kept his eyes closed he was fine.

♥

EVENTUALLY LAFAYETTE LOST HIS WIFE ENTIRELY. IF THERE WAS A part of him that thought of his courtship, their marriage, the cornbread smell of his young wife's hair, her thumbprints on his biscuits, the red flowers on the quilt her fingers made him, that part had been caught up, tangled in the mess of his guts thrown up at the birth. That part was braided in with a third of his dumb boyish innocence, a third part of fastidious ignorance as to the aftereffects of sex and sperm and blood. What was left in Lafayette was something else entirely, something that had hitherto been obscured: the opening to a dank and tomblike rodent's burrow. And once Lafayette discovered that hole, tumbled into it, he liked it, liked the stench, the warm comforts, the tender pink. The comfort of ancestors, garrisoned in the luxury of plantation blindness. Needs met at any cost. Huddled down there, Lafayette found the source and began to suckle.

♥

THE TWINS ARE UNCONCERNED ABOUT THE APPROACH TO THE front of the house. There is a road a few hundred feet off that offers a turn into their windy graveled lane. People come to the house from the town and they can't help but bring out the sound of the gravel—it carries the news of an arrival into every room of the house and the sisters peer from upper windows, behind bushes, above the rail at whoever's coming. It is their mother's job to greet them, and for whoever it is—bringing a dying or crazy relative for the hospice, delivering groceries, selling something—Maw always has an answer, kind or mean, and the twins leave the boredom of welcome to her. It's the river behind that causes worry.

When they were very small, the twins used to dare each other to lean over the long white porches at the back of the house, tempting the river. It was Sweet Marie who had the idea to feed whatever was down there and so the girls collected scraps of compost in a bucket and dumped it over the railing before they went to sleep. But even in sleeping they kept long stout sharpened sticks next to them in bed.

❦

SOMETIMES THE GULF GIRLS INVITE LAFAYETTE INTO THE THREE-walled room, the room whose fourth wall is a window made of the thinnest, clearest pieces of glass. Outside the glass wall are a few chairs and on them sit a small number of people: a man alone one night, drunk and laughing, or a stiff and somber pair half hidden by ridiculous hats or scarves. If there are first time men on the other side of the glass they either begin by being very quiet and then becoming loud, or the other way, where they sit down raucous and then vanish into solitary silence, eyes hooded, rapt at the unfolding goings on. There are tunnels that connect the white brothels to the black brothels, the color lines criss-cross under the tidy town but once inside, there's no telling who might turn up. Erections of all colors. Pussies to all tastes. Anus and penis and orifice that seem to ask no questions about what goes where, and why, or why not.

So when the Gulf Girls invite Lafayette into the room he pretends he is blind and imagines himself vanishing completely and forever into their bodies. He might run his tongue, slow, up inside along their bare crack of ass and while he tastes the hole he thinks he's small, just a small mole or a snake, and not a man at all. He can pretend that his penis is all of him and that when it's inside their mouths he himself is dancing down their rosy throats and feeling the billowing curtains of their lungs with his fingertips. And all is pure.

If a man buys his way across the glass sometimes Lafayette is told to stay and sometimes to go, but when a rough and hungry cock finds its way to Lafayette's hole, to the hollows behind his fundament, then he imagines himself an eternal tunnel, a spiraling expanse of inky closeness, an intimate and blind embrace, and all is pure. Lafayette shivers, winnows, burrows, nestles—anything to ingratiate his way to disappear into a dark and wet opening where there's nothing to see, where no one can follow him, certainly not his wife, his girls, certainly not them.

♥

A LITTLE OLDER AND STILL THE TWINS ARE WORRIED ABOUT WHAT might climb up at them from the ravine. They make a list of weapons and maintain their defense against the river on daily expeditions.

From the house, the river must be approached in a series of twisting paths that cut around knots of trunks and limbs, down narrow perilous gullies where the water has washed the dirt from between the rocks. Over the stony topsoil is a layer of leaves and bracken that can slide down the hill unexpectedly—to climb down requires a low crouch and to dig boot heels well into the loam. The girls have tied lengths of rope at treacherous points along the way and lower themselves down like fiddleback spiders.

They leave traps and pitfalls along the river. Rusty nails planted point up, lockjaw poised beneath the soil. Rotten teeth fallen from the mouths of dead people. Dung disguised as rattlers. Cow bones arranged in crosses. A mattress—shot to the banks by the river— riddled with rust, springs ruined, contains the skull of a fractured dog, all its flesh sucked clean in the cold harangue of winter.

The girls keep one large secret from each other, the part of the river war that isn't talked about. Sweet Marie guards the river so her father can't escape it and return. Whitey guards the river so it can't steal anyone else.

♥

ALL GIVEN THE RIVER IS SUNK TO BOTTOM, OR SPREAD TO SHORE. Arrogant, struck by its own grandeur, the river could rise up and climb, claw its way in a glorious wash of power over the shore, the banks, up the ravines and past the trees and pastures—laughing, gloating— and take the town in a wide rapacious lunge. Pluck babes and pops from porches, crush gables, kitchens, roofs: the river steals their eggs, their sperm, their first and last born, unborn, next born, next of kin, all the cherries from the prized amongst the virgins, then belches.

Sometimes the river falls in love and sweeps the body up and carries it, valiant, until its own rocks smash it, or roots ensnare it, and then comes the river's harsh and violent weeping. The river knows all there is of love. A woman feeling the same in lovemaking would set her jaw and sink her nails into her lover's yellow viscera, draw the meat from her lover's bones and shove it into her open mouth, veins still red and hanging—the hunger content not just with flaying. The river knows that need. When the river takes a lover it drags it off by the hair, holds it down chin back, ribs heaving, heels chopping like cleavers into the rocky bed, gasping.

For the pained and harrowed lover flows clear water, and clean—the sweet water of juniper and watercress, violets and ladyslipper. Liquid filtered free of snails. No watery sweat, no salt, no silt for the weary worldworn lover. And for the innocent lover, the lover open to the fold, the water seduces with funk and madness, danger—swirling eddies of green brown muck—that draws them in, curious and unsuspecting, *why not?* The undertow exotic, the way it flattens the surface to a gorgeous sheen, begs for entry, why not a toe, and arch, an ankle, the hip, lungs and brow. W*hy not*—a whirlpool in the stagnant shallows, a queer eddy without rapids, some odd effluvium of yellow bubbles at the beaver dam—*why not investigate?* the river murmurs.

♥

THE GULF GIRLS WASH LAFAYETTE IN A DEEP ALUMINUM BASIN, boil him, with his knees up nearly to his chin. They have two kinds of soap: sweet soap, and bug soap. They use the bug soap first and it hurts. Inside the soap are rough bits like bark and sand, and it smells of gasoline, turpentine, and lye. It burns, makes Lafayette feel like his cock is a match, as though one more rub and it might erupt, engulfed with flame and ash. After the bug soap the water is a murky black, brackish, and the Girls help him up so one of them could take a turn.

Lafayette shivers with the wet and they wrap him for a moment before using the sweet soap, which sometimes makes him cry when he is tired because the water is clean and nearly clear, and the Girls' fingers are slickened with soap as they dart around his balls and back behind, gentle, and since they're making fragrant amends for the injustice, their sweetness reminds him of the few bad things that have happened to him in the house: a farmer's climactic thumbs pressed down so hard against his windpipe that he felt it give a bit and crack; the fright of a scarlet stream of blood that poured from his haunches unexpected; the last night of his favorite girl who screamed and screamed, stopped speaking, then took pills; all these and a gut drawn sickness bring themselves to the bath hoping to get washed away. And so sometimes Lafayette cries when it comes time for the sweet soap because he knows its sweetness won't hold against the black tar that smothers, or against the sticky sludge that clings.

♥

WHEN THE GIRLS BEGIN TO BLEED THEY HAVE GONE DIFFERENT ways but Sweet Marie can't hide her flow from Whitey, who steals her sister's rags and sews them with her own, ties them before storms with wire to the bark of trees in the ravine, hoping the scent might draw their father home.

To Whitey, she has rendered Lafayette a wolf man with a wild, beastly fierceness who was drawn in battle with the river to protect them.

Sometimes he is a giant snapping turtle who swam to find the source of the river and put it out.

He is carnivorous, her father, ravenous, and certainly subject to the bait of fresh girl blood.

When he returns, lured, Whitey will stalk and trap him. If he displeases her she will flay him for a winter coat. Use his skin for moccasins, post his head as a warning to others.

And if he's suitable, even if he comes back wounded, vanquished from the fight—skin torn, missing hair or teeth, limping or dragging an appendage, then Whitey will tie a rope around his waist and reel him up over the banks of the river, wrap him in rags and hoist him up the ravine, taking care that his body not get beaten against the rocks. If he's suitable Whitey will find a clean soft bed for him to die in and she'll watch with him for death, victorious, laughing at the river down below.

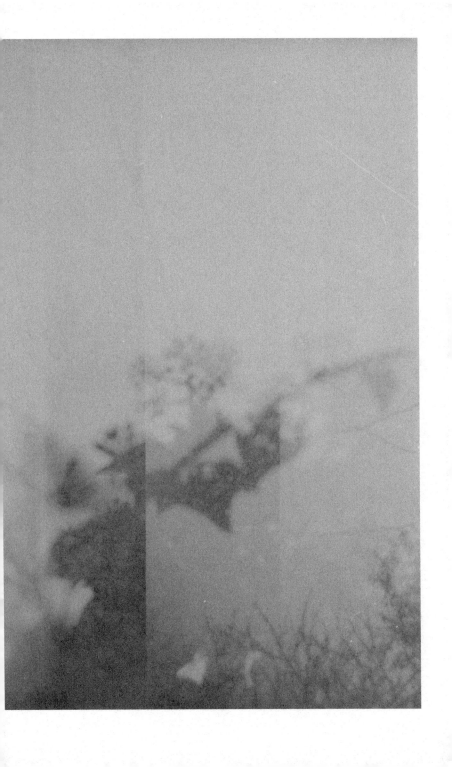

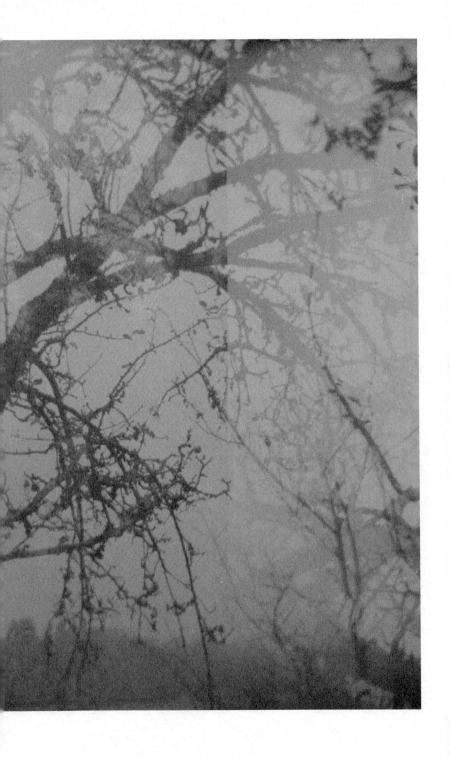

REQUIEM FOR WINGS
IN THREE-QUARTER TIME

OF THE THINGS SWEET MARIE DISLIKED WHEN SHE WAS A GIRL, there were strife, anger, noise, sadness—even too much gladness was too much for Sweet Marie. When Whitey played Ma Rainey on the radio Sweet Marie would disappear, choking off the sound beneath her blue flowered pillowcase and soon falling asleep, her lungs and heart filled with feathers. She hated music. It was too much.

As a grown woman, her best times were when the door was closed and she was in a room alone. Any room would do. She had her own bedroom, but wished it had no windows so she would not have to sense the changing light of the day. The light at dusk was too painful, particularly on Sundays when the seasons were changing and she felt the rush of time howl past her from the sky to the soil.

Time, with its reapingcutting power, ok to remove that, but there's still something strange about time. With its reaping power? Yes. I think, "with its reaper's power" or "with it's power to reap" or "the reaper" or whatever. Maybe the first – "with it's "reaping power". Or "with its dangling, dirtied scythe", was not her friend ; each morning she still felt the raw slice of the new day as keen as a page torn from the spine of a daily calendar.

Sweet Marie was a friend to sleep. In the parlor after supper when Whitey and Maw would have their nightly arguments, Sweet Marie would wake later to a dark and empty room and sense the slowly dissipating ghosts of hard words lingering behind the curtains and in the oily velvet folds of the sofa.

Even the air, soiled by emotions, was enough to force her quickly to her bed and off to dreaming.

❦

SWEET MARIE'S DREAMS WERE OF GREAT WHITE WINGS TIPPED with pale blue—the tips of these great feathered wings merging into the cold white blue of the skies. In her sleep she could believe she was never coming down again, not with these sinews stroking the air to keep her aloft, aloof from the earth she had no use for.

How ugly the exposed soil. How hideous the way people's hair grew out of the tops of their heads, long fibrous strings that turned white and then yellow, stringy, falling out from their ugly skulls.

These things Sweet Marie saw in her sleep as she flew: The rotten leaves on the tops of flat roofs; clutched huddles of ragged folks behind buildings, reeling, women with skirts up and men fumbling between their legs; bald and ancient heads twisted to ridges by forceps, or else flattened by days spent neglected in the cradle.

The only beautiful things were the trees: giant clusters of interknitted veins reaching higher than human grasp, seeking the sky, poised to climb ever higher, ever taller, barely held to the earth by their thin stems of trunks, obviously eager to break free of the very ground that fed them. Drawing their source of blood from elsewhere.

And when she got older, she would stay above the clouds and see only the cotton batting of them, their foam and mist, or the simple, pure colors of the sky that changed from black to gray, then pink, red and orange, then blue, and then reverse it all to make night.

The only place Sweet Marie would go to rest—when she was flying— was somewhere in the topmost branches of the very tallest trees at the crest of the highest hills. And that only for a moment.

♥

I<small>F</small> S<small>WEET</small> M<small>ARIE</small> <small>TOUCHES HER OWN LEG SHE FEELS IT TO BE OF</small> some other body and no part of her. Brushing her own hair seems as if she is brushing out her sister's—she cannot feel any pull where the strands attach themselves to her scalp. They say she has never cried except for when she was born—but it's not true. Even Maw admits that one daughter cried for them both, that one of them cried in shock and separation while the other—she doesn't know which—fixed her eyes upon the corner of the room as if in a strange and stony resentment.

And throughout her youth she never cried when she should have: when she fell from the apple tree and her arm hung limp from her body for months. She was *brave*. She didn't complain when she never fully regained its use. But she was neither brave nor afraid— perhaps she didn't complain because she didn't notice. Or if she did notice, perhaps she simply knew that no one would really care. She certainly doesn't care now. Things come and go—she notices, in a way that suggests she has moved on.

♥

T<small>HEY CALL HER</small> S<small>WEET</small>, <small>BECAUSE SHE IS SO SILENT AND BECAUSE OF</small> her delicacy of body, her thin wrists, long narrow nose, the strands of her hair vaporous, so inexplicable and soft. Skin so light they say she is made of golden brown bottle glass, *and so pretty*. Sweet because she doesn't impose, doesn't take up space or force anyone in any way. They like that. *Because life is too contentious already without adding difficult women to it.* They liken her quietness to sweetness—something that goes down easy with no strong flavors or rough edges. She smiles when she is smiled at, she does that for them.

But contrary to what Lynchburg thought, Sweet Marie's manner was not actually what they saw. She was not a beautiful bottle of glass filled with the rarest of gold and amber. She knew her gold had evaporated, and left the sediment of illusion. She wasn't made of gold but of the thickened chaff of air at harvest, of useless dried out pollen in autumn, falling into a fallow soil. That the gold that once filled her had fled. That it lined the vestige clouds of a sunrise she would never see, and had fallen gently into a harbor she would never reach.

No, this bottle glass woman named Marie didn't exist at all. *Sweet*, they call her, *Sweetie*. She knows she is not sweet, not at all. *Sweet. Sweetie.* She has learned the artistry of evaporation: she sends each cringe into the clouds, and replaces it with a smile. She learns the ones that satisfy others. And then, while her truth ascends upwards, she looks, she observes, she watches how they mistake the simple movement of lips up and over and past teeth for expression of contentment and comportment. How they gain pleasure by turning her performance of obedience and servility into sweetness and goodness, how need it her to display it to them, and so they all create it. And inside she hates them for it, and she lowers her chin deeper with a tilt of compliance while inside her skull, her eyes lift from the crux of her head and think of the gold lost beyond reach in the heavens. She looks, she observes, she watches their ignorance, their collusion in her illusion, her destruction. Her contempt nestles its beak into the feathers of her gut, a soft dark place where her loneliness, her grief, and her rage sleep with eyes open.

Everyone wants a good girl in that family.

❦

SWEET MARIE WAS NINE WHEN SHE REALIZED HER FATHER DID not exist—certainly not as a man, and therefore doubtfully as a father. She knew this creature named Lafayette was not "gone," he was imaginary. She knew that Lafayette was only an ivory idea, a desire, a need, a tradition of his time carried forward with the tongs of time's sadism, and that besides, that bizarre desire and need belonged to her mother and her sister—not to her. She had no need for father, only for some kind of rootball, a mother lode, a twisted inextricable knot of growth and nourishment that existed so far underground, where no human hand could destroy it. A caress from her mother, that her mother hadn't been too far gone in tragic determination to give. A sister less oblivious to subtlety of emotion. But a father? No, she had no need for that, and in her own secret way was pleased that he had gone.

Sweet Marie knew that what Maw told her and Whitey about him were only stories— twisted figments of a damaged brain—each episode in the saga merely a page turned over to the next: on one page Mary is raped by her god, and on the next page a new god is born, and a cracking spine of faith holds the tale together.

❦

Sweet Marie knew that if she had no father, and her mother wasn't there to care, then she was no true daughter. No one had possession of her, or noticed her, and she wasn't even entirely alive. She was too white for negro, too negro for white. Too alone to belong, and so familiar to the secrets of the South that for all her visibility, she remained invisible. For if a few cared to look at her, certainly no one cared to see her. And without an auction block and tally sheet, her life would not be valued. She could no longer be bought or sold. No script exchanged on her behalf. And so if no one any longer cared if she lived, it was proper and right that she did not inhabit this earth. This was no place for her kind. Sweet Marie couldn't see any point in living for herself: she felt nothing, and meant nothing to herself.

She would lie still and quiet in the lane but nothing and no one would run over her, the travelers swerved and keened, as though her life, her undesired life, was worth sparing. How peculiar.

All this time there has been nothing tethering her, no family line to trace back down to the ground wrapped around a spool held by a warm strong loving hand.

And she has known that it's just easier for everyone to believe that they're not alone— it's easier to believe they matter.

It brings them comfort, but not her.

She likes to be the only one to know that nothing, no thing of it, is true.

❦

In spite of everything, Whitey's random passions fix themselves at times upon her twin whenever she sees her other half turning into an ever more distant and winged thing, a foreign creature who flies away and leaves Whitey behind to face the big house all alone.

Whitey cries and rages, then pets and purrs, anything to keep her sister incarnate and at her side.

Sweet Marie watches Whitey studying birds in lonely desperation, burning their feathers in her secret pots in the basement, or in the light of the waning moon. Goldfinches, starlings, scarlet tanningers, all come under Whitey's fixed scrutiny as holding the answers to rooting her sister, keeping her anchored to the funk and muck of the earth from which Whitey's witchcraft draws its power, and away from the ether that climbs up into the unceilinged sky, into which she might rise and rise and never return.

And sometimes Whitey's spells work, and serve to tie Sweet Marie's wings together for a time and force her to the ground. And she lies gasping on her side, dark plumage heaving, patiently, silently plucking at the restraints. But only for a time.

SHE BROKE HER TEETH OFF
AT THE ROOTS

WHITEY LIKES THE BEST THOSE IN WHOM SOMETHING IS A LITTLE wrong, the ones kicked from the litter. They have things floating loose in them that aren't yet sewn down, needles still left in their spines, rusty tacks pulling together the dark parts—legs and arms knotted and tangled with memories and desires. She goes for the light, bright ones whose faces seem open as a cow's. She tries the ones so sharp they might be cut from aluminum, pocked and dinged from wear. The fat and the thin ones, the young and old, even those as weird as nature makes them.

It's the first flashing glance that does it, tugs her in. Hook in her mouth and line held fast between her teeth, lips parted, Whitey comes at a lover head first and open. She goes out swimming for their hooks.

She only needs to love a lover once. And it's the anticipation, the raw appeal that's the best thing—the peculiar stink, a rank particular odor of their minds. The way a gait rolls or doesn't, an early starburst of wrinkles at the corner of the eye: a rebellious sideways tilting chin or an arrogant wean of the hip. Any of these is sufficient to light the fire of her consideration, a certain thoughtful deliberation: *What if...?*

If the road runs just a little out of the way or a shy-voiced wanderer of the back woods slips a little liquor in with the lemonade, then it's bound to end with Whitey in a cool damp bath and a half-shorted radio whirring in the gloom, one night's lover in the bag.

Every so often a lover vanishes from the make. Whitey shudders each time the line goes so suddenly slack. Her sweet generosity plays itself out to its takers, yet she is surprised to come up empty, time and time again, to a smooth clear lake of nothing that she can work with.

❦

IN THE MORNINGS WHITEY PREPARES FOR WORK AT THE HOSPICE. She washes the hollows and rises of her face, puts pins in her hair and a clean dress on, then out her bedroom door and down the hall, to its once majestic rooms and rooms and rooms of the now nearly dying. Her fingers trail the wall and pull back slightly at the arrival of every bedroom door. Each door jamb surrounds a frame which is wider than the beds inside to allow for their easy removal. On top of each bed is a patient, a human, a person waiting for something or other from her.

For Whitey there is a stability in their fragile ongoing needs, their plaintive and stubborn lust for nursing. For her. Each morning they need her to look in on them, and cluck or frown or sigh, laugh—and whistle or tut-tut, tell a joke or toss a spray of honeysuckle onto their beds. She comes by to distribute her drops of belladonna, perhaps to remove an ominous discolored washcloth from blankets dampened unexpectedly. They need her to look into each of their rooms regularly and search for signs of life—they are afraid of passing unnoticed. Of beginning to smell. Or of dying broken-bodied on the floor, their nightgowns over their heads and dead buttocks, or balls, or breasts sprawling exposed for hours. They need Whitey with unmitigated desperation. When they do die, they trust Whitey to be the one to smooth their crumpled skins and put their bodies in clean underthings. To wait until their beards have stopped growing to shave them, so the families, even the ones who don't exist, see them looking good.

She knows how to take care of a body.

Whitey moves from patient to patient with impunity. No matter how bad, they neither frighten nor harden her, them or their illnesses. Whitey has never known sickness herself, not one day in her life.

She's never had knotted bowels, felt something wrong in her limbs, no troubles of the organs of any kind, nor headaches, rashes, pallor, worms or chills. Just fever, once, and a short-lived sort of ache that went away when she moved her bed from under the ceiling beam.

She likes their hollow, feeble bodies curled awkward against a bank of pillows.

She likes the tiny mews they make in the late afternoon, half-asleep.

They never call for her mother Maw, and no matter how angelic they consider her sister Sweet Marie, still the patients call out just for Whitey, and she comforts them with the dry click of her tongue against her teeth, a sound like dog's claws that carries even down the hall.

Yes, isn't it hard, she clicks, *but you're so strong.*

Most can't even walk without her arms to hold them.

I've got you, she clicks, *come here.*

❦

BUT IN LYNCHBURG, THEY SAY, SHE'S GINCHY, SHE'S GIVING, SHE'S *googy, she's gone, she's funsome, she's fish-fried, she's forward, she's flown.*

They say, *She's horse-hot, she's horney, she's hoggled, she's hootch.*

She's sneak-eyed, she's steamed up, she's stone gone, she's swung.

❦

WHITEY DOESN'T TAKE A BODY TOO SERIOUSLY, THAT'S THE GIST. She comes to one guileless, open to its folds, where other girls might hunker and run.

In the hospice, the widows and veterans have skin of wax and horsehair. Though the women would not admit it, they long await a bath from Whitey, whose palms smooth down their boils and hard spots, straighten toes, and ease the fascia knots. Whitey has a white metal pail dipped in porcelain—blue, with the smallest drops of white—enameled. Whitey fills the pail with water and with fragrance, or with herb: cucumber peel in strips that leave a residue of crispness, the starched-flat skin of youth; chopped verbena, tied in muslin, is a young mother's kiss of kindness; on Fridays there is hyssop—no sweeter weed is known—and the dying bathe in lavender, or chicory dock and rone.

❦

IN HER SHORT LIFETIME OF MINISTERING TO THE SURREPTITIOUS sexual needs of the secretive citizens of Lynchburg, Whitey feels as crucial to them as she feels to her sick and dying, and similarly gracious in bestowing her favors. And although she won't flatter herself that her lovers worked particularly hard to win her, wracked their souls in lovesick wonder, she knows they sometimes soil their beds with moonshine all in the throes of her.

But she wishes they knew themselves fortunate, special in her care.

Whitey gives, gives all the way down to her marrow and sinew, and they seem appalled by the gesture.

What Whitey intends of her loving is a comfort—a quiet easy comfort, some short safe sanctuary from the world—and while the dying folks put a price on it, she feels the living in Lynchburg sense a threat in her, a taunt to their well-being, and she can't see why. It's not that she's asking or wanting, only giving—generously, at no price—for something alchemical that so many of them take from her, but will always deny.

She knows rumors follow her—what is whispered behind her back by the women and tossed about by the men. The short time she spent in school the one thing they worked hard to teach her was that everything about her was wrong: where she lives, who bore her, who sired her, which family won't acknowledge her, the unspeakable mysteries of her origin. Her father's people crazy. Evil. Or patriots. Martyrs. Rapists. Slaveholders. Her mother's people awkward, lost and unlucky. Negro. White. Or liars. Passers. Skin magicians. While others have *hard times*, her household is *poor*. And not just her household, but her body, her self. Her attitude is poor. Her appearance is poor. Her hair is wrong in all ways, as are her clothes. Too bright, too dark, worn too loose, too low, too short, too tight. Her words are overly loud, ill-timed, wrong even when she says the right things. In Lynchburg there is always anger behind their eyes, even behind the smiles. It hardly seems to matter, they smell something wild on her.

The boys in town claim to have found her in the barn with a mule, behaving crudely. It will never be entirely disbelieved.

Yet the Lynchburg boys persecute even the good girls' innocent silences too, those good girls with their obedient hair and shapeless clothes, and their refusal to give their bodies until bound by God and law to do so. The boys hate Whitey for giving at the same time they hate the ones that don't give an inch. And she watches the boys torture but later marry the held back, held in, held off good girls, and then she watches the good girls think they've won.

And then, afterwards, when it is too late, she watches as the girls find out they haven't won anything after all.

❦

AND RARE IS THE MAN IN LYNCHBURG WHO DOES NOT THINK OF Whitey and then of his love-stalk, his love dart, his lily, his lark. His bowsprit, his broomstick, his bird dog, his bark. His sternpost, his short arm, his spigot, his spark.

Of her acorn, her apple, her all's-well, her ache.

Her copper, his clovemeat.

Her coupler, her cake. Her pudding, her plug-tail, her pinter, her pant.

His gardener, his grinder, his gimcrack, his gap.

Her cuntache, his todger, her tonguer, his tash.

The words that they used were inviting.

❥

WHITEY STILL THINKS OF THE FIRST ONE SHE EVER LOVED. AND SHE sometimes thinks of that skin, as burnt brown as butter at the bottom of a pan. And those eyes—two bolts of lightning seared into a face of otherwise mortal flesh, those Christ-like teeth glinting in the sun.

How she was followed home from the Lynchburg ABC, was trailed around the dusty corner and down Green Street past the river, how she ventured past the buck-eye grove and was caught up with at the old springhouse with a grin. She gave an invitation, slowly, glowing, to go in down under her skirts. Hips nearly unhinged they were that happy. Her back bent so neatly over the gate, the one hidden by the high stone wall, where the rusty water that condensed off the ancient iron of the lock left a square-patterned dull of orange on her blouse.

And later, Whitey remembers a moment of despair, a lapse in the letting of her monthly blood—nothing between her and a tiny growing lily of a something. How suddenly he'd had no restraint, no patience or want to grow it, and she'd stood and listened to him for a moment, just stood there, then slowly walked home to drink her pharmacy tea of sticks and molds and timothy weed. Whitey waited while her belly turned to sump and mulch. She stank of it—the reek of decay wafted out from between her pores and then she told him about the sixteen different sorts of herbs you can put in a certain cup of tea. Once more she buttoned up.

And although he left ten purple blooms on her arms, even now there is still—underlying her fury at the cruelty of it—a glimpse at the first idea of love: a stalwart, supple, eager man with a handful of morning-glories waiting at the last light of that Friday night, whiskey in his pocket and a few dreams twisting in the wind.

❥

HER SWALLOW, HER SUGAR, HER SAMPLE, HER SPARK.

Oh, how his cock was a wick for her lighting.

♥

AT THE WHITE HOUSE, WHITEY'S FAVORITE PATIENT ALWAYS LIES in the arbor room, the one where the grapevines curl all across the window panes. Nobody realizes she always has one she pretends is her father. It doesn't matter which man it might be, or how long he might stay—she takes him as her own special charge and keeps Maw and Sweet Marie from having at him. While Whitey doesn't know where her real father is, she imagines where he's been gone to for so long. He's just like her, each footstep following a beat of his enormous heart, his unseasonable needs—she understands that deep down he just couldn't stop himself from reaching out, from touching people. She's heard the whisperings loud enough to carry. Not just one girl, one wife, but a hundred, a thousand, and each of them different from Maw in her way.

Whitey knows that kind of secret wandering curiosity of lust and love. She must have gotten it from him. This is why she is so misunderstood—there is no place for her, as there was no place for him. She will take care of him here, lavish the kindnesses on him nobody lavishes on her. And now, when some kind of fit comes on her false father, her make-believe invalid, the man who loves her, Whitey is the one to rub his back with oil.

She watches the hairs on his back take on a thin shine and she blows her warm damp breath to cool him down along his spine.

♥

AND IN LYNCHBURG, WHERE THE WOMEN LAFAYETTE LEFT BEHIND live out far beyond the edges of the map of what should be, and their house is a place to drop the near-dead destitute, everyone knows the wilder twin is useful for a bit-of, a bunk-up, a bop, a rumble, a rhubarb, a romp.

A plowter, a plug-nup, a pranger, a prowl.

A tumble, a transom, a tickler, a trowel.

And they say to her, *Let's sump, let's saunter, let's sally, let's suck; We'll wrestle, we'll pestle, we'll bundle and wump; We'll baker; we'll butcher; we'll fixer; we'll pump.*

♥

WHEN IT COMES TO WHITEY, LYNCHBURG IS A TOWN TENSED AND ruthless as a cat. The townspeople who think kinder things often say that Whitey is naïve. They think she goes with so many different men because she keeps hoping for the one that will work out and be her husband and take care of her, take her away from the white house and her rundown family. Or they think she does it because she is foolish and keeps getting taken in, taken advantage of, preyed upon. She used to try to defend herself against these suppositions but she doesn't bother any more because she knows what she knows.

Men, lovers even, who are aware of her activities often tell her that she is more a man than a woman. This makes them uncomfortable, because it makes them suspect an unbearable thought: that they are the woman in the relationship. God forbid. She makes them see themselves in a poor light.

There are women who are not unkind to her. The woman who owns the diner—with her big bust and her hip-cocked lean against the countertop, she picks the disreputable men from their eggs over easy and leads them up the clapboard staircase to her rooms—and hasn't ceased from saying *Whitey's just the generous kind.*

At the Lynchburg Steam Laundry one of the women sneaks her children's clothes in with the loads—no man wed but five children, each with different hair and eyes, some skin sallow and some pink, none of them much alike except in manners—she gives Whitey clean bandages for free.

And a darkskinned and silent woman, once, who stopped her kids from taunting Whitey in the lane. Though nobody respectable talks to the girls who work the third floor of the factory, one of them said, *They ain't nothing wrong with Whitey being friendly to no man*, though soon after the girl disappeared with a suspicious tumor, swept to the doctor's in a wash of blood, skin ashy as a stove and Lynchburg left to wonder.

Whitey stands out. Lynchburg claims to itself her dress is somehow different, brighter, tighter, that there's an unnatural sweet stink in her underthings, that she once wore a hat of white fur in summer though she had no money for it. Nobody else in town looks quite like Whitey. *Strange*, the ladies explain it to the children when it is necessary to do so, or *unwell*. On the weekends, the Lynchburg Military Cadets punch each other and swear down low as they can in their new young throats when they pass her on the street, and ask the Diner woman if she maybe has a little friend in need of some companions.

They might have been sympathetic if she was repentant but since she is proud girl there's no excuse. For a Lynchburg lady, passing Whitey on the street is an event—

If someone were to say anything bad about her, they'd be glad.

Cathy, the sweet-faced, rose-dewed woman who runs the Ladies' Aid Society with vigor and raw zeal, gives lectures on special lamplit nights about the call to act to save the fallen sisters, speaks soaringly of her compassion for women of ill-repute, mixed-blood, dubious reputations, takes collections from her audiences, tells them to lift up their eyes and hearts and find the mercy in their hearts to heal the wounds of these girls' sin-blackened flesh. Her hands are smooth and pale, her voice sure, and the town listens piously to the eloquence of her words. Her column in the Lynchburg newspaper never falters in its rigorous pleas for society's betterment: the women living in sin, the wages of Satan in their pockets, rotten teeth in their mouths. The liquor pouring though the streets, violence in the places of the night. Give money. Give prayers. Give of your indignation. Moral-less hussies. Heathen children having children. Blood swelling and growing with the wrong blood. Devils and devil babies. Oh give of your pockets. Women standing in the shadows, and the men who find them there. Give money. Do not give them money. Give Cathy money. See how she rattles the can of coins. Avert your eyes, wash your hands, keep your own self pure and put money in the palms of Cathy's dewy Christian hands.

Yes, Whitey's mouth has been on her husband, too.

❦

OFTEN, WHITEY DOES THESE THINGS, SHE GOES WITH THESE lovers, because she is curious and she likes to feel at the edge of things, poised, ready to fall. Bystanders worry for her safety. But Whitey is never afraid. She knows she is indestructible. She has secrets at her core she knows her lovers will never touch, and that is her defense from them. The only ones who can destroy her are those who know all of her, and there is no such person. Nor, she thinks, will there ever be. If she is rejected, if she is abused, it is not really her. It is only a part of her, and not reflective of the whole. *I might take that part of me, afterwards, and hold its head under the water until it stops kicking, and then it might not ever be seen again.* Or perhaps she takes that part aside for a while and she tends to it until it is healed, or at least better, and then it goes back in with the rest of her again.

❦

THESE DAYS WHITEY DOESN'T HARDLY LEAVE THE WHITE HOUSE anymore except at night, and that only to get hold of what she needs, carry something somewhere, and then back again.

At times it seems to her that the bulk of life is hampered: shoved down in a hollow underground place without water until the need dries up, blows away.

And in those days, many join her grief in telling themselves, *Dry the notion, kill the zazzle, rid the red-eye, fix the greens. Drop the aspect, stop the goo-goo, lance the blister, break the bat. Axe the mashy, bind the brim-band, kill the gaoler, scrape the rust. Snip the fizzy, cut the daisy, bind the cow-tail, knock the jump.*

♥

WHEN THERE IS NO WORK LEFT TO DO FOR THE UPSTAIRS, WHITEY
fills her orders in the kitchen down below, underneath it all in the
cellars where the red brick slave shade clings to her ankles. She
prepares her medicines carefully in the quiet and dark underground.
Bars still on the windows. She burns herbs and the sad-eyed cat
watches the green smoke twist into the air and escape to freedom.

People often discount Whitey's wisdom, her sordid basket of stories,
but inside it is her store of experience.

Men have war, she has this.

She has much knowledge that few women want, but most of them
need. Whitey can make a spell to order. Sometimes they stop by
for a packet of this or that, quiet, in the morning, early, or well into
the end of evening.

In a pantry in the cellar below the kitchen Whitey keeps her jars neatly
labeled: coltsfoot, yarrowseed, lady's slipper, teeth of drained sow
red thread, sumac wood, barley water, catclaw, pennyroyal.

In old shoeboxes are ready made packets and bottles—LOVE REMEDY
FOR A POOR GIRL or *right back at what got you*—and they take it
from her quick as they can, without stepping on her threshold.

♥

EVEN MORE WHITEY BEGINS TO WONDER AT HOW MANY PEOPLE
are slowly drying up and flaking, crumbling away, both upstairs and
in town, finds it hard at times to help them, touch them, figure their
ailing out. She can't herself have everything she wants— especially
not with other people. It seems the more she touches, the more
disintegrates. That people aren't really living, but just wads of dirt
and lath plastered over and cleverly painted to seem more solid
than they really are.

Surrounded all day by the ancient people who can't even seem to rub themselves into a state of happy wetness, Whitey must keep herself from thinking of their bodies as stagnant things, not even hardly real. The sore-hearted girls coming for her cures, half- crazed or crying above their delicious curves, as gone as branches scraping in the wind.

So more and more, though still wild as a spring onion, Whitey can't as often find herself eager to go near lovers. Of course it never lasts, her lack, but the lengthening spaces between when she can't and when she can mark her very worst times. And yet this one who walks down the sidewalk, that one who staggers from the barroom, lost in a haze of sickness—any one of them wandering through her world could contain the laughter and the prize, possess the clue to a well being.

In between times, and now even during her love affairs, an aching dullness seems to rise always higher in her. A dangerous remoteness of vitality and desire, of goodness and joy, hope and pleasure and of dancing through fields of green and yellow, of color and tastes exploding on the tongue. The frozen winter snap of a cattail. Cracking through the razor- sharp white mica of an egg and feeling the otherworldly temperature and texture of the slime within. That delightful shock of the odd. She longs for a jolt, a person or a place or a thing that doesn't make her feel unable to pick up her feet, to feel herself ever more tangled with each move, choked off by stringy white membrane and some hideous dark shape getting larger and larger as it approaches along its web.

❦

It makes her frustrated, her need, and when she's frustrated even the tiniest insurrection of the biscuit dough or pencil lead can fill her veins with the torment of a thousand gnawing ants until she's hurled herself against the pantry corner—or struck the baking sheet against her head, six or seven times slowly, right above the hairline where the red won't show—or taken the tine of the good silver serving fork and driven it just under the half-moon of her fingernail—only a little farther will change the pain.

❦

THE SUN SHOOTS DOWN ITS RAYS FROM STRAIGHT ABOVE AND THERE is no shade, no twilight, no evening, no night. The patients complain and Whitey takes her knife to the summer garden. She gives the old folks cold melon with salt.

It's at such quiet moments now that something flashes inside Whitey, bright white as a photographer's bulb, and it records for her an image in her brain, a sort of vision where she sees herself wrap the dead folks tightly in strips of clean white cheesecloth, press the fabric close against their skin and slightly tighten it, hoist the tender bundles over her broad shoulders and carry them out to the smokehouse where she tosses them up and onto an empty hook. The smoke is thick and fragrant in the summer. In the draft from the open door the bundles sway slightly, heavy and dense, as the heat and fire cures them.

She leaves the skin on and they gnaw it, hungry, till it's gone.

❦

Get a jigger— get a yum-yum—
blow the coin from the bed—

Play at pickle-me— play the mud daub—
Hunt the kit in the staff—

Put the wick in, put the fire out,
put the devil in hell.

THE TEXTURE OF A HAND
UPON MY HEART

THE MANNER OF FINGERS UPON FLESH. THE SLICKNESS OF LIPS upon a nipple, her own nipple, her own small circle of flesh rendered to a point of peculiar beauty, a small rosy tower of ache.

An arc of leg, her own leg, pressed against some other leg.

This came to Sweet Marie in sleep, and she woke, crying, and did not remember.

A faceless girl—her own sleeping breath in short gusts against this stranger's naked back. Breast pressed to back, leaning along her spine, breaths following one another, up and down. The winged thing that lives in her gut takes them away to a place where

The dream girl smells of swampgrass and amber and mulberry blossom.

❤

THESE BEAUTIFUL ENCOUNTERS SWEET MARIE UNDERTAKES WHILE sleeping, and in the morning the winged thing that lives in her gut takes them away to a place where she can not remember them. Where they cannot be destroyed. Desires and ambitions that live inside her, secreted away, hidden away, tucked into the crevasses of her intestines, wordless but not quiet.

Safekeeping, under the beak.

And like a hoodoo, Sweet Marie sleeps without memory—a certain internal silence.

♥

SOMETIMES IN A FAMILY, ONE PERSON IS APPOINTED TO HAVE ALL the feelings for everyone. And sometimes, one person is required to have none.

♥

SHE'S NAKED IN HER DREAMS. WARM. SWEAT. THERE IS A GIRL. This girl is a one-night lover—she will not be remembered in the morning. Every night the same dream girl returns. This secret night hoodoo Marie is a being somehow unreal and yet embodied, and full of fear and promises. Possessive, flawed, suspicious, seductive. So close to real. Naked. Wet. An instant's sleep for Marie before the dream girl leaves, the secret dream Marie and the dream girl curl together each night, for just an instant, before the girl slides quickly, quietly to the dream door, accidentally slams it behind her—Marie wakes, the girl is gone, nothing but the slippery damp between her legs to cause her question.

And just when Sweet Marie thinks the girl left nothing else behind, no trace of the space they twisted into one—just then Marie finds the salt of the girl's saliva on her nipple, that small circle of flesh. Almost small enough to go unnoticed.

♥

MARIE LIES AWAKE IN HER ROOM OF VIOLET DARKNESS, WINDOWS covered with cardboard and flour sacks—no difference between eyes open or closed. Anxious. Her small cool ass is clenched anxious against the sheets. Her small golden fingers narrowed to beams emitting light.

The lonely power of being the only one awake. The struggle not to feel.

Anxiously clenching her small cool ass, and surrounded in a dander of down, and the feeling an instinct to remember, to stay with herself, to feel, even though she knows, she knows otherwise.

Marie has a secret sense of the sentimental. A longing to enter some kind of haven and not feel shame for embarking upon that most dangerous and unreasonable quest.

Romance.

Of being lost.

Of seeking to be found.

Of finding.

❦

THE VULNERABILITY OF A SLEEPING BODY.

❦

SHE PREPARES FOR HER DAY, AGAIN, BOTH TETHERED AND untethered to a life as yet unmoored. Why find belonging in another and then fear the loss of that love, face again the grief of lack, avoid mirrors so as not to see again her face as one abandoned?

❦

AND THAT NIGHT, DESPITE THE BEDROOM'S ETERNAL DARKNESS, Marie cannot pretend to sleep. Her hairs count the years of her survival in the world. Sweet Marie's hair is shot with too-soon gray that betrays the existence of time. It moves—her hair, time, the hospice, the flow of monthly blood, desire. It moves away. Everything pulls away from her. Tonight inexorable loneliness and desire have banded together, have blacked her eyes, broken her fingers. Sweet Marie fights against them, as always. She lies in the bed breathless and defeated, her body crumpled against the victors. She can't think of it directly, but something's there. Something is at stake for her, something that comes to her in dreams, something small and frightening she's fighting for and something bigger and scarier she's fighting against, and she wrestles with her mysteries in sweat and sleep and bourbon.

And after her winged thing is loosened by drink, up from below comes the sense that tonight she wants someone in the bed, a woman with an engine of indefatigable arms to curl into, arms that she will be able to feel, iron or steel, someone whose warmth and strength she will be able to feel. Someone to lubricate her neck, unlock her shoulder, someone with those dreadful eyes of love that suggest *Yes, I can give this thing to you I can discover you and I can take you and keep you and you can be with me. I feel better when I'm touching you—*

♥

THE ONE BARE LIGHT ABOVE HER IN THE BEDROOM HAS GONE DARK. She dreams she's on a train. The train is going north, her window faces west, and the east—the sun—is on the other side, invisible. It's dawn, but her sky is dark. Some crazy sliver of joy. Fleeting. Insignificant. But no, it's more than that—she's kissing the girl and she's poised over the void, unbalanced by desire, toes pointed inward like a schoolgirl, unsure—fingers clenched and sweaty—shoes buckled in shiny points of leather and steel, firm, solid, deceptively fierce below her liverlike heart that clenches, frighteningly delicate, unmuscled—where to go—jump or stay—she's kissing the girl, the river-eyes of green unknown.

It's a miraculous dive to the center of a soul—downhill, a desperate quivering.

The wheels on the track strum notelessly, the strum of brushes on the earth's steel drum. Sweet Marie has been plummed, her depths softly excavated by someone's hands and tongue, deep in her unknown places: she plummets into sadness. She's been lured to the ledge of love and fallen into it, unbalanced by desire, she falls down deep into the hollow of her own unsightly needs.

She is buried with them in a distant unmarked grave—they make her ashamed, her need to be loved, and to love.

It is Sunday, a holy day, and even asleep she knows Monday's cold blue hollow is rising to her right.

Crying, Marie touched the dream girl's knee and found it warm—firm and smooth and warm as chicken eggs. Its uncanny sweetness made Marie scream as the dream ended, leaving her once again alone. It's the middle of the night and Marie's hands are on her belly. There is a whistle, low and smooth. It's a sad note, winding into the sky, thick and sweet as hope nestled deep into despair.

The Sweet Marie she will wake to—that Marie is obedient, responsible, and small— only focuses on the crumbling rock of the dying, shoring them up, attending to their needs. Scientifically. Diagnosing and treating.

Knowing when to pull the sheet over a face.

How familiar that moment, knowing what comes next.

NEITHER IS THERE ANY REST
IN MY FLESH

THE FORCE OF WOOD AND GLASS WHEN THE HINGED WINDOW comes torn from its latches and is struck again and again against the side of Whitey's bedroom wall, the sharp motion containing something animal about it: an animal not begging but forcing its will on the thing it wants, breaking zippers and buttons as it strips its prey and rips the meat from off the bone.

The morning storm has woken Whitey, and before she rises to tend the patients' bodies, Whitey first checks her own for errata, aberration. Automatically, unconsciously.

She notices more than anyone thinks—is more aware than anyone knows. She understands the necessary rituals of care, for without them things change, things fall apart, they turn rancid and decay. But for now the soft faun skin around her nipples lies lustrously revealed, a plump support for the dark dots of her milk ducts.

Sheet creases leave grim fissures along their route to her ribs.

Inside the white house she can sense a wary nervous tension. She can tell there are too many people in their beds awakening with worry. Wondering *why this?* And *what comes next?*

She will bleed tomorrow or in a day or two. She can always read her own time by the rising ache of ripeness in her breasts.

The dying. She can assess the weight of their memories, tell their unrest or their peace, the fullness of their bellies and how well their meals digest. Feel their struggle to stay alive, their desperation for reprieve, their confusion or relief at having to finally surrender. Their fear for the impossibility of release.

She curls her compassion round them, keeps them warm.

A scratch along her cheekbone and her above her upper lip—left by a frantic cat. And the single bruise dark and nearly perfectly square upon her left bicep—*from where?*

One shoulder stiffened by thin sleep.

In her water glass a dead fly snared and sunk, trailing a filament of spider web from its hind legs. A black shoelace strewn along the floorboards is not a string at all but a long dark line of ants come to nibble at the pale moonlight trail of her in the dried damp inside her underthings. She will give them a washing with rosewater in the basin.

❦

AFTER ALL THESE YEARS, WHITEY CAN RECOGNIZE THE FINAL DYING. She feels something click inside her on the last morning that they wake. The last bright sparks of their minds brings her pilot to flame and she heats and begins to boil.

Their fear slinks from their beds and down the hall to find her light, comes creeping through the cracks and settles along her blankets, edging its way to reach her underneath.

A dream of some sharp thistle imbedded in the palm of her hand, no one admitting to its insertion, nor willing to help with its removal. It travels through her body just beneath the skin, an errant mapless traveler ripping through her on its path into her heart.

Feel this, say their fears, pressing her hand to their foreheads.

❦

THE SONG OF THE MOTHER:

Feel this. Memories not yet robbed from them: the names of long lost children, names spoken only in trembling dreams they can't quite wake from.

Feel this. The dull mourn for a flower garden left to the neglect of niece and daughter-in-law. The forsythia's lurid bloom unchecked. Rhododendron mawkish without a pruning.

Decades of concern about coals rolling from the fireplace, worry too ingrained to cease now the hearth is gone to someone else's care.

So very much ironing—prostrate in a heap to wait for the heavy pressing that would take all day—

all those tiny tucks and pleats—

all the short expanses of cloth between the very smallest of buttons.

Such knowledge with no need any longer; the equal and opposite torment of listening for the baby's croup and of not hearing it. *Feel this.*

❦

AND THE SONG OF THE LOVER:

Upon their brains rests the dent of old desires.

The adored's embrace in the night, lying together under comets long since passed. The pattern of his breathing forever memorized, the beat and rhythm of the air inside his throat.

I still feel this.
The scent of that one lover's sweat: sweet apple cider. Her yellow cotton shirt opened at her breastbone.

This.

Such memories with no future—

the soul-clenched strain for the beloved's touch (the beloved now buried, the strain still alive). *And this.*

When their fingertips wakened lips and sex—

Like this.

♥

AND THE SONG OF THE SICK:

Feel this, resting her thin fingertips on the bulging tumors on their necks.

♥

SO WHITEY GIVES THEM HER COOL PALM, HER FINGERTIPS, HER warm young self to feel with. They fill her up with their emotions, they bank and store them in her, will them to her and feel comforted, knowing when they have passed from the earth their vestiges will carry on inside her.

And they pay for it—a wage, not more, a wage paid the tall strange woman of the white house.

May we have water. A whiskey.

Everyone pays dearly for it.

That letter—read it to me again.

Again.

A fee for her human kindness, because—although if they were dying on the road someone would try and save them—dying slowly in a bed is not an honor often lent for free.

♥

As the lightning fades slowly into dawn, Whitey watches the ceiling in quiet contemplation. The sheets are damp beneath her, pillows cast onto the floor. Her scent is high and full and she can feel the hairs growing slow beneath her arms.

These are her moments alone. Not moments of peace, but of something like it. Something nearby peace. That brief period of time following a rare pure morning storm, while the world remains caught between half-light and half-dark, and the day ahead as yet belongs to no one.

She closes her eyes to better feel the lavender gray air the birds seem to swim through rather than to fly.

She reaches her slim fingers between her legs and rubs slowly, tenderly. She can steal herself these gifts. They belong to no one but her. The thunder grows distant beyond the greening fields, beyond the pastures and mountains, rolls past the hollows and on westward to escape the rising sun. Her coming dances in, hand in hand with the dawn, a great glowing thing that expands to fill the heavens themselves.

Four in the morning is a new-birthed baby, lungs still full of mother wet, poised in balance for that instant before the tears.

THE SCENT OF COPPER
IN HER BONES

THE TASKS OF MAW'S DAY WERE CRITICAL. FOR SHE LIVED IN A house of industry. There was no sitting quietly, no periods where the vibrations of her hands and brains didn't cause the air to stir in great swirls and gusts around her. In the winter, when her quiet despair began dripping out of her in a clotted sludge and stained the carpets, she took on more old people for the home, or told Sweet Marie to pick up shifts at the Confederate veterans' home, or made Whitey take on more desperate girls lurking at the basement door for her secret female remedies.

Some years Maw expanded to animals—and then as if by accident, in springtime, there would be a profusion of livestock and wildlife breeding from the wayward creatures she had gradually found herself accumulating throughout the winter.

Maw wondered about the ladies who had no work to do—they must not be desperate people, or else they would be unable to endure the endless wastes of it all. Leisure in which minutes upon minutes marched on, the internal emptiness matched in step by an internal emptiness. Tick tock—

♥

TICK TOCK. AT LEAST MAW HAD BANDAGES TO WASH, AND instruments to clean, and meals to prepare. That took up the day. And at night she had the woebegone sufferers she went to treat in lamplit barns and toolsheds, or else the pointless mending in her basket, or long walks back and forth across the porch at night listening to the noises of dark water down below. She had endless tasks to which she fled at any opportunity—their narcotic escape luring her from one hour to the next.

And Maw had her aging hands to keep her busy. Cleaning, cooking, knitting, sewing, repairing, dismantling, scrubbing, all these actions she took upon herself to do without ceasing. She enjoyed the encroachment of arthritis that made each task take longer, and required additional endurance of discomfort. She clutched her knotted hands with a devout pleasure in their breakdown. Time was leaching out from within her very bones—that's how deep it went, to her marrow. She was getting older. The disease was satisfying to her. She sewed together her days with strings of doing and was content, in waking, to see the unraveling that had been done overnight.

But still she felt herself tremendously alone.

❦

ONE SUMMER MAW TRIED HER BEST TO HIDE A FEARSOME excitement at the arrival of Claudine, whose third birth had been an unfortunate one, the baby with the color and formlessness of a bruise. Claudine believed the baby had taken all her blood—there had been a lot of it, and it kept coming. After the burial she raised her head again and went about her life but her husband saw a great swamp spreading out inside her. A thick stickiness of her soul—the way he'd seen in dogs he knew were watching him but couldn't be stirred to raise their heads or wag their tails. There were many causes for it, but none of the effects were good. People failed when the spring inside of them went sump, all the current gone from their stream, and their eddies would falter into this salty swamp. He knew whatever it was he had fallen in love with was still there, but had gone stagnant in this funk. She was in danger, her shine was turning to a rough dull brown.

Her husband watched as the heat of sorrow cooked her swamp to breed stinging gnats and biting insects: if he forgot to move the boards from off the new grass her anger could slice him open quickly before it vanished, leaving him bleeding with no weapon to defend himself against. His wife's tears were secret and hidden from him but he could detect them in the texture of the mare's mane, in the new soap that never seemed to rinse completely off, even in her scent when he licked between her legs. Everything of her was festering. There was no option but to take her to the women in the white house.

That June, Claudine arrived in pale lavender. Maw admired her red hair, the Irish in her still new and glistening, not tarnished to the patina-gray ash of most of Lynchburg's white folks. Claudine had no tarnish yet. She was young and new. Speaking to the husband Maw heard him tell about the small secret swamp inside Claudine that could not be visited, but Maw knew the rot had not yet had the time to sink in—the penny had fallen into the muck, but Maw could retrieve it yet, and burnish it to orange on her hem.

For three months the two of them would lean together, gray hair mingling with the red, laughing sometimes (a victory!) at the titillating jokes Claudine would tell after her laudanum—Maw engulfed in grins, giving herself a gift of innocence and of maturity: she had made those jokes once, or heard them anyway! She was a married woman of forty! She had born babies and lost a husband. She could laugh at anything she felt like! Claudine told her secret gossip and Maw listened.

Listening. That was new. Maw entertained ideas from Claudine she had never thought to tolerate before—Claudine had been raised in the city and learned piano from a European woman whose fingernails were as long as garter snakes, who wore six red lacquer sticks in her hair—*like this!* And Claudine stuck young firm green beans into Maw's dirty bun and they laughed together. The piano teacher had lovers and didn't marry, not a one of them: at Maw's age she took in a boy not over eighteen and offered no excuses. She gave dinner parties and sprayed rose perfume onto the plates to give the chicken taste. Maw listened with ears pricked up high as baby corn. At night she dreamed of lavender boys with roses for eyes, Claudine feeding them to Maw with tea in the afternoon. They tasted delicious, like powdered honey and orange blossoms. She would wake smiling, laughing at herself, and go to check on Claudine. *Was she resting comfortably? Had she heard the one about the girl who tried to pick a mushroom?*

Maw swaddled Claudine in an attentive rapture. Whose had been the mind that shuddered and slacked? Who had been the one whose husband saved her? Who had been the one to bear the bruised-skin baby? Surely it had been Maw. They had discussed the matter until Maw knew the texture of the dead baby's skin as well as she knew the back of her own teeth.

Maw looked younger every day, fuller, more handsome.

Years dropped away when she wore Claudine's lavender dress. Her hands no longer ached—she missed the child, but she could have another, soon enough. It had been Maw's bruised baby, it had been Maw's sweet natured husband, hadn't it, who had seen the swamp overtaking her and had rushed strong and proud to care for her so honorably, so attentively—

In September the husband came to retrieve his wife, her skin plumped out and pinker now, a ripe shine to her eyes and no graycharcoal lichen sucking at her features. He was still very much in love. Maw found the two of them together in the washroom, Claudine pressed against the tub with her ruby-centered breasts exposed and sparkling in the sunlight. Another baby would come to pass, Claudine was sure of it. She had two small pearl earrings now, a gift from her husband. To Maw they looked like eyes without pupils staring back, triumphant, at her. *We will watch over her now*, they said blindly, *we do not need you any longer.*

❤

WHITEY AND SWEET MARIE GREETED THEIR OCTOBER MOTHER as if she had never been gone from them. They hadn't resented her delusions, her happiness—they didn't care about Claudine one way or another…a fairly stupid girl who got worse as soon as her sorrow lifted. The girls passed the mashed potatoes to their Maw. They set the gravy tureen at her right side and refilled the salt seller. *Is there any reason to believe they will let the new school be built*, they would say and let Maw's silence go unremarked. *No, they'll just argue about it til there's some war to spend the money on,* they'd reply and let the conversation spread out and drift, letting their words trail moss-like behind their Maw as she got up from the table and slowly left the room, went up the stairs, down the hall, and into her bedroom. *They will pay themselves better instead,* the girls said as they heard her heavy body settle hard into the bed above.

AT NIGHT THE SKY LEAVES SPACE
AROUND THE MOON

ALL THE LAFAYETTE WOMEN FELT THEMSELVES TREMENDOUSLY
alone. They had each other, but even together the three of them
always felt insufficient—felt themselves to be insufficient, and felt
an insufficiency in one another.

Every so often one of them would reach out into the void that
surrounded her as if the blood coursing through the body was
suddenly without surrounding veins, and didn't precisely remember
the veins but missed them nonetheless, and felt that veins should
be there. An internal bleeding, filling the unseen cavities with red.

Every so often over their eighteen years together—and less so as the
years progressed— one of the women would reach out and there
would be the shock of a thin, chill hand clasping back, but most
often there was nothing, an empty clasping at nothing. One of the
others, gone to for reassurance, would be too busy putting up pickled
melon, or stripping stains from the floorboards, or repairing some
hole in the siding, or it would be just before bedtime and the woman
in need would suddenly seem selfish—or worst of all weak—in her
need for consolation.

The timing was always off.

The women were not unkind to each other—their tracks just didn't
join anywhere along the line. The best to be hoped for was to catch
a glimpse of one another from a fleeting window, passing by.

♥

The existence of their family felt precarious. Anyone could leave at any time. Somewhere along the years, their rock had become all cleft, and they could fall through—all of them, or just one.

Just one, falling through to the void all alone…

❦

THIS WAS THE TROUBLE ABOUT THEM. AT BREAKFAST IT WAS ALMOST a surprise for each to see the other two gathered in the kitchen, and when all three were there at dinner it was a surprise again.

Their togetherness seemed accidental and temporary.

Anyone could leave at any time.

There was no tension to their surface—if the milk of them spilled it could run on forever without pooling, it could simply turn into a viscous smear and vaporize.

❦

THE GRIEF IN THE HOUSE WAS NOT ARTICULATED, BUT IT WAS ancient, it was larger and longer and bigger than the women, it went back to ripped apart continents, to the center of the earth, it fed on magma of loss, its lava the only trace of injustice in the void, every inch a measurement of grief, felt in the morning upon rising or in the evening as the light changed from thick to thin and a part of them, unconscious, wondered, each to herself, unspoken and incoherent—did the world contain this pain for all people? *Is it just us? Or is it everyone?* The inchoate question couldn't be answered, but it seemed to matter terribly just for that instant. If everyone was starving—every soul on earth—then there was at least some solace in the companionship. But if it was just the three of them—as they grew to sense—three forgotten and inept souls, beyond the reaches of navigation, abandoned by patriarch, in the world and yet pariah—then there was a new grief to be added to their sorrow and confusion, and then they had been cheated somehow—either by themselves, or by the bitter blood of their family, or by the hardness and impassivity of their fellow beings.

Take one stick and you can break it, the old dying people would say, as they died alone. *Bind many sticks together and they cannot be broken. That is family.* Sweet Marie and Whitey heard these words in wonderment. *Family.* As if it was some entity, some marvelous source of strength. *Cannot be broken.* If such twine existed to bind the women's sticks together, the twins would knit it until their hands bled from working it. But they hadn't found it. Not even when they were young, and less and less with each year that passed: any one of them could fall to hell itself without another passing down a rope, nor shedding tears to watch the rope catch fire and burn.

Each of the women had something to which they could attribute the void of grief and opacity of self, but it was never love. Love was something that, in a moment of conscious confession, none of them would recognize enough to see she knew it lacking. Or be able to define. It had been gone so long—if it ever truly had existed for any of them—they didn't know enough to feel that it was what they missed. For their heads were protected by a good strong roof, and there was always ample food, and the needs of the patients always seemed to fill some sort of void. Whitey had her liaisons with local lovers, caught here and there when she needed a bit of touch. And Sweet Marie gradually weaned herself from any need entirely, for anything: New Year's Eve would pass and she would occasionally realize she had little or no recollection of what events had transpired for her, and she didn't care—one day, perhaps, there would be something to remember. And Maw was entangled in a thicket of fears and beliefs so knotted that her attentions were single-minded: her single-minded sense of survival, anger and betrayal, bereavement and isolation were of such constancy they had grown unnoticed as breathing.

Had it always been like that? Should it be?

Each woman poured herself another teacup of bourbon and the question was quickly submerged in the brown waters. And perhaps as the porcelain cups slowly cracked and stained, each day too imperceptible to notice, perhaps resentment lingered and grew: should there not be laughter and golden lamplight and full heads of wild curls gleaming, bouncing, as they raced up and down the stairs to tell one another the news of this or that? Yes, there should be a thick, sweet skein of love and adoration that could not be cut by petty arguments - who had broken the handle of the good broom, who had spilt coffee down the front of the sofa and not confessed, who was petty or vindictive when she was tired. They had more than enough to go around.

Yes, they thought, yes, it should all be like that. That is the way we believe it should be. The way it is for all others but us.

They were wary to discuss why it was not this way. To name the man and the mystery behind his absence.

Shouldn't a house of mothers and daughters feel full? Why must a man be necessary?

But they were as wary of this question as they were wary to leave the house or let go of one another, even though when they felt the cool limpid touch of each other—or of the walls of the hideous old house—it was like touching the unfeeling crepe of a corpse. A form from which something solid and happy had, taking precautions, departed. As the patients died and their bodies were carried swaying out the door, such was the sense of constant suspension—of questions, of answers, of truths. Anything suspended they hung on Lafayette whether they realized it or not. For all three of them, Lafayette was the point upon which they hung the bath towels, their nightgowns, the rakes and shovels, their wet stockings, their blood-soaked bandages... Anything that was waiting, hovering, delayed indefinitely, unresolved was Lafayette.

For Maw and Whitey, there were often daydreams. Lafayette himself had returned! And all at once, they discovered how and why it was his absence that had done it to them, and how it was his return—likely or not—that had undone it. They could not leave the house, not now. After they had waited this long not to see the end of it—so much invested to just walk away—to give up on a resolution—any resolution—felt impossible. The last, most unendurable defeat. And so they waited, and they watched, each of them in secret.

It was as though the miasma inside the house was a living being that held the women firmly to the fearful face of waiting, up in the white hospice on the hill. And this miasma kept them evenly spaced from one another, at a great distance, with nebulous fog that hid their souls from themselves and from each other.

♥

THEY NEVER SPOKE OF HIM. NOT ONE OF THEM, NOT ONCE OVER all the years.

The twins never once asked *what was he like, how did his voice sound, what was the color of his hair*. They knew better, or they knew it somehow already—they added up what parts of themselves were unreflective of their mother, and attributed it to him. Lafayette had held their joyous innocence, and taken it with him.

He had held the music, and the summer nights beneath the stars, and wild curls stirred by wind. He had been the one who read poetry secretly at church.

He had allowed butter to drip down his chin when eating corn, and he had white flashing grins suitable for every occasion.

He had cuddled infants and had been the champion of ridiculous birthdays. Lafayette had been the one to light up the house for Christmas with candles and tin votives and a thousand smells and guests.

It was he who sat on the porch, or in the barn, or on an old chair in the yard listening to every heartbreak and triumph. He had been a sentimental old fool, that Lafayette. He had given sweetwater goodnight kisses on their foreheads right as the first snowflakes of winter were falling.

He was buttermilk, rich and golden and salted strong.

He had taken laughter and burnished it into a swinging orb and run through the house with it like a censor, letting it drift into every highest corner, seep into every crack, wind its way up the stairs and into the attic.

That was Lafayette—they didn't need to ask any questions.

♥

IT IS DIFFICULT TO DESCRIBE AN ABSENCE. FOR BY ITS VERY NATURE it is something not there. A something nonetheless—a quality or presence lingers somewhere distant but it's out of reach, forbidden, banned.

Things are so often known by their contents: a kitchen for its labors and equipment; a baby by its smell and sounds and need.

By what is a nothing known?

An unfilled hollow in a crib, perhaps.

A kitchen stripped of food and scent.

PART TWO:
THE RIGHT ATRIUM

PLACING PINS WHERE
THE COMPASS POINTS

FOR A LONG WHILE, SKINNY JONES LAY AWAKE NIGHTS CHARTING out his entire past before him on the bedspread and placing pins in it worriedly, without being able to make much good sense of any of the routes he had taken, how he had gotten to this point or to that, and where he would proceed from the unfamiliar place where he now found himself paused. Although Jones deliberated about all the possible itineraries he might take, in the very beginning he also deliberated about whether he wanted to continue at all.

Skinny Jones locked up the Black Pirate during these months, and then he unlocked it after he had found his answer. He resumed business with his few customers, answering none of their questions. He had thought he would need only one or two drunken, misspent days to destroy his love for Whitey. And not even that one day, but rather just a few hours locked alone with his heart would be sufficient. Instead, that day dragged into months of long, slow weeks where instead of killing his feelings for her he only seemed to feed them. And eventually he accepted his prognosis. He had waited long enough in life in solitude, made enough errors and missteps, and now at the age of thirty he would proceed without caution and with full courage into the terrifying architecture of the heart.

It might have troubled him to know that while he was building the rooms their love would inhabit, Whitey had not even begun to address her problematic conceptualization of the nature and existence of love itself. But even had he known that, perhaps Jones would still have opened the Black Pirate after a sojourn into contemplation and gone about making himself the man he wanted her to love.

❦

Skinny Jones had been born to indeterminate parents of indeterminate heritage or history. They had either died or left him— either way, he was alone at an age before memory. He was raised in more houses than he could count. The houses came with people inside them, as though each of his home environments was part of a series of dollhouses purchased at a shop.

There was a clapboard house painted green, where the winters left snow on the roof so thick it took several months of sun to discover the roof again. The green house had contained eight people—all blond, with green eyes that matched the house. He was the one who did not match with his black hair and skin so copper in the summer. They spoke quietly, and the ones not called Mother and Father were all called Brother or Sister. Jones had been placed with them through their church. He labored.

After a year had passed, the green house people were replaced by the brick house people, whose numbers were as difficult to count as their names were impossible for Jones to set in his mind. Their ages varied with their sleeping places: cradles, drawers, sofas, beds, graves. He had fit inside them as undelineated as a mote of summer dust. He was fed, he was clothed, his hair was never cut yet he went to school with whichever children were in the house and at the end of the day a sleeping place was found for him amidst the many.

There was the house that looked like a barn. The house of whitened sod and fists.

The house of ableached stone.

The boarding house, infested with an angry red grit that burned.

❦

AT SOME POINT, RELATIONS—OR PURPORTED RELATIONS—WERE located for him and he lived in the colorless wooden house in a region of the country where the earth was very flat and the nights were dismally silent of any comforting kind of calling thing and the people spoke little, as though influenced by the silence around them. On the train journey to this flat place he was hoping to finally call home, the boy imagined a door opening to reveal people inside who didn't seem to have emanated from misery but who rather were live impassioned beings with his same long determined spider's arms, dangling in wait, and his large hands, his same flat pelvis and scarecrow legs, his high thin neck and agitated eyes.

He felt at his own already-tall form in the train. His ears: small and flat. His nose large and straight. His feet bumped along on the floor, tapping. His people would have big broad feet like his, and toes that seemed more like thumbs. Shoulder blades like his—scythes, sharp, to bring in a harvest of belonging. Wide chests, with collar bones to support in all dimensions. But when the door finally opened, the wooden house harbored no more vision of kin than any of the others. Just people who once upon a time had had a place, and then had survived that place, only to be taken from it, the land left profaned and propertized. These kin were not kin. They were of his people, perhaps, once upon a time, but they were not kin. And after it came six or seven more attempts to bind him to those to whom he did not feel bound. But by that point, Skinny Jones was nearly a young man and had long stopped experiencing any excitement about families or belonging or what pleasurable surprises might lie inside.

❡

HIS MEMORIES OF THOSE YEARS, BESIDES THE HOUSES, WERE THAT he did not particularly exist yet, although someday he might. The women in the many houses fed him and fed him, but if they noticed they despaired for he grew no fatter. He disposed of their food in hidden places. When they weren't looking, plates of sweet potatoes were placed in pigsties. Perhaps he ate them. But there were, perhaps, pigs inside him that gobbled up the goodness. Buttered beans tossed past him, losing themselves in a golden-green arc into a meadow. Cabbage soup poured through him carefully between the cracks in the cellar floor. When they took to starching him, he balled up the bread in small pellets and sent it, gluey, down the sink of himself, where it stuck, and provided none of the nutrition he needed.

❤

HE RAN ACROSS OTHERS OF HIS KIND FROM TIME TO TIME, STRANGE children in strange situations, and he watched them become new people, reinvent a successful identity at this place or in that. Some died. Some took to drink. Some married and achieved a patina of truth that wore to blisters at the hidden places. But he knew or wanted nothing of their slight of hand tricks. He would be skinny, and slip through the world undetected. He would pass like air through the hands of love. When he was ready, when the time was right, when he was grown he would emerge from the darkness and be found. And she would find him there to hold.

For during this time there was always a she, a her, there for him. She dwelt in his head in a place no living female took it upon herself to occupy. And he looked down at his slight and ghostly form and didn't try to move himself in any girl's direction. Skinny Jones looked in on love from out in the street. He felt himself nearing the structure but would still himself before mounting the stairs. Many nights in many towns he watched from outside as first little girls and then young girls and then young women and then women nested inside their homes.

He grew with them, but separately.

At a great distance from them.

❤

HE WAS LONG, FULL OF LONGING, THE ROAD WAS LONG THAT led to them, everything stretched out taut as a plumb string, and he wanted to snap it and leave a trail of blue across the world that would lead her right to him.

❤

Was he different from other boys? They groped and felt at the thighs of their love or lust in barns and fields, behind walls or trees. Skinny Jones watched that, too—how the other boys worked their hands, how the clothes were pulled at here and pushed at there and bodies were revealed in entirety or in part, how some of the boys made their girls happy but often made them cry. And how afterwards nearly all of the boys kicked at things in triumph or despair or ignorant animosity at the huge confusions of their worlds—Skinny Jones watched that too. Was he different from them? How would he touch the skin of the girl who had chosen him—would she be smart and kind, and happy with him? Fierce and pretty, and surprise him?—he didn't know. But he wanted to chose a field and there would be soft sun or else starlight and his face would be tangled in her milkweed hair and the silence of the hour would be filled with smothered kisses and laughter. He would marry. He would carry this girl across a gleaming wooden floor and set her feet down firmly on the strong smooth-hewn floor of their future together where dreams would creep and then crawl and then walk and eventually run across and out the door into the wild sweet arms of their future and Skinny Jones and his girl from the field would rock back and forth naked in their bed, in their chairs, in one another's arms until the end of their days.

❦

WAS HE LIKE OTHER BOYS?

❦

WHEN SKINNY JONES WAS A YOUNG MAN HE LEFT THE PROGRESSION of houses for a life without walls. He slept with his work—he found labor along the southern train routes, fixing track, hauling cargo, filling crates, riding lines, whatever work needed to be done. He was all bone, but unbreakable, and he traveled from ocean to ocean and back, the peaks of glaciers in his view one month, swamplands the next. He learned bits of French, and Spanish, and Italian. He owned so little it would be considered nothing, and when he lost anything another thousand already existed in the world and could be easily acquired for what he already had in his pocket. His dark skin further darkened from the sun, and his entrenched silence deepened, and his reputation as a good and hard worker largely sufficed for the words he didn't care to express.

Whenever the trains pulled Jones through the eastern parts of Texas, he admired the deception of flat land that often contained subtle mounds, sensual forms that revealed themselves only when the light came down at side angles. The women of Texas were alluring—confident and loud, full-bodied and rich with life, noses always a little sun-scorched, muscular asses that rose high from walking broad-paced and heel-first.

Even in the graywanness of winter it seemed like summer, how the live oaks remained green and the diffuse light was only moments away from breaking into bands of warmth across his arms.

When he was introduced to Marisol, she introduced herself right back to him, *so happy to meet you,* looked into his guarded eyes and peeled them back, wide opened. She laughed into his face. She took his hand. Her awestruck captive, she led him into the sweat- soaked dances; her damp, dense body didn't so much fit with his as impact it.

Their lovemaking was quick and large, for she took him in fast and he turned himself this way and that and thrust about inside her without ever finding the end of her. It was her first time, and over before he realized it had entirely begun, but when he landed on his back afterwards and they lay there sweating together in the still dark air, he felt strands of her hair strung across his nose and mouth and when he tasted them he knew them to be salty and sweet at the same time. He chewed at them silently, wishing her to sleep and not notice, and his wish came true, and he spent the night awake next to her, smelling her, tasting her hair, and watching the moonlight rotate in a bright joyous path around the bedroom. He was inside, he was inside, oh yes, he was inside it *all...*

He left her many times to carry the trains across the earth and each time returned to her. While he was gone he sent news, his love, plans; he told her about new secrets of his body and mind he never failed to discover and relate. He wanted her to be magnificent and tremendously mysterious and powerful with him, and for them, together, to finally carry something he couldn't have replaced.

♥

MANY YEARS LATER HE WOKE IN A BED FILLED WITH LIQUOR bottles and he was twenty-six and his gut was sick with roiling bile, ash and dust, narcotic seepage, and his skin was rancid, each pore an exploded universe, and he didn't care. Money came to him from unknown places—in the morning he was broke and in the evenings there was something there he could use to eat or sleep or forget, and he trusted it would be so. There was some mercy in the world for drifting—the winds took seeds and deposited them where they would, and the same held true for humans. And Skinny Jones was a wisp upon the wind and let it do with him what it wanted, and he told himself whatever the wind wanted for him, he would accept as his own will. Had Marisol been right, or had she been wrong? She had lost interest in his dreams, or she had slept with another: a mechanic, a grocer, a preacher, none of them, all of them, she had scorned his innermost secrets, something had been done and then couldn't be undone and then everything had been broken. She had dismissed him from her with accusations of this or that, an apology, some explanation—perhaps. Maybe not. It was all a blur. She had used him. She had not loved him. He had taken his thumb and smudged and rubbed and then used his fingernails to scratch and pick at the memory until nothing remained but the seeping fact that once a long time ago he had gone out of Texas a love- starved boy and later wandered back into Texas in a haze of heartbroken disarray.

He had first gone looking for the green house, the gray house, the house of stone and the one of brick, and found nothing. Searched for even their ruins and again, nothing. But he found the people who had once inhabited them—they were everywhere. The doll people, with their sightless eyes and their jointless polished limbs and cold, clubbed hands and wooden heads—they were all around him. While he had been laboring under the illusion of happiness with her, cardboard boxes from shop windows had broken open all over everywhere and these matched people who were nothing like him had once again overtaken his world and convinced him, for a moment, that he was of them too.

But now he knew himself alone, with a new finality. He had always been alone but had held out hope, before, held out some vague inarticulate and buried belief that there would be an earthly reward for his boyhood loneliness—that *she* was somewhere and she would find him. But now he returned to his drift, and he abandoned his maps, for he knew that not being alone had been an illusion, and at night when he was drunk and had fallen into a liquid heap in a place no one would notice him he felt at himself as he had when he had been a boy and discovered those same small warm ears and long desperate arms and painfully tall legs that had taken him across the continent and he curled his feet beneath him and knew he would wake again soon enough and untangle himself into the afternoon and go about the business of moving his lonely quiet body through this world.

❦

AND THEN ONE DAY, TIME AS HE HAD KNOWN IT SIMPLY STOOD still for Jones, and then dropped away from sight. The new kind of time was warm and quiet and with a kind of furious turmoil, and all the leaves rustled in his life. He was in Lynchburg when that happened. The wind that had propelled him, rootless and seeded, stopped carrying his hollow weight and dropped him up against the pale eyes of the strange wild woman of Lynchburg.

The air was hot and thick, and the wind that had always blows him all across the map of the continent now blew through him instead, and seemed to clean him out.

Skinny Jones leaned against the counter of the Black Pirate for a moment, gathering his strength, before he opened its doors, and sat in the tall wooden chair behind the desk, and waited for everything to start.

HOOKS AND EYES
FOR EDGES THAT MEET

It begins with tenderness and curiosity, a touch of idolatry. There is the desire to please and to be pleased. Hearts beat in unison by instinct. All goes well and is in concert.

And then the much becomes too much. Sweet Marie looks at the doctor across the room and cannot be moved by him. His small hands darting around the edges of his plate. The night before, he worked late at the county hospital—she had wanted to cry she'd needed him so much. And then she had wanted to push his head beneath the water and hold it there, for a time, until it was all over.

Sweet Marie had gone to work at the hospital. It was her one effort to bring herself out of the old white house with her mother and sister—to join society, to be part of the accepted—the only true effort she had ever made at anything constituting change, improvement. Her one charge against passivity. She had seen her life laid before her, long and prone: childbed, deathbed all in that house, all behind the same windows, the same doors opening and shutting against her with their dull inevitability, her face acquiring a faint powder of plaster dust as she walked on between its walls, shut in on all sides.

Then the newspaper had listed an advertisement for the new Nurses' College, and the door had opened a crack.

She had gotten in on a scholarship and bought her first medical books—the pages were thick and dense, with small type and etchings to illustrate the physical orders and disorders she'd seen since she was a child—but they had a dignity now, reposed against the printed page, named and numbered. She could escape to books and new teaching, to this talent of hers—a real nurse, modern, with a paper hanging on the wall when she was done—she would frame it, put it behind glass, watch the gold seal shine in the sunlight, the signatures of patriarchs in thick ink—and her knowledge would be better and newer than that of her sister and mother.

She washed her hair more regularly, and put pins in it. If her hair wasn't clean, it would leave a residue of gray inside the white edges of her cap. She found that distasteful.

Disinfectant was her new perfume of choice.

Astringents. Solvents. Antiseptics. Antibiotics.

A host of exciting liquids to poison the dirtied and diseased.

She liked to sit in the classroom with the other silent women in starched clothes and smart shoes, feet pressed firmly, quietly, against the linoleum floor, sharpened pencils with a ruler next to them for underlining critical passages in the appropriate medical text. She did it neatly. If the line she drew was crooked, she would erase it carefully and begin again. The books were holy things to her—had she an ark she would have kept them there. How to fix a bone properly, so that it hadn't the hard bulge around it her mother's set might have.

She learned the same things again she already knew, but this knowledge she respected more. It was official. It came to her in Latin words and Greek; she ministered at the hands of men instead of mother.

The order of it all pleased her. She aligned her books one on top of the other in a progression from large to smaller, set them at sharp right angles to the corner of her desk. Leaving the classroom, she would touch the blackboard surreptitiously, and walking down the hallway admire the sleek white pearl of chalk smooth as talcum between her fingertips. The marble path of learning. It was burnished, Greek, it had passed through the ancient hands of learned men: it was far superior.

♥

IN SWEET MARIE'S FIRST CLASS, DOCTOR WILLIAMS HAD WALKED into the classroom of women and she admired his air of focused erudition. He did not nod or make eye contact, there was no *How you ladies doing?* or comments upon the weather. He was an esteemed and elite surgeon. He flipped through charts. He pointed, he illustrated, he chanted through the body's systems like a priest. Sweet Marie longed for his mind—she wanted to run her fingers over its whorls. Dr. Williams was nothing she had ever known. He was not a man, not like the ones she'd known. He was a being above contempt, carved from a block of the cleanest white marble, chiseled with cold crisp water and polished to an immaculate purity, as satisfying to her eye as a clean china cup or a white enamel basin freshly washed.

♥

HER FIRST DAYS AT THE COLLEGE PASSED IN THIS CRISP PROGRESSION of well-organized pathways, clearly marked. The schedules had her days laid out in disciplined systems of order: new skills, new services, new knowledge. She forgot about her prior listless days of crying, the torpor of nightmares that had tormented her before she had clawed this new opening. She took furtive pride in her accomplishment at flinging open her life—fresh air flowing into her lungs through doors and windows she herself had pushed and strained to edge wide.

Alone at night, when she recalled her days before the college, she rolled over in her bed and faced the faded pink wall of her room and dug her fingernails angrily into her palms. She hated herself, and how weak and hopeless she was. She willed herself to stop thinking about it all—when she looked back on her former self she felt a rising tide of nausea that nearly made her run to the bowl to vomit from the secret animosities towards Lafayette—dissipated perpetrator as father—towards Whitey—outrageous and unkempt twin—and the angry dark goddess her mother with the black iron keys and whiff of old spilt blood.

From a candle-lit place she had entered a bright sunlit place and she would never return. She would never return, though she still slept nights at the white house, her spirit had risen up from the shameful dregs entirely and she felt she slept on a clean cloud of snow overtop the horror of it all.

♥

IN THE SPRING DOCTOR WILLIAMS WAS HER TEACHER AGAIN. HE stood in front of her throughout the lessons and she studied him as carefully as any other subject, his hair was the color of beeswax, and cleaved in a clean slice always four inches above his left ear and an equal four inches above his right. Each morning closely shaven, and each afternoon closely shaven. Teeth white, eyeballs white, fingernails neatly trimmed and buffed as alabaster. The creases of his pants and the break in his cuffs lining up in utter precision with the pointed tips of his shoes. Fresh stiff collar. His back never touched the chair, she imagined, for there were never wrinkles in his linens. Or did he know something about how proper people sat that she did not know, and could not even properly imagine? He wore his clothes in a way that made one forget his body, or that he had a body, refined, noble-garbed. He did not smoke. He did not drink—if he did, she couldn't smell it on him. Not like she could her father, if she'd had a father.

She did not see him smile, but she imagined he had more important emotions because the lines were there faint upon his face—dignity. He was professionalism. Power. Authority.

This is how it is done by the important people of the world, she thought. *This is how I shall do it.*

At night she has a recurring dream. In the classroom, Dr. Williams has chosen her the brightest among the pupils. His back to the blackboard, he calls her name to come forward. She can tell he admires her white stockings, notices how she has learned the mysteries of starch and pleat and crease. He draws the attention of the other women to her fingernails. To the order of her brows and lashes, the bright even spacing of the hairpins along her white cap. His eyes glisten their approval, and his words speak of the superiority of her intellect, her attention to his lectures, her assiduousness at the assignments, the thoroughness of her dedication to standards of hygiene. He hands her a scalpel. *Demonstrate your knowledge to these women*, he says, and motions her to climb atop his desk. *Kneel*, he says, *open my brain and show them what I have taught you.* She cuts into his skull along the pale pink line of his part. Carefully, as only she knows how, she neatly splits his skull in half and reveals not the wet granite ridges the women had expected but instead row upon row of shining silver cabinetry and shelving, held within it knowledge glittering in rows, ingots of gold and bronze. The heat and light issuing from within his head is unimaginable. The other women avert their eyes. *Come in*, he says to her alone, and Sweet Marie steps into the cavernous library of his cranium. *Everything you need is in here*, she hears, *everything you will ever need.* And Dr. Williams reaches up with his own hands and closes the halves of his skull together and, with her inside, threads suture through the needle and effortlessly sews himself closed around her.

❦

IN APRIL SWEET MARIE ASSISTED THE DOCTOR IN HER FIRST SURGERY. She attended him. He was frowning all the while, then when it was done he threw the implements on the tray and ripped himself from her assistance. She could hear his soft soles padding angry down the hallway. A door slammed. She did not know what to think.

The next morning his note summoned her to his office. Eyes focused on his feet she listened. *Concern* she heard him say *proper focus* and *unbecoming* and *I'm afraid I simply have to question your* and then *unacceptable ignorance of basic* and *see some improvement* and she felt herself choking off again. Hadn't she tried? Wasn't she among the best—hadn't these tasks been her own excellence, in her mother's house, since she was old enough to thread suture? *No.* No, she was wrong. She had been wrong. She and it was all wrong. *And what is this shabby...garment...you're wearing. And your...hair.* His face twisted in disgust as he pondered the halo of frizz and kink surrounding her face.

She tried to will the winged thing insider her, command it to fly herself high up in the corners of his office, on the top of his highest bookcase and close her wings around her eyes, the things that had always worked for her. Wrong. *Your absurd and ignorant attempt at—*

Fly up to the corner and let the anger wash below her, swirl in nasty eddies far below. But he reached up and grabbed her fleeing wings and pulled her down again. *Important,* he said, *if you want to continue in your studies here,* he said, *too many unforgivable mistakes—*Sweet Marie's feet dropping through the linoleum, sinking, sinking—*you will be severely reprimanded—*her smart shoes now stupid.

There were now spider webs she could see behind the door. Coffee stains on the Doctor's desk. Ugly hairs sprouting from her forearms—they disgusted her. She disgusted herself. Dust on the window ledge that cushioned dead black mayflies: one, two, three of them. Four. Five. One on the floor. Six. It was all of it wrong.

The doctor leveled his pen along his paperwork.

Listen very carefully, he said. He snapped his fingers at her.

Listen. You will have to put your trust in me and do exactly as you are told, he said. She would not walk inside his cranium. Not ever. This was the doctor, closing her precious door.

You must not waste time. You must let everything go but what I tell you, he was sewing himself closed with her on the outside, *if you are serious about your success here. We are already making exceptions for you.* She heard a slamming sound, a crush upon her bones.

You will assist me, and me only. She would be at his command. If he spoke it, it would be so. *If you drop an implement, you will be gone.* Gone.

If you move too slowly, the death of a patient will be on your shoulders. Shoulders. Shudders. Doors open to her then closed. Closed to her then open.

I will not waste my time with an idiot. You will do as I tell you to, and do it well, and one day I may determine you to be a nurse. Do you understand?

Yes.

Yes. Sweet Marie hunkered in her chair. The chair was too painful but she sat up in it and cast her eyes down upon the floor. *Yes.* She had never dropped an implement—she would not do so now. His face carved from a Hippocratic stone. She would not move too slowly. Her face carved in fear and stupidity. It was meet and right, what he said. He would provide for her, the discipline, his disciple, his student and daughter, she would read his book and re-read his book and when she was done anyone would see—she would be as a page torn from his great book of medicine and wonder.

Yes. I will brace my very soul against this door to keep it from closing upon me.

Do you understand.

Yes.

Do you understand.

Yes.

❦

THE TIME PASSED WITH HIM—BEDPANS FULL OF VOMIT AND feces and wound waste, and he would watch her. *Clean it again.* A pus-soaked bandage thrown at her. *Bind it properly.* A hand on her breast—where it didn't belong—his. Then, a reward, a commendation for good service.

Into the classroom again came spring. Tender, the light a new urine-green the color of stripped pinewood. The light came straight down—sharp as scalpels, cutting pinks and reds into pale skins newly uncovered. The air frothed with pollen, everything swollen for more months that it would seem possible. Dr. Williams chastised her in his office a second time. She cried. He sat her at his feet and placed his hand, heavy and forgiving, on her nappy head. Because she is special to him. Because she has something the other women do not and he will strengthen it in her. Because of the warm dark line of her breasts that lead down into her new uniform—because of that he cannot concentrate. He will examine her to make certain all is well. In warming months the pods of all seeds burst. The night brings open windows. The day brings closed shutters. Behind two of them Dr. Williams lays her on his desk and parts her legs, thrusts himself into her, a terrible ripping of flesh.

Do you understand, he says.

Yes.

That will be all, he says.

Thank you.

♥

AFTER THAT CAME HIS TENDERNESS, A TIME FOR SWEET QUIET. A strong softer summer hand, warmer than the angry bones of winter or the violent skin of spring. His mother dying, he took her into his house as nurse. Now she was his, above reproach. No one questions a doctor.

Sweet Marie was there in body but she was also gone—removed from the hospice with Whitey and Maw, and removed from hospital and school with classmates and patients and libraries, she found herself with only her wings, and they were fixed within this new place where some days her knowledge was greater than her strength, and other days her strength greater than her knowledge. Neither served her properly.

Her brain bowed under the imbalance.

She sagged, succumbed.

The precise and shifting weight of him atop her. That uncertain pain between her legs.

A love brings loss. This she had learned in girlhood. This her unwanted lover, this her unwanted loss. *You can return to classes in the fall,* he said. Top of her class, she had been top of her class. Once. She was to tend his mother all day and then wait for his arrival in the evening.

She understood everything was always to be tidy. Her heart tidy, her brain tidy. Her hair tidy. Her housework tidy. Her eyes tidy, and her heart, although ideally she should keep it stilled at all times. Her lips tidy. Her tongue. Her teeth. She wasn't frightened of the discipline. It was love. This would be love. There are always consequences. This god among men, this doctor—before, she loved him. A distant being. A god. Jesus the rape of Mary? She is not to say. She is not to say what the shutters saw. Keep them shut. Batten them down. Let no one be the wiser.

But there is difficulty with the seal of it—the heat of love flows in but if by some betrayal the vessel is too cold, the glass cracks. Fissures form. The passion pours out, water everywhere.

❦

THEY CALL ME *Sweet* BECAUSE I AM QUIET AND BECAUSE OF MY delicacy of body. *So pretty.* I smile when I am smiled at. *Sweet* because I don't impose. Skin so golden he says I am made of bottle-glass. I have found no pleasures in myself yet, but he does. *Yes,* he says, *you certainly are sweet.*

I have done my tasks. I have ordered his life. I press his pants, I wash his mother, I serve him his dinner, I open my legs.

The knowledge taught me, I cannot use. The knowledge I need, I do not have.

I like to be the only one to know that none of this is right.

❦

THE DOCTOR IS HAPPY NOW, HIS HEART FILLED WITH TENDER caring for Sweet Marie. He feels a quiet ease around her, in his house—he speaks when he wishes, remains silent when he feels it. His touch is always welcome to her. She has gratitude for his attentions. For his exceptions, made only for her, and for his graces in improving her. He can raise his voice at her and she obeys. Her body ever at his access, and she acquiesces. She is made for bruises. He studies them, developing on her skin from the first dusk of rose to the last shimmer of green and golden mist. Her voice low and soft. No tears. She doesn't need a constant reassurance of his love or an underlining of his anger: she cleaves to him, he need not show any larger rationale to her. He comes and goes as he pleases—his actions unquestioned. His house a palace of sweet freedom for him.

❦

SWEET MARIE WAITS FOR THE AUTUMN TO START, WHEN SHE can return to the college, and then in winter, surrendered to imprisonment, she simply waits. Waits slowly for the last of her love for him to bloom into a complexity of emotion that only the winged thing inside her knows so well how to grow. She feels it inside her as sure as she feels her lungs and stomach. It is an extra organ, her hate, left off the doctor's charts of systems.

She knows how to hate him, for she has studied him. Each thing that holds the most meaning for him, she will despise. His neatness now contemptible. His knowledge of medicine a cold cruel science. His power now repellant. His authorities unearned. She buries his pills and tinctures and nurses his mother with herbs she steals from Whitey—his despised witches' cures. She wills the mother to heal, or to fail. Should she kill the woman for being the mother of a monster, or heal her to prove his medicine a lie?

❦

SOME DAYS SWEET MARIE LIKES TO PRETEND SHE DOESN'T HATE
him. She goes out of her way to please him more, nursing her
disdain in secret, because that is more cruel, more powerful. She
wants to obey his wishes because it's pathetic that he knows her
so little as to not imagine the black fetid moss growing higher and
higher in the well of her disdain. His breath smells like the muck
of a sty. It makes her smile inside.

And some days there is a perverse shielding of him: her respect
for the man worn so bare that she thinks of him now like a child
missing half its brain so that it cannot comprehend the simplest
of instructions and thus can hardly be held accountable.

Her power is that she shelters him from her truths.

What a beautiful day, he says.

Yes, she lies.

*I am so pleased with the care you give mother. I know it means so
much to her to have a good girl in the house for once.*

She passes him the corn.

Thank you for saying so, she lies, *it gives me such pleasure.*

❦

A RELATIONSHIP BASED UPON DISHONESTY. SHE DOES NOT TELL
him of what grows inside her. She begins the tending of her many
secrets. A thousand tiny untruths told each day simply by the willful
omission of detail, of pertinent fact. What did you get at the store?
Nothing. Do not mention the seeds for the herb garden. Do not
mention the coltsfoot. The forbidden kitten I have hidden in the
kitchen where you never go and will not discover it.

The secrets themselves are unimportant—they are kept because it is something to hide, and she believes her power is in the hiding of them. She has some territory of her own.

He has access to her body, she holds tightly to her brain.

Look what I know and you do not. Look how little you know me. I have things here that you will never find, not ever, and if you wanted to hurt me you could not. What he loves is only a woman-shaped shell of lies and simulations.

She tells of her secrets without telling. She is too quiet, too reclusive, he cannot read the signs.

She comforts herself with the familiarity of her unhappiness.

❦

ALWAYS, THE CRINGE IS THERE, TRAPPED IN THE FIBERS OF HER neck flesh. How he kissed her there and she recoiled, saying that it tickled, and not that she wanted to get out of bed, walk through the door, through the next room and its door, out the house and down the lane and wash his touch off her skin with a mortician's vigor.

❦

NOW IN THE MORNINGS WHEN HE LEAVES, SHE CONSIDERS HIM lucky. She waves him off to work with a loving smile. She would like to throw things at him—hard breakable sharp things, like teapots or vases—or butcher knives or hatchets. Boiling oil. Fill him with flypaper tea.

Now that she has lain with him for so many months since he first took her, and now that her mouth has been on his cock night after night, she wants to see him drip with blood.

It is not good for her, she imagines, this secret hating. The lichen of the body— this crust spreading through her body, hardening and flaking, cracking, peeling. Parasitic. Not a scab, protecting a hurt, healing it, but a leprous burn. An active rot that leaves dead ash of flesh in its wake. A sumpish, crusted, bog of dying tissue that spreads a bit more every day.

♥

This is her fantasy: a lover who wants to know her entirely. It is a warm evening, and they are happy together. We have eaten a good meal, our stomachs are full. There is some wine, but not too much. I am told, *I want to know you. All of you. Every sentence of the stories you have to tell, every step you have taken that brings you here.* And I demur. There is not sufficient time beneath these skies for such pursuits. But my lover insists, and fingers my hair. My lover swallows some liquor slowly, and smiles as me. *I will tell you if you tell me. Yes,* my lover replies. Some people would say that's something that would only happen in the beginning of a love, when it seems necessary to seduction, not months or years or decades into one already consummated. But I want someone for whom curiosity is never too late. And so, honored by this interest, I begin to tell about myself. For the first time. And the hours pass and some things I tell quickly, and some slowly. When I speak of my father perhaps I cry, perhaps for the first time ever. And I speak of my hidden darkest things. And of things I worry will frighten my lover—they do—but we continue, for my lover has faith now and so do I. And the sun is rising and I have more to tell but there are other days and we both know this and this someone, this someone takes me off the sofa and pulls away the blanket and my clothes and lies between my legs and licks my warm darkness and my lover's full mouth is filled up with me and then rises up to kiss me, and fills my mouth with my own liquid. *This is how you taste,* my lover tells me. *This is who I love.*

THE BLUE AT THE BASE
OF THE FLAME

SOMETIMES SKINNY JONES COMES ACROSS THINGS ABANDONED here or there. He almost drove right past the old pig knuckle jugs, the ones where the hole is tall and narrow and just large enough to pop the knuckles through and pour in the pickling liquid before stopping it up with a piece of towel or cork. He was halfway home to the Black Pirate with them before the smell woke him to it, rot as thick and soft as hands around his hips squeezing him to slime. He flushed thirty-odd pickled rats out with a hose and long-handled fork before getting his five dollars each for the jugs.

Before he turned it into a junk shop, the Black Pirate used to be a bottle factory. Its rear plunges down into the river whose water they once used to cool the glass. Skinny Jones bought the crumbling place outright, traded it for twelve cracked and speckled diamond rings. He liked having exchanged diamonds for junk, for a pile of disintegrating clay and rust and rot and mildew, and for the pleasure of filling it with the vast ever-accumulating detritus of a society he feels no part of.

The top floor of the Black Pirate is where Skinny Jones lives. The third floor is for household goods–anything fragile and light and small and easy for him to carry up the three narrow flights of stairs. Things like cracked lamps and baby buggies and dressmakers' mannequins. It's where the women climb to, and he can watch their asses shift back and forth beneath their skirts as they ascend. Not that he cares. But they're there, and it's something. The hands go round the clock.

The second floor is where he puts books and magazines and all the things made out of paper. Old newspapers. Comic books. School books. It's the place he thinks most often of setting a match to, late at night, when the sparks would catch as sharp as firecrackers and the heat would separate each sheet of paper and lift them up glowing into the air.

The first floor is for big things, heavy things, and things that people might want to look at more than they would necessarily want to buy. Things that might only catch their attention enough to draw them through the door where he could watch them, spiderlike, from behind his counter. Rarities and freakish things, like the two old electric chairs Jones bought on the cheap when they fixed up Eastern State Pen.

And in the semi-secret basement of the junk store is the unmentionable, the frightening, the secrets, the hidden things. There is pornography, French cards, photographs, books, stories, carved and molded strangely chiseled things from Africa and India and the haunted parts of Europe. Dildos of leather-wrapped wood and stone. This too draws them in. For Jones, iIt's curious what people are willing to exchange for a commodity they desire.

❦

ALTHOUGH HE IS IN LYNCHBURG NOW, IT'S NEITHER A MEANINGFUL arrival nor a place he plans to stay. In each town he used to begin anew. Located his hope and fed it, forced the old tired blood from his veins and replaced it with the gentle hand of morphine, or poured liquor straight into the huge empty pockets of his heart—but somehow never with enough relief, just a variation in the timbre of his torment. But recently, Skinny Jones has flung himself into town after town, seeped into villages and poured out of them in liquid misery, gone running to or from a girl, a dream—shot himself down each lane and later crawled his way out bent over sticks and rocks and spitting phlegm. There in the abandoned factory Skinny Jones has finally fallen off the edges of his world—that explains the scars on the palms of his hands, the cigarette burns on his forearms, the absence of a foreskin, the way the soft hide of his testicles seems in danger of peeling or cracking and spilling out its contents all over his feet…Embers inside him that once burned red and sent him spinning fierce and furious through the world now seem to lie there grayashen and heavy and hard as kidney stones, a dreaded quickening that stops up all movement inside him and fills him up with a rancid vinegar.

And now he tells himself not to try, but it's hard—in a business such as his—for Skinny Jones not to secretly search for something, somewhere, buried deep and well-disguised amongst all the worthless trash, something tender, beautiful, and sentimental to cut through the sadness in his heart.

Jones is waiting for the wind to rip it all away, but the wind just blows through, and passes on leaving it all sadly intact.

And night burns brightly in the rich black oil of his soul.

❦

HE KEEPS HIMSELF OCCUPIED. HE HANGS A NOOSE FROM THE rafters and contemplates it longingly for hours, feeds rats in the crawlspace and keeps the cats out, then watches the cats sleep grinning in the sun. Looks for the lizards' loosed tails, spends the interminable afternoons cataloguing the length and texture of the black snake's sloughed-off skin, all the while looking for something he cannot name. He has smelled the thin flat air within the bones of birds. Sought answers while chopping cords of cherry poplar, seen how their flesh has grown tenderly around barbed wire.

None of it gives him any tranquility, and he's not sure what he would do with it were it there. Is peace just another form of sadness? What kind of soul is his?

And at other times he believes that every last thing is meant to be a mystery, and he is the spider at the center of the web, spinning unknowable things that string between the branches of trees, the corners of rooms and in between the petals of the daylillies.

❦

On this flat-hot summer day he watches the strange woman, Whitey, walk towards his store from the field in the folding light of late afternoon. His thick blue uncoils in a moment, wrangles itself into what has become an unfamiliar interest. In his brain is an incantation to the forces that despise him and array themselves against his happiness. *Let her be as I am,* say these forces, *let her be something to me.*

He has these hidden things inside him he doesn't want to think about and barely understands. He wishes he could spill himself. Into someone else. Into a toilet. A box. A crack in the floorboards. Somewhere where he would vanish from his own sight completely and eternally. He doesn't want to collect himself any longer. He knows he cannot rid himself of himself. Instead, he wants to combine himself into a large experiment in which everything broken becomes useful, and all the fragments coalesce into an unseen display of fire and light and heat. He wants to meld himself with another being and become greater - not so much whole, but rather magnificent. She has a face. Witch. He sees this woman walking towards his store. He could drop into her with the plaintive mew of a litter of baby squirrels dislodged from the rafters—he could fall—fall down freely unimpeded and crash open inside her.

He could simply stare down at the narrow hairlessness of the backs of her thighs bent below his shoulders, feel her heels tap against his spine, feel her breath on his neck.

He watches her long slow walk across the field and soon his semen stains the floor, and white roses spring up in his damp.

❦

When Whitey comes in and walks up to the counter, proud, asking for something from the downstairs section, Skinny Jones sits back on his haunches and lights a cigarette. He considers her from all angles and finds his lungs pressing wider in his ribs. His stomach heaving, thrashing beneath his skin.

He hates her for eliciting this response, in an instant he hates her, and hates her quiet witch's gaze from above his head. He will not sell anything to this woman. He will in no way serve her. He makes his face disdainful. He will not take her money or give her junk. He decides to treat her rudely. Pretend he didn't watch, with his irrepressible need, her slow walk across the meadow. He feels angry now. Skinny Jones scratches his back beneath his shirt and then examines what comes off underneath his fingernails, a waxen slate grime he rubs away between his fingertips, a seamy expansive gesture. He will treat her like someone she is not to him, he will be cold to her. Deny that his delicate wrists wanted to reach up high behind her butterfly back and wrap around her.

Jones pulls down a half-filled bottle of gin from the shelf above his head and his gesture releases an armpit full of dill weed and mulch, molasses and warm cedar trees, everything in his dark armpits acid and oily as crop dust. He sees her nostrils flare to take it in and senses the sweat of want breaking out on her flanks.

He has decided to forge smoldering words upon her and watch their burn sear across the fragility of her small face. He wants to distance himself, to give himself relief, to dislodge the weight of his pain and want, to hurry her along. He senses dangers everywhere with her. He could lose himself in this new woman. He could get lost and die.

I don't think I can make the time for this kind of business, he says, and rests his hand on the mound in his pants. He scratches himself, his eyes narrowed to slits. He lets his throat release a dull grunt, spreads his legs a bit and jerks his chin in the direction of the door.

And she begins to laugh. The sound of her is slow in bubbling up, wet and thick, with a dark bloated quality to it—a raucous lilting angry sound.

You need the name of a good whore to take care of that for you, she says, *or else take it to the butcher and get it removed if it bothers you so much.*

And suddenly he laughs, and she laughs, all he wants is just to talk with her, to ask her questions, to know her awkward and unexpected ways. To wrap her in his arms. To see how quick she is. To see if she can see him in his quickness. To surprise her with his kindness, give her a pink enamel heart on a tin chain. See the light in her eyes change from wild to won, responding to his gift. He wants to know her. And know how his skin would feel against her skin, and how the morning light caresses her ribs and shoulder blades.

Jones nods his head, a simple, quiet, downward motion. For now, surrender is all right. He asks Whitey *in or out*, and she shocks him when she chooses in. He wonders at her choice, surprised—is it because she knows? Because he knows. He knows now. What this thing is, between them, and about the pink enamel heart, and about the blood that has dried and crusted on his paws.

❤

ALONE INSIDE THE BLACK PIRATE, WHITEY AND SKINNY JONES sit side by side in the electric chairs, smoking, Whitey lost in uncharacteristic silence.

At their feet a stack of French pornographic cards pucker in the damp, weighed down on the counter by a rock, the girls on the cards shuddering in the breeze, all slicked up and sleepy, pulling at themselves and their transparent clothing. In Whitey's lap a similar book has fallen open on its spine. There are cigarette burns on the cracked red leather cover and a pressed gold image, a guitar-torsoed naked woman, her nipples floating in the guitar's wooden surface, one of her generous hands coming down to press the strings, her other hand poised above the large dark hole of the body. A long lean nose, lips rouged and curling into a scowling pout, eyes painted dark—closed and absent but the eyeballs flickering fast and rolling up behind the lids; a seven fingered man, stroking the strings with an unsettling condensation of intoxicated hate and peace.

Whitey asks Jones why he thinks the pictures are always of women, the naked photographs and naked paintings and drawings and prints. Why the naked girls dancing in halls and on stairs and sitting spread-legged in chairs. Why their slits exposed, the cracks of their asses wet with cum, why not men as well?

The low-slung snub of a fat white man, the nub tucked under a pendulous belly like a thumb, like a hard-rubbed clitoris, protruding only enough to make itself seen and no more. The long thin cock, bow-strung to the left, a pointed arrow, its swollen vein running straight down to form a ridge, then turning westward and running out at the head with the desperate clutch of a foreskin barely covering the small eye at the tip, puffy and thick, pink and clenched as a rosebud.

The pale slice of wet scar on a circumcized obsidian penis, halfway down the shaft.

The ones that are small and then huge.

The ones that are always small.

The enormous ones that don't change.

The defiant thick ones.

Jones says, *Because there is a lack of imagination. In all things.*

She asks him how, with cunts so familiar to the world, cocks are rarely undocumented and never just reduced to a commodity, each entire manhood remains to her unique and individual, seems to evoke a mood, an emotion, to convey a certain kind of feeling to its beholder, as distinct as the odor of a particular house or the expression on a face. The common ones: dignity, eagerness, the soldierly self-satisfaction of an officer. The subtler, more specific ones: the self-pitying cock, the reproachful cock—almost resentful of what it is about to undergo— the frightened member, the innocent stalk.

The ones that seem soft but go in somehow and stay put for a time, but only for a short while, not nearly long enough. And the firm live fighters that won't go down after they've blown open but stay strong and beg for another ride. How some men have hips and tight-nipped waists like women, wide ribcages, a hollow pelvis flanked by hips sharp as blades—as if a woman would get cut riding them—the cock jutting up from this valley in a slim climbing vine from which hang balls high and hard—rich ripe grapes. Some balls swing low as cherries. Or the swollen testicles that seem fermented and close to bursting. The ones that beg a picking. The ones left too long on the stalk and droop, as if spoiled. The hairs that spring up and out, a shock of red or brown or blonde or black, straight or curled, flat or tall. The forested ones. The ones that smell of rancid cat's milk. The ones with hairs that cluster in paranoia around small red bumps at their roots, tucked into a lover who didn't know better, or didn't care. The shaved ones, smooth as bone, as wax beans grown in a cellar.

When Whitey looks at the pictures, she remembers certain men's faces when they speak to her, their brains crouched back frightened behind their eyes, a dull rebellion above a thirst that increasingly disgusts her—a wheedling, begging, craven need, like an addict's frenzied search for the liquor bottle. Jones is not like them. Same as how some patients shriek for morphine and create more pain just to get it. Again, she does not see this in Jones. All the desire without end, the parade of greed. He seems above this, somehow. She is suddenly so scared. What is it, exactly, for which she has been so desperate all along and just never allowed herself to feel and name it?

Whitey and Jones consider the endless variations of private masculinities and femininities, those throbbing wholes with many parts. Bodies severed from hearts. Their own. And most likely many others, are cut out. Separate objects. Neglected. Mistreated. Devoid of the sublime. They sense themselves so strangely small and big and young and ancient and full and empty all at once.

She says she is a reed of grass, hollow and bowed, barely attached. Transient but permanent. He says he feels his feet penned in and frustrated, fractured - he is restless and stunted. She says she been searching all wrong—nothing, no one, not a one of her lovers or patients or mother or sister has held what she thought she needed— he says everything comes to an end, all lives and loves cross him and then leave him or he them, and he is left with the ashes, the smoke, to carry inside him forever. She says instead of only fire in her womb she now senses also ashes, smoking whitened cinders.

Silence falls between them.

Jones feels an unbelievable sorrow for it all.

Whitey doesn't want to carry these things, these old dead things, inside her any more.

Nor any part of them.

She wants no more touching, no more touching of her body or other bodies, and she will give herself to no one any more.

He had hoped—and needed—communion. Sanctuary.

Without knowing, they have shown to all the world a brutal, arbitrary gaping maw of hope and need. Here it is, reflected in their eyes that they each avoid—in the end the act of living is hopeless, it's hideous—is the longing for love, for home the same as well?

And they look at the body parts on the postcards, and they wonder that everyone has been grasping for things their whole lives, not for a whole but for parts, clutching at tiny morsels to take the edge off, grasping at one night of approval, at a moment of escape. At a little security. Solace. Greedy for acceptance, flattery, excitement, distraction, loneliness; for power, for control, for fear.

And inside Whitey knows—through all of it she has fucked wanting something. Somehow starved for it. As if this *something* could be pounded into her, poured into her; as if she could suck it out of someone else and into herself—as if a body could suck an absence right out of someone's body.

This thirst of the heart, this darkness at the core of it all, this tunnel of aching, Jones wants nothing more to do with it.

He wants the sublime or nothing.

He sees Whitey is exhausted, tapped out. Dried and burnt. Her body is death. All bodies are death. They smell of mulch and old blood and oil. They smell of rotten hair. Kerosene. The grave. But he knows she wants to wash it all off her skin, and then wrap herself in soft cloths and put a sweet brown velvet hat on her head, sit in the sun, make salves and poultices and tinctures in the sun—she wants only to touch green growing things, little seeds, look at the cherries and apples growing on the limb.

She wants to hang, warm, from a long clean stem.

♥

SKINNY JONES WATCHES WHITEY FLIP THROUGH THE STACKS OF postcards and sees wounds in her, sees sorrow surround her in the ghosts of people she has nursed to death, and of her father, of her mother—in the pain of those who cling crying, barnacled to her ankles and he wonders if she can see them, can see how everyone has clustered around her, how the air she breathes is filtered through a thousand ghostly fingers clutched around her lips, pulling back her flesh, tapping their hungry bones against her teeth.

Can you see them? Can you feel them? Do you feel penned in, frustrated? Are you like me? Don't you see I understand?

And he sees there is so much life around her too. He wants to protect it, to rescue her while it still exists. He wants to tell her that the two of them should go away, leave here. Wants her to scream and let herself go.

He wants to tell her that they should go away, leave this place to live in the freedom she needs: he doesn't want to have to share her with her cares or with the world.

He can tell her womb is about to give forth its offering of blood and he wants to lay within that promise of life, lick the purple juice pumping from her heart and womb from between her legs: taste the slippery rat tail of her slit, suck the bloodied button whose string ties itself tight around her gut and nipples. He wants to milk her ovaries of eggs, kneed them and gently squeeze their fruity pulp in the palm of his hand. He sees she is surrounded by the weight of death yet still she floats and grows with life. She has the life he wants. Her sap. Her breath. Her milk. He wants to hold the life she has in the palms of his calloused hands.

❥

WHITEY AND SKINNY JONES SIT IN THE ELECTRIC CHAIRS. HE blows smoke into his Coke bottle half-filled with gin and clamps his hand over the top to catch the smoke inside. They look at it twist and swirl in the dirty glass. The ash settles to the bottom of the bottle. She is sucking on one of his dropped cigarettes but there's nothing left of it, she just sucks on the paper to taste the burnt tobacco. She asks him something, quietly, but Jones says nothing, just hands her the bottle and puts her hands over the top. She decides not to ask him again so instead she says something small and meaningless. He doesn't answer, doesn't say a word. In his head he is thinking how he would like to take the old empty coke bottle and press the neck of it up into her to fill the wet and lonesome opening between her legs. He would like to feel her muscles take hold of the bottle and grasp it, push it out and then draw it into her, his hand around its base, the neck of it high up in her and filling the wet and lonesome opening between her legs. It would be tender. He would fill the bottle with her wetness and cap it and keep it, a holy relic, a sacrament of life, her holy water, it would cleanse him and he would be blessed by it.

And Whitey.

Whitey and Jones look at the smoke inside the bottle twist and swirl within the dirty glass. She is sucking on his dropped cigarette but there's nothing left of it except the taste of burnt tobacco. He asks her something, quietly, but she says nothing, she doesn't respond, doesn't say a word. After a few minutes all the smoke has come out through her fingers and the bottle is empty again.

NOCTURNE FOR THE HOLLOW SWAN

UNLIKE THE OTHER WOMEN IN HER FAMILY, SWEET MARIE DIDN'T particularly care for drink, but she found it interesting; the scent of gin in a bottle just opened reminded her of winter, of dead trees.

She was drinking it on a rare swift trip to New York—temporarily freed in order to retrieve a new patient—when something unfamiliar stirred in her: the way the dirty snow formed a blanket of quiet filth across miles upon miles of striving city life, the way the drink went down cold with ice as the train quivered on its tracks, the juniper taste of it, the cut-branched moan of the crushed ice in her glass and around it the dull hum of the tracks and the passengers' voices muted together in a loose paean of communion: strangers together, canned as summer apples, a grim cigar streaming smoke in the lounge car, old wool damped with sweat, the sounds of longing, of striving to reach city and money and luck—

All that from a glass of gin bought for her in the dining car by a jazz girl she shouldn't, she should know not to—but Sweet Marie didn't care about those things even though people thought she would, from the outside, thought she would care about the rules of society but she was too gone far out of the reaches of the world for that. And besides, the gin stirred something in her, swift and shivering liquid. Or was it the girl who stirred her?

The Jazz Girl shouted out to her friends, loud, often, head back and mouth cracked wet and wide, arms flung, cigarette in one hand then the other, lighting four cigarettes in her mouth at once for her friends and passing them down the line, eyes crinkling into a slow wink, a wink surely directed at Sweet Marie, and kneeling down beside her, suddenly a hand on the smoldering crease at Sweet Marie's hip.

Oh, how this bright shining copper-colored girl spoke to her—expansive, huge, thickly low-voiced, as tremendous as the sea at night, mysterious and glistening. The Jazz Girl and her band were on their way to the next gig, a club somewhere in Harlem, or Greenwich Village, or somewhere—the girl's rhythmic intonation of the city's names and foreign neighborhoods as remote as heaven or hell to Sweet Marie—deep within the pockets of the South she had no idea of their import, but sensed their resonance.

The Jazz Girl brought Sweet Marie another drink. She carried their two glasses in long wide steps, heels sunk down into the carpet with each step, mannish, as though even through the floor she still sank with purpose into the mud of the earth. Her front teeth slightly gapped, white and wet as a mussel shell cracked open, a smile glowing in the light. She shone. Luminous. A midnight water snake, she swam closer and closer to Sweet Marie, encircling, whirling, mesmerizing her, was it all happening very quickly or very slowly, or was it not happening at all?

As the girl spoke softly to her in that smoldering tobacco voice, Sweet Marie inhaled unevenly, trying to catch the girl's breath, trying to capture it, that fire-flung scent, what was it, so rare: syrupy and strong, warm brown thing, a forest smell caught up with salt and sea, a Carolina coast of swamp and saline and cypress woods.

The Jazz Girl carried a saxophone and a violin. She showed Sweet Marie the block of golden wax used to calm its strings. Her hands were rough but small, capable beyond her narrow wrists. Her fingers long, their base and tips callous-skinned, small cropped fingernails flat and shiny as picks. The bones of her face cradled the instrument, exquisite to Sweet Marie's devouring gaze.

A man's cotton shirt half-concealed her breasts, rich and full—heavy, soft, rounded. So perfect. Sweet Marie imagined her nipples like the nubs of antlers on spring fauns. A velveted firmness.

Eyes centered brown, burning out to a young green. Keenly intelligent, and sexed.

You are song, the jazz girl murmured to Sweet Marie, *you are soul.*

And suddenly Marie looked down in fright at the girl's small, beautiful hand resting on her own pathetic stretched-then-shrunk dress and felt tremendously sad; Sweet Marie was another bit of the world's detritus to this girl—this girl could see no more song or soul in Sweet Marie than in the shred of lint at the bottom of her pocket. The girl was like the others—how could she truly know or care about the secrets of Sweet Marie.

Sweet Marie grew so afraid: she wanted this girl, and yet she had trained herself so well to scab over, to tend to her leprous numbed parts. To be hard and fierce and unfeeling. She feared what it was to love—to be part of something great and passionate, important and powerful—when she herself was so strange and alone, so easily and thoughtlessly blown down, trampled, and forgotten. Sweet Marie had learned to use her cold exterior to slowly extinguish the warm and tender vulnerable thing inside her that she once knew. This girl, something about this Jazz Girl's coal fire touch, the focus of her eyes, hinted at the presence of something unexpectedly amazing—there was a rare something illuminating her from within—something that could utter a call that would bring forth what Sweet Marie had long concealed. In the face of that, Sweet Marie felt herself dangerously humbled.

But somehow Sweet Marie accepted the girl's drink, and felt a strange low vibration carry through to her heart as though from a very great distance.

❦

IT TOOK TWO DAYS TO REACH NEW YORK CITY, AND ONE NIGHT. Sweet Marie had planned to sleep in her seat—her body had formed itself to its armature over the course of the day— but then she began to feel less comfortable instead of more and she went to the lounge car. She denied any desire to see the girl.

The Jazz Girl sat in the seat across the aisle. The musicians were talking quiet and high in the car, the windows dark against the night and the passengers' faces, shining with oil, reflected, became spirits peering in at them.

The Jazz Girl was polishing her saxophone, rubbing it down with a purple velvet cloth worn bare in the places where her fingers often went.

At dusk the train had crossed state lines into Maryland, and now those awake at night could rise from their seats and mingle, the dark skinned and the white, and those whose flesh fell someplace in between. Sweet Marie and the Jazz Girl talked into the shared air between them, undisturbed.

❦

I KNOW THIS JAZZ GIRL COMES TO ME IN BOREDOM, FROM A PASSING need for contact, not caring who or what I am but rather idly curious to see what pleasure I can provide for her, what pleasures my body might have to offer. I have found no pleasures in it yet, but this jazz girl, this singer of the city, thinks she shall teach me something new. But I know all about love already. I know its hollows and its deceptions. She will teach me nothing.

They come looking for my vulnerability and they happily find it whether it's there or not. They always somehow want a power over me. The great need the world has to create a defenseless woman. A plaintive unfilled longing for the protection someone kindly shall provide. But I do not want protection, and my absence of self is my power: I shall tell nothing, I shall feel nothing, I shall want nothing. No one.

Sweet Marie, she will say, and smile with knowledge, and stroke my hair back from my forehead tenderly, as though she cares.

❦

A sleeping car cost extra but the jazz girl paid with change. Sweet

Marie saw everything about her shining, the brass of her saxophone, the coins in the girl's hand, the sheen on her teeth and damp lips.

The Jazz Girl touched Sweet Marie like a note, drawing blood into her body so she felt a sudden heaviness of breast and thigh, the way it is the first time water courses through the copper of a new pipe.

And then the girl's hands were an electric storm enveloping her body, crashing and howling, a crescendo snapping branches and hurling sticks and leaves into the drowned air.

A pelting of embraces. Fingers so deep in Sweet Marie's muscles, pulling her leg up, behind the knee, and locking her fingers there in the hollow.

A hurricane tumble.

And Marie falling, falling into the rain, becoming a droplet, a stinging nettle of water mixing with this jazz girl, pouring wet, dripping, Sweet Marie's own pale rain running down the back of her thighs, her dress wet—this was new, after all, new—

It was suddenly not like anything before, hailstones falling, a shower of pearls. The girl's lips large and sweet, hungry, delicious, endless— they held Sweet Marie above and below, released, took hold, these active live and lovely things—Sweet Marie had to feel the girl's mouth, run her fingers along the ridges of her lips, feel the wetness, the groove down the center, force them open to run her finger along the surface of her teeth, feel them suck and bite.

This was completely new, completely different.

Sweet Marie's body shook, skin plucked and strummed, pummeled by new feeling.

She became afraid.

♥

Marie's wings bore her away from the Jazz Girl, took her the great distance to the corner of the car and lit upon the curtain rod, perched there to watch the Jazz Girl at her work. The swan watched with detachment the girl's fingers touching, stroking, exploring with her muscled musician's hands. The forest scent hung above the two bodies—nothing more. The Jazz Girl's body christened Sweet Marie's hairless skin with sweat. They slid in it together, thighs grasped between each other's thighs. Their tongues swam the rivers between their legs.

The swan watched them both from the ceiling, the ridge of the Jazz Girl's spine pressing out through the layers of her skin, the softly glowing tissue in the darkened hollows of her knees, the lovely soft pink soles of her feet. The swan saw the map traced on the Girl's skin from sun and cloth: the subtle fluctuations of hue between arm and ass; the ring of shadows where her sleeves and neckline had been. The swan could see how the Jazz Girl rested her weight on Sweet Marie. Turned her over and held her ass as she would an orange, an apple, or a peach, gentle, possessive, appraising. How she grasped it with her hands. How she spoke to Marie slowly in small words, in soft compliments and demands, and the great spaces in between she filled with breath. How Sweet Marie arched upwards for the girl, offering lips or breasts or belly. The Jazz Girl's eyes were a deep pool of kindness, her hands smooth. She cupped the woman's breasts and drank from them.

Up in the corner of the car the swan flapped her great white wings tipped with blue and watched Sweet Marie's body behaving unfamiliarly. These narrow hips and thin calves, the pockets of these shoulders and the arms writhing within their sockets. Heard her thinking about this jazz woman and wondering, worrying.

Oh, the swan knew many things. Like how the Jazz Girl knew Marie only as a body, but Sweet Marie was so much more; her body was complex, pained, full of knots and sorrows, repressions of hope and above all so many pushed-back longings—the Jazz Girl did not know Sweet Marie. The girl had entered Marie's city and wandered alone through the shuttered streets of her flesh. The swan watched the

Jazz Girl on her journey as the muscles of her narrow naked back contracted and flexed, as the girl delved into the hollows between Sweet Marie's legs.

And the swan, sentimental, was strangely sorry for the Jazz Girl's mistake, for the lovers' clumsy ignorance of one another, for the fact that Sweet Marie would fade away into the singer's forgotten memories of a friendly fuck. But for now the swan, saddened, merely wished them pleasure—pleasure would have to be enough.

Down below, the arches of the girls' backs rose and then flattened, then rose again.

The swan put her long sharp beak beneath her wing, and fell asleep.

❦

SWEET MARIE'S DREAMS CHANGED THAT NIGHT. IN HER DREAM she counted off *two- three-one- two-three* with the Jazz Girl's band.

❦

THE NEXT AFTERNOON SWEET MARIE HEARD HER DREAM SONG playing from the radio at the boarding house. She washed her face to the sounds of New York City, its songs from far- flung places where people knew their bodies in different ways—she watched the foreign women move themselves down the streets, letting their smiles and frowns run rampant across their faces, the sounds of their heels tapping a fierce new rhythm into the world—she was too ancient—she would never—

As though unaware, she walked to the Jazz Girl's club the following night and heard that low throat crying out to her in a deep rhythm of sound, a furious torrent of feeling—it was too much.

She felt it try to drag her to her knees—the sweet saxophone, the soft brushes against the skin of the drum, skeins of song wanting to weave themselves into the tight white warp of her flesh. The sounds that demanded some kind of response from her, that tried to enter her ears without consent—those notes, these things with wings that flew through the air unimpeded.

Did they expect her to stand there in the lights and the smoke, open her lungs in new ways? Count off *two, three, one-two-three* with the jazz girls, someone blindly fingering the piano, metal tacks in the velvet pads striking wires?

She was not these people.

She would not wear red, and her hair would not hang down smooth and she would not be one of the people of passion for whom words alone were not enough—who needed beat and note and sex to make their point, to carry their hope and pain outward in a great wide throb.

The only beat she knew issued from her heart—it seemed capable of merely a distant muffled nothing.

What would she sing? What would she play? She knew nothing of the complex mechanisms of scale and tone. She had spent her life locked away, and the locks were rusted shut. She wanted to run to this girl, but the girl wouldn't want her, not want who she really was—difficult and complicated and possessed of a mind even more than of a body, full of blood and gut and want.

That night she passed by the bar, heard the music bellowing up from the hollows, and chose to keep walking. And the sounds that floated by her, that carried through her air slowly dissipated, and faded away—

Never. She ground her fingernails into the palms of her hand and walked back to the train station faintly nauseous, the swig of gin no longer rinsing in her stomach. Alone and empty, floating, one slight and angry woman flowing through the world in an invisible wash of air. Empty. She was a lung let go of sighs—deflated, and not knowing how to find the sense of full.

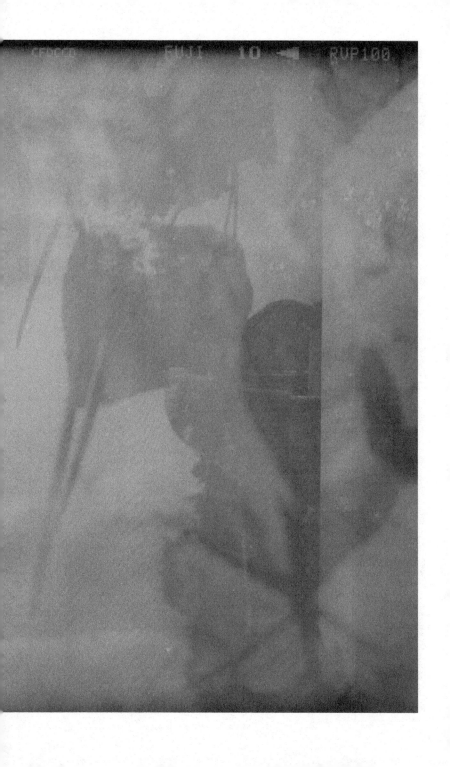

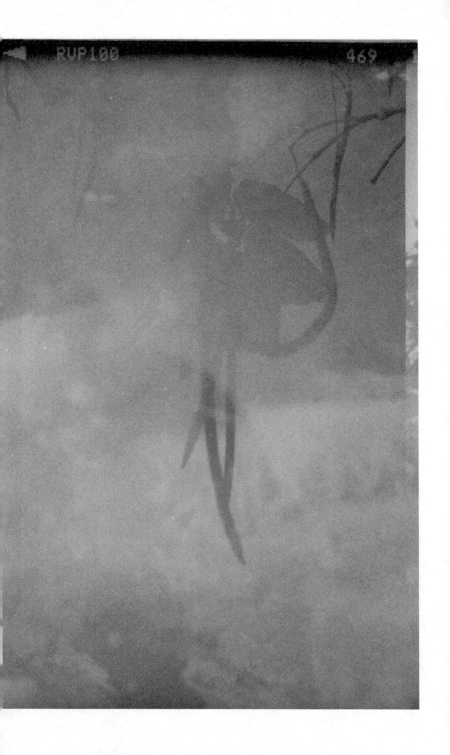

HOW THE LOCK FEELS
WHEN THE KEY GOES IN

First Whitey had felt the immense wind in the grass.

And then out of that came an unknown man whose presence struck against her, as if she herself was the wind that after passing through the tall dry grasses came up sharp and strong against him, a wall of fire.

She sought for cracks, for holes or missing rocks and finding none, was pinned.

She fixed on him hard—held there, flat out, to understand where he pulled at her, where he stopped her despite.

Contact was suck-the-marrow-from-the-bones deep and hard with him. Wide and long.

Veins hurried in her body.

Here was a man—Jones.

Heart set spurs to flank.

She saw a huge, empty, perfect bed—there—she and the fire and the man and the immense wind blazing in the grass—but she was not the kind to know how to settle down quiet by his side.

❤

IN HER DREAMS, JONES KEPT COMING BACK, RISING UP, HOT, AND rising again, to meet her like a wall of fire in the tall dry grass.

Whitey was afraid that if she didn't close her teeth, clench them, there would soon be nothing left of her, not even the breath from her lungs, hanging there to swept up in the wildfire too.

And so she wondered if she should flee, leaving him standing there licking and burning in the tall dry grasses.

❧

THAT NIGHT WHITEY DREAMS SHE IS IN A ROOM CARVED FROM dark stone. There is his enormous hand, and she sleeps within it. Her long dirty hair flowers, falls down and hangs there between the massive fingers of his enormous dirt-dark hand, the skin on his hand as dry and cracked as August loam. And all that was closed was open.

When she wakes the sheets are coiled between her legs, snake strong, turned stiff as steel.

❧

BOILED BY THAT FIRE IN THE TALL SPRING GRASS, THE SAP HAD begun to rise and Whitey felt her flesh risen with it, firm and plump as a starter bread filling out the bowl in the coming sun; she had felt her veins stir and wake so fiercely that she took herself gone out to the grove of standing sycamore trees and scratched at their bark until it bled. She dug madly right down through their pale gasping sinews to find the bilious green sap and she filled her fingernails and hands with the stuff and spread it over her face and breasts. Broke a green new-growing branch and rubbed it between her legs, drew it across her hips and back until she was as young and new and spring-drunk as the grove, bucking and swaying in the spring wind. Even the moon looked raw, burning white, forever uncooked, parboiled as rhubarb with its rich pink milk. Her own breasts filled with the moon and the sap, and they ached as they grew fuller. Her legs seemed to grow longer, her feet wider; the muscles pulled away from her bones in an attempt to escape with her nerves and sinews—everything within her wanting to get out to the edges of things, press for a new bloom, breathe lungfuls of yellow pollen and float up buoyant into the outstretched air, light and pure and porous as milkweed.

♥

AT NIGHT SOMETIMES SHE DREAMS JONES HAS COME TO LIE WITH her, or in the early morning before dawn, or in the orange and lavender water of dusk when her dying patients are downstairs in the parlor eating leftover ham and drinking bourbon. She doesn't know to convince herself that he has arrived to her bed, to love her kindly—she wants to tell herself it isn't another vision, just another of her well-formed vapors come to torment her into a rekindling. That he has climbed the three stories up the rose trellis, pulled up the sash and slid in over her rosewood bureau, knocking over stacks of stockings and cologne to slip into her dirty sheets and kiss her plaintive nipples? Whitey doesn't know, doesn't know how to ask him to come and go without really staying long enough to frighten her. Is the beating of her heart fastened to his so tight that it doesn't bother to consult with her as to its speed and strength?

Whitey doesn't know.

She has dreamed for so much of her life, hoped for so much—she is laid down so low and brought up so high she knows it could be god itself who brings these dreams to her in pity of her torment.

When he comes to her in dreams she feels her skin crawl to him from across the room. When he comes to her, she hears the breath in her throat gasp out tall and loud from deep within, feels her laugh ring out from her chest in golden swinging ripples of shining light.

He seems to hold her up to the sun and magnify her—she feels the light refract in her, through her the brightest spot of light focuses upon their bed. She blows it gently into a flame.

When these dreams come to her she seems to swell out of her dress, her bones grow larger beneath her skin, everything fitting too closely it has to come off, everything has to come off. Her face relaxes into a smooth plane of hope and satisfaction.

When he comes to her in tenderness she learns expectation: a new understanding of how she is built, what she desires, her unknown hidden names.

And satisfaction. Fulfillment. Satiation.

Communion.

The velocity of the journey to the heart. Veins hurry in her body, strung and quivering as the strings of beautiful violins—her blood untangles to dance in channels through her open, flexing flesh. An internal light from a thousand love-illuminated cells, tiny angels who glow red as ancient planets. Her opening heart--the quick clotting at the cut, red sap that—though split—still can heal. Corpuscles. An ever high and low tide of life's force, that tidal caress and slap. The pummeled form of meat and heat.

What burns and holds her, a viscous liquid punch, spring-drunk and plummy.

Oh, sweet and salty syrup poured in her delicate vessel—

Rush of wildfire, of lightning. This gorgeous gnaw and tug of her good juice.

♥

FOR TEN MONTHS IN THE PREVIOUS YEAR WHITEY HAD BEEN lovers with a stolid man from in town. Her body was quiet, it arrived in the affair stillborn and choked-off, blue. He had come to her, but not in the night—no, he came to her in the day, arrived civilized in an automobile, stepped out with hobnail and cracked leather feet, gigantic, stinking of salt and old soil, his fingers—broadened and flat-knuckled—laid forth evenly, calmly, upon her spine: no force, no thing to restrain, once a week a quiet knocking against her closed cervix, a measured handful of even, numbered knocks. In him she had found rest.

No one knew of the affair. There had been no witnesses.

The first time he came over, he had purchased a new hat for her, no gift of passion. On the front porch they shared a slice of red velvet cake—that was their greatest moment, hands entwined on the rocker, a few words echoed from the lover's script. Her dress was always on, she was never naked, her skin under the cotton felt thick and white and starched, her ribs like hard spokes of corsetry bearing her up under him. After lovemaking she felt the nearby passing of Solitude. She kept Solitude in the spare room.

During this time he knew her as a kind of kitten, looked into her eyes and saw a fierce milky mystery and turned averted from it, longing only to rub his face into her fur and lovingly feed her fat with store-bought powdered milk.

Under this care she grew and grew. But each day she knew him loath to see her fangs come in, broken through the tender lining of her gums. Talons in her mouth—vulture clenched—she thought she would break them off in the back of his neck by accident. Each day her claws hardened and became opaque. The milk was not enough. She wanted blood. She drank the powdered milk he made but she was thinking of blood, longing to pounce and feel the sinewy resistant give of a vein in her mouth, feel her throat fill up with some other being's pulsing juice. The milk soured in dishes left out on the floor. When she drank it, starving, she threw up; the vomited milk remained in the saucers. Flies came to investigate and she swatted them with a hungry paw, but caught, their bodies offered up only a brittle crust, a husk of empty breathless shell that caught within her teeth in a hollow snap.

❦

FUELED BY THAT FIRST WIND IN THE TALL SPRING GRASS, IN THE days and nights that followed with Jones, Whitey was lit to a blue heat, glowed hot from within, her marrow reddened embers hollowed out from the inferno of he with the immense wind in the grass.

How did this junkman come to hold the fuse to her explosion? To carry the match to set flame to her destruction, if it came to that; or to her creation? It was *her* match, it was the one she had always held, the box of them in her pockets flagrant and infinite—oh, the blazes she had lit without knowing, the blazes she had lit without knowing what the wood felt in burning.

Now she knew the shudder and warp, the swelling and rupture, popping of fibers, the hiss and moan of ring after ring of growth: tough outer bark—the first to give itself up to the brutal heat, the damp stringy hidden white parts exposed to flame, bloated to bursting by the steam. The magnitude.

She longed for him to crack his match against her teeth, set it to spark, make flame, force this fire out along her limbs and down through the cracks in the pine boards beneath them both—let him take down her woods, her thickets, let him torch it all in the same blaze he held her twisting in—let him take it all and leave her satisfied. He was glorious to her. His eyes held all God's glory. His proud chest contained a fire Shadrack could never resist—Meshach and Abednego too would burn helpless before his furnace.

❦

By half-light, she imagines his hips against her hips, next to a cup of water, spilt, the water soaking through the sheets. Five bruises on her thigh from his fingers. She has come to know his long and calloused fingers and felt their whorls and ridges along her flesh. *This is enough*—for she doesn't need light to see.

She rides on his hips as he rises up and his strength sustains her weight and his own. Then above his mouth her hips. The velvet of his lips is enough to convince: her love has spilt and she tastes it on his lips beneath his fingernails and around his tongue upon her teeth.

Whitey will not wash their pale stains from off these sheets.

Upon her lips his hips, in her mouth she tastes his juices.

I will never get enough—

Even now, with their sweat soaking through these sheets, her weight joined to his, above her head his hips. Give her.

More.

Against her hips his hips, again and once again they've spilt upon these sheets.

❦

IN THE MORNING THERE WILL BE SALT WHITENING ON HER along the lines of his hand print, sweat left by his skin, the water evaporated by this heat. She will need to kneel and lay her naked breast against his palm—press her bared form against him, wait for his touch, silently.

❦

THORNROSES CLIMBING A WOODEN FENCE. A TOMATO, SWOLLEN on the vine. Wet seeds of an opened watermelon. Virginia clay soaked to bleeding. Rhubarb with its rich pink milk.

More.

A crimson moon teasing the flesh of the horizon. In all things the sap has begun to rise—a violent blossoming. The short soft hairs on a berry. The plush of warm lips, a scissoring kiss, skin filled with flames. More. Firm plump wetness of a trout bucking in the stream. Raw ore boiled at the center of the earth. Sweat's salt whitening in the lines of the palm, the water evaporated from the heat.

The need to kneel, to feel the scarlet shock of a palm against a breast. How the lock feels when the key goes in.

❦

WHEN THIS PHANTOM MAN IS GONE AND SHE WAKES, WHITEY

still finds his hairs in her bed and curls them, fast, inside her palm. She records these traces of him, artifacts of his presence, enormous fingerprints left in the cornmeal face powder snowed across her dresser top.

♥

AND NOW INSIDE THE CAGE OF HER RIBS THIS FEROCIOUS MUSCLE burns. On the days that follow the nights when he does not come to her, she cannot bear the town. She cannot go to the part of it where he is, she cannot submit herself to seeing him.

She cannot bear the town. Without his reassurance, absent any trace of his love within it, only the horror of his unavailability to her, the buildings howl vacant, in danger of falling, his bones the very beams they need to hold them up.

The sidewalks of Lynchburg buckle and crack under her, the ground a file that grates upon the soft quivering curd of her feet.

Without him at night when the sun is gone Whitey crawls through the town on her hands and knees. Looking down at the boiling, buckled sidewalk she sees she has left her handprint there with each next move, and next to them his handprint appears; his body invisible, his phantom skin nonetheless searing its mark upon the stone. She sees their coupled handprints on the town, their palms pressed against the melting soil.

The nights when he does not come to her she listens but his footsteps do not call from the porch; she is buried there under his hands and the wind will do its best but only stirs the heat that has laid down upon her skin.

A sudden desiring of death in that hollow country, the hills the shoals of an ancient ocean, the white house cradled in a warm palm: because she does not know which day she will find him returned to her.

She cannot forget the shape of his broad and perfect hand upon her.

WHEN SHE CANNOT MEET JONES, CANNOT SEE HIM, WATCH HIM turn her dust to flesh, inside her ribs it is nothing but mincemeat. A fistful of ripped tissue, ugly clots. A miscarried heart—choked-off and blue—no longer even gasping for breath that will never come. Stopped knocking on a door that never opens.

A string of beads with no string, beads with just holes, a strand of emptiness.

♥

WHITEY, ALWAYS THE ONE WHO RULES. AND HERE, JONES, THE lamb whispers sweetly to the lioness. Damn him—damn him. To be in love is to be homicidal. To desire his blood under her fingernails and in her cuticles. His dried blood in the crevices of her joints. To wash out her hair in a tub of his pink water. To take apart his golden brown body, wring out the bile from his liver and leave the organ curled around the spine in a dead heap. Let the lungs go black and brackish, fill their balloons with yellow vinegar. Pock the stomach's raw lining with holes and cigarette burns. Twist his fingers into thick wrinkles, purplish swollen knuckles bloated as pig's feet. Leave him out to dry, two kidneys shriveled on the vine, cords tied off with muddy twine. Skin thin and waxen as old toenails, embrittled. Laugh at the snailshell of his ear, let the smoky brains go to the sluggish worm that lives inside.

She has curdled. Left too long on the boil she has spoiled. Rancid and bitter, full of sour curds, unstrained. Damn him. Damn him all to hell.

Inside the cage of her ribs this ferocious muscle burns.

♥

Whitey dreams she has opened in herself that gasping fissure between her legs.

She is in a room carved from onyx stone the color of the new moon. She is within his hand and she writhes inside his broad palm, the curls of her filthy hair twisting between the massive fingers of the hand whose dark skin is rough and loose as August loam. The hand curls around her anguished coming, the contractions of her muscles and the quiver of her shanks, she's wracked with it—a tightening of her passageways, a dull thrust, push out, tighter still—a searing wrench. Until at last a dull dark purplish mass emerges from her, warm and damp, bloody, squeezed to throbbing; a uterus, her own heart. She pulls it into her lap. Heavy but not still. Awkward as a calf, her womb. Deflated and yet full, a living muscle.

His reins tighten and slap along her flanks.

Far afield she's grazed.

She wakes, not knowing how long this great loving muscle can remain inside her—she pushes it deep in. Commands it to stay there, just so.

Then begs it.

What is to become of us? she cries.

How is it to remain inside?

SALT ON THE SKIN
NOT FROM SORROW

THE JAZZ GIRL HAD POSSESSED A THROAT THAT CONTAINED ALL the water and sand of the oceans, bodies of water Sweet Marie had never set foot in, for she had never seen an ocean in her life. Still, she thought of the girl's voice that way, like she thought of the girl's river- snake back sliding liquid above her own, her sweat dripping onto Sweet Marie's face as the girl moved back and forth above her, sounds of yearning in her wet and sandy throat. Like swimming at night in unfamiliar places. How the girl's palms were heavy and smooth on her flesh, worn silky; how they skimmed down over Sweet Marie's stockings without catching, without causing snags. And then the calloused tips of her fingers slipped deep between Marie's legs, where she dripped onto the girl's warm, burnished fingertips.

The Jazz Girl read Sweet Marie's sex as a song, the syllables of slit.

Her newly swollen sounds—she played them out, lips spread, and Marie took them in.

❦

The saltwater from the Jazz Girl's sweat had dropped down onto Marie's dry face and clung to her eyebrows, ran down from them to her lashes where it gathered around Sweet Marie's eyes and, glistening, mixed with tears.

The girl had asked Sweet Marie why she was crying, asked her there as she rocked her whole hand deep inside her, as the train car rocked back and forth in the thick Maryland night air.

She had asked Sweet Marie why she was crying and with a level gaze Marie told her evenly, coolly:

I am not crying.

And so to hide her tears Marie closed her eyes and the Jazz Girl's sweat continued to collect along Sweet Marie's lids, and the girl didn't ask Marie again.

❧

Her hand a boat inside Marie, a boat in her canal, traveling through this her red city. How Marie drew her in, past her many bridges, along her sleek wet banks.

Sweet Marie recalled, when she was back home, after she had returned from her trip—

How the Girl had glided through her waters, then so suddenly, painfully let go of her legs, moved her lips away from Marie's hips, and vanished forever into the metropolis:

How then Marie's hollow-boned lightness quickly shot her up to the surface again, sadly buoyant, as though the dark mystery of the ocean's depths had no further need for her and returned her cruelly to the air where the light refracted against her from the sky. Vicious. And she gasped at it.

Marie's eyes were never the same—in a moment they had accustomed themselves to the darkness of the sea that had been the girl's weight on top of her, the girl's voice, and hands, and lips. Her fierce tenderness. The elemental scent of her. An unspoken promise of more than anyone had held for Sweet Marie before. But now, living again on the surface, Marie seemed to have to squint all the time in the daylight, as though it was too bright, as though this return brought some unwelcome clarity. She closed her eyes against what she felt but it was of no help, for the Jazz Girl's face nonetheless appeared: wide, curved lips, curiously pointed chin, and a glint of something further in her eyes.

❦

THE JAZZ GIRL HAD CARESSED MARIE'S LEGS ON THE TRAIN, TRAILED her tongue along the swollen ridges between her legs, reached up to caress Marie's nipples—and it was too much—the Girl pushed Marie away, turned, pulled her city clothes on quickly, over her head, and did not even latch the compartment door behind her as she left without a word.

Yet now, when Sweet Marie closes her eyes it is only to find the girl's eyes still there, looking into hers, widening and widening and widening, catching her gaze each time she approaches climax.

❦

SIX MONTHS LATER, SOMETIMES, OFTEN, WHILE SHE WAS WORKING at the hospital, she wondered how it would have been to see the Jazz Girl in the different light of the nightclub.

She imagined her on a stage, a small stage painted black, in a black room, with blue and green and red lights shining down on her. Painted women in handsome dresses in the room, lipsticked and glistening, dark handsome men in brown suits, sweat-stained underneath, hair oiled back against their heads as they jogged to the music Sweet Marie found too overpowering to listen to.

She saw the Jazz Girl in the center of it all, howling out her mysterious self. Her broad feet tapping hard against the drum of the stage, leaving a scuff there by the end of the night that would be washed off or painted over in the light of day. What the Jazz Girl's face might look like, if her eyes would widen for the beautiful women of the city, if her lips would curl at them, or for the notes, or for both. Sweet Marie wondered these things without knowing where her ideas sprang from. She had never been to the city, to some velveted womb of a club where she would walk up a thickly carpeted staircase with mirrors on the walls that would reflect nothing, for there was no light in this staircase—she would wear perilously high heels, and the long small muscles of her calves would rise up at the height of the shoes, rise up and up her skinny legs, making her ass rise up, and her back curve in, and her breasts jump up until she would suddenly reach the top of the stairs propelled by her own shoes, her own curves—too quickly, much earlier than she was ready for but what could she do? Linger on a dark stair?—and the club would be dark but the Jazz Girl would still somehow see her and those eyes, those god-awful wonderous ebony green eyes would flash at her. Sweet Marie would lick her lips, accidentally. Shiver in the heat. Embarrassed. Quiver. Knowing it could not really be a wink, only the stage lights blinking in the Jazz Girl's face. And then it would happen again, with the girl's face turned towards hers—a sweaty shining conflagration of a face, with salt liquefied upon it, pouring down into the dark, low cleavage below her glistening collarbone. Sweet Marie would feel that damp sexed heat rising off the girl, who would jerk her head slightly, grinning that dangerous tiger's smile from the flower of her mouth. Some smoke- obscured figure would take Sweet Marie's arm at the elbow and guide her to a chair right at the front, in the center. She had arrived late. All the other seats were taken—but this one had her name written on it neatly, in a woman's firm hand, on a white card, propped against a dripping glass of gin with tiny bubbles rising up from the tonic. When she sat down her dress would turn blood red in the stage lights and she would find herself to be one of those people, these people—for once alive amidst the living—and lift her lips to her drink, and when she set it down again she would see the print of her dark lipstick left there firmly pressed against the cold clear rim of the highball glass. A kiss on glass.

To leave a mark on the Jazz Girl—as if she truly existed, for the first time.

And in the smooth electric darkness she would feel, in each note the girl sang, the shape of the girl's body pressing hard against her own.

❦

AT THE HOSPITAL THE BANDAGES FELT AWKWARD AND FOREIGN

in her hands. Thick and pasty, starchy from the dampness of her fingers and palms. It all grew more distasteful by the day. Rolling them, unrolling them, applying them. Day by day they seemed to get heavier, more like plaster than cotton. As though she were preparing the strips to mummify herself. The injections she gave not medicine, but embalming fluid shot straight into her own dead veins. She didn't want that anymore.

Months had passed since New York, and it was spring. Sweet Marie sweated now, and could smell herself sometimes by the afternoon. She would bathe in the morning, longer and longer each time, and even searched out her mother's old lemon verbena soaps to wash under her arms and between her legs but still, by afternoon, she could smell her ripeness. She went to the wash room and smelled herself and a rich hot odor surprised her, a darkening gamey smell at once marine and fecund, a swampy summer scent that wouldn't wash off and could not be disguised.

She tried to keep a few feet more distant from other people. Stand with her legs firmly together and her arms down hard against her side; she was deeply uncomfortable reaching into high shelves for supplies or standing at someone's bedside, where she knew the patient's head was positioned at a place where she would be unable to hide her mark. She thought of it as a mark. A mark of what? She asked herself but couldn't find an answer to which she was ready to admit.

There was something, some thing, alive in her, awake, growing. She wasn't sure if anyone noticed, and certainly couldn't ask—and besides, they would think she meant a distasteful, unclean smell, whereas she had begun to find it not to be so unpleasant after all. Conspicuous, without question. But when she caught the trail of it rising up from underneath her she was startled to need to breathe it in deeply, to sense its new beauty, to find her breasts and nipples slowly run through with a determined charge that spread down her abdomen and nestled in the burrow between her legs, twisting and burning and humming there like some live thing.

♥

AND SOMETIMES AT NIGHT THE JAZZ GIRL'S BODY STILL FEELS SO close, but it's in some other bed. Sweet Marie longs for it, for her, splayed and dreaming, warm and spread, an ocean's flesh floating heavy.

There is a new aching she's never known—for the Girl's head against her shoulder, her sleeping hand on her breast, dream words whispered into her ears.

Come here—take my breasts again. Your graceful ocean tug. Feed me the oyster of your mouth—let my tongue know the salt of all your teeth.

❦

IT WAS A MONDAY THAT SWEET MARIE BEGAN TO SHOW. It was an early spring Monday, and she had known for some time, suspected, that something tiny and good was growing inside her, *a low note…* those words rolled around in her head like a lozenge. *A tiny note. A low note baby.* Part fist, a musician's hand wedged up inside her, filling her, making her swell. A knowledge baby. A *wake-up-now-and-get-it-on* baby. Morning after morning she sat across the table from Dr. Williams, pouring his coffee, tidying his paper, with the refrain *jazz baby, tiny baby, tiny jazz baby* in her head. But the song did not progress, whereas her strange pregnancy did. There was something the very idea of jazz had planted in there, deep inside Sweet Marie, that refused to die, even though the note she'd heard was long, long gone. Over the years of her slow sad life Sweet Marie had calculatedly killed every craving part of herself in order to survive, had willed herself to dissimulate, to deny; to manipulate, submerge, obfuscate, repress, ignore—she had buried just about every natural part of herself simply to prevent her sanity from being stolen away by the pain she felt in living. She was well-trained, and she could accept, if not admit, the swift departure of the Jazz Girl. But this new-growth fighting thing inside her was the kind of creature that told her to stop all that running away. This was a scat baby, and it took what it had and asked for more: it cried out with urgency not of need but of passion. A bee-bop love baby. It was an idea baby—a freedom baby, a no fear baby. Liberation baby. She longed to see the Jazz Girl, to tell her, to make her smile and not run away this time and say *Yes, ain't it cool what we've created something special, something new...* Wouldn't she?

No. The Jazz Girl had long forgotten Sweet Marie, the hillbilly passing flotsam-jetsam riding the wrong direction on a wrong-bound train. But what did it matter. The girl was gone: completely gone. But she'd left this little quarter-note spooning into song inside Sweet Marie. A rat-a-tat-tat child, soon to be a half-note kid. *Gittup.* A three-quarter note brat. Get you goin' rat. A wake-up be-free kinda baby.

♥

SWEET MARIE LIKED THE SPRING MOONS OF HER BODY, WHITE and slowly rounding, and she would keep this freedom baby, let her swan float on the tides the moonbaby drew out of her. *Lavender blue, dilly dilly,* she sang to the child without noticing, *lavender green.*

She sang for the first time in her life. A song she had heard her mother sing. *Lavender green.*

♥

SHUT YOUR MOUTH, I'M READING, SAID DR. WILLIAMS. *THE ONLY decent thing about you is your silence.*

♥

THIS WAS A JAZZ BABY. UNRULY. THE FIRST THING THAT EVER WAS hers, something strange and sweet that seemed to eat away at the bitterness, hatred, anger and pain, seemed to munch on her sadness and rejection and turn it into a rambunctious kind of joy that nobody, *not nobody,* could take away.

♥

HE BEAT HER, CAREFULLY, AS ONLY A DOCTOR WOULD KNOW HOW to beat a pregnant woman without causing suspicion. He shoved her down onto the sofa, applying swift and accurate pressure to her shoulders so that she would bend down almost naturally, almost as though she had only sat down too suddenly after losing her balance. As though she had tripped slightly on the rug which had been upturned at the edges by a passing housecat. Almost as though she hadn't been shoved there at all. Before she could rise he took his belt in one hand and pressed her, back down, against the sofa, her ass up in the air, legs spread. He took the curtain ties and bound her and his belt came down across her thighs and back and ass and crossways against her cunt, again and again, drawing deep mean lines that soon bloomed with blood drops.

Get up, he said.

There was a white swan in the corner, on top of the bookcase, too high to be touched. There were vivid red stains on its wingtips. It collected its feet beneath it, its long black stalks of legs.

Get up, the doctor said.

His hair was parted as if chiseled. His thin white arms were covered in wiry hair. Down below the angry man took the woman, yanked her up by her wrists, her hands tied, already bloodless and rendered a frozen, ghostly shade, and hooked her wrists onto the top corner of the opened door, her feet swinging not even an inch above the floor, limp.

This was not beautiful.

The swan had a beautiful elongated neck, which it arched up in a pained frond. Blood ran down its wings and dripped onto the floor. The swan looked down. Long parallel, diagonal lines were being drawn with surgical precision against the woman's delicate back.

Over the next hour blood ran down two grooves on either side of her body, ran down the slice of her buttocks and along the insides of her long thin legs, and twisted around the bones of her ankles and collected in a pool at her feet.

And then the man lifted the woman off the door, untied her wrists, and left her in the bath.

In the rising light of morning, the water slowly turned a wan pink, a small swan swimming gently in the liquid at the woman's knees.

❦

WHITEY WAS THE ONE WHO BANDAGED SWEET MARIE. ROLLS OF gauze wrapped her torso, and covered the bruises. Once scabs had formed, Whitey rubbed comfrey into the slices several times a day to keep her sister's back free from scars.

Below the bandages, Sweet Marie's belly rose up, still ripe with a female sea of life.

Bop.

Be-bop.

A warm live thing, this baby ate her pain and sang out songs of love. It sang jazz to Sweet Marie, so faint and low she could not even hear.

❦

WHITEY WENT TO DR. WILLIAMS' HOUSE TO GATHER SWEET Marie's few possessions. In her strange dyed fur costume and feathered hat, eyes drawn on thick and black, high tight boots waterstained and manly around her doll's feet, Whitey clearly adhered to her own peculiar holy host and, perhaps intimidated, the surgeon did not offer threat or excuse.

Whitey wanted to burn him down to a charred skeleton of a man, to slice his neck from ear to ear with a slice of broken bottle glass. However, in her wake Whitey simply left snake eggs in his cabinets and behind the bathtub. Black widows and brown recluses in his drawers. Hornet's nests in paper bags deep down within his closets. A copperhead beneath his pillows.

She had promised Sweet Marie only this revenge, an introduction of pestilence. Surely anyone's God would understand.

♥

THEY SAID TO ME:

Wrap your arms around me

Their requests split me wide, I was an open gate

Which let them

Pass through.

♥

FOR WEEKS SWEET MARIE WAS NEITHER ALIVE NOR DEAD. SHE was no longer numb, and yet she could not yet feel. Her heart beat more slowly than it should. Her blood was thick and syruped. She felt no stirring in her belly, but nonetheless there was something uncoiling, unwrapping itself from around her spine.

The jazz baby, knowledge baby, freedom baby—that still awake and still alive baby tap-tapping

scat-a-flapping

In Sweet Marie's head the notes the Jazz Girl played still scratched at her memory.

There is a piece of jazz lodged inside Marie, reminding her of something more that still ought to be.

Should come to be.

Rattle that cage, mama—

come on out.

❤

And sometimes Sweet Marie is more awake than asleep. But her awake state is a dream state: she shudders to see the Jazz Girl and the doctor in the faces of everyone. Smells them everywhere, and feels revulsion. Listens for the sound of their low live voices and hears them, sinister and smoky in the bed next to her. Feels their fingers laid heavily against her breast.

Her heart slowly pounds one-two-three-four against her chest.

Sleep had always comforted Sweet Marie. Solitude brought clarity, distance, detachment provided peace. So what is this now when her sleep brings dreams of violent touch—the only touch which has ever come to her—the fist and the belt, the abandonments, the demands and the goodbyes. Her eyes and their eyes, her hands and their hands, their force and her cunt, their words and her silent breath.

❤

AND THEN, MANY MONTHS LATER, WHEN THE SLICES ON HER body had turned smooth and upraised and shining, in this dream state come the high long notes of a violin. The instrument cradled beneath a chin swathed in darkness. The player makes it long and low. She pulls its strings like she's tugging at flesh itself. The wooden body glows, it is the glow inside a conch shell, it shines, a scarf of copper silk. She plays it in the bedroom to a baby laying upon the bed. Lying naked on a summer bed while the musician plays overtones and harmonies. Syncopates. Pizzicato. There is a pitcher of milk with honey next to the bed. The sun is filtered from the west. The breeze blows in the window through soft amber curtains. That is the east. The light is shadowed through amber curtains, and tints the room in dawn's patina. Sweet Marie slides the bow, it arches up, rises and falls. The notes pour out.

Yeah baby. Yes. Please.

It is this she hascraved.

Somewhere inside Sweet Marie there is a happy voice, a pure unheard-before voice that murmurs quietly along to the notes of the violin. The notes are impure—sometimes burred, or blurred, a flat here instead of a sharp. The vibrations move through her in waves of moon and tide. She can't tell the difference between her voice and the violin. Sounds. They are all so kind and new. Pure. And her hand gently pressing the neck, softly, carefully, her other hand on the bow, loving, calling it, her hand holding the fingered strings, drawing notes. Her baby lies on the bed naked on its back, its belly rising up in a firm round globe and Sweet Marie stands her music against the baby's fat form and plays for it. The air itself vibrates. And there is a wet and salty love there, lapping at the two of them in the bedroom and the notes cry happy in the curtained summer air. This will happen. She knows it will.

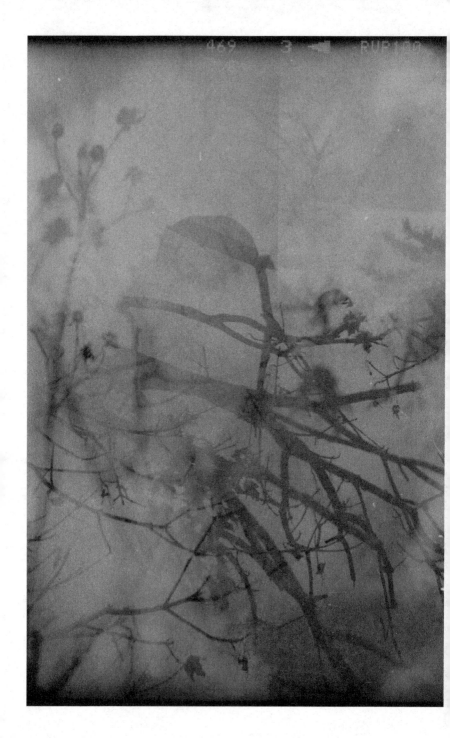

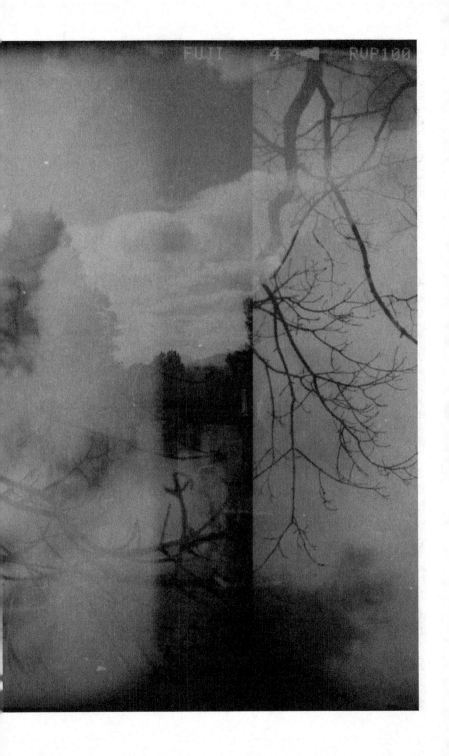

THE KEROSENE IN THEIR KISSES

SKINNY JONES' LONG THIN FINGERS DRUM UPON HIS THIGHS THAT stretch out far past the edge of his chair. She marvels at the length of his feet, and their broad flat expanse. Whitey is able to pick out that string of a sentence from his knotted skeins. She is surprised. She warms, realizing her body had, before that, become chilled.

She is tired. A day at work—nursing people she doesn't love is work. Bodies to heal and to please and roll from side to side, manoeverings, decipherings, comforting, listening, worrying: it never ceases. Bodies of the young and old, minds mostly in pieces. Her own body exhausted, beached out.

And this man beside her, thinking a relationship with her is possible, when she is so shattered—she wants to start over again, yes, but she wants to do it right.

Whitey looks at Jones there next to her, her beloved, sees him twisting a stick in his hands, his crooked skinny knees pointed upwards as sharp and strong as anything she could imagine, and she knows him to be someone who she would carry on for. She is afraid of him. He is the one she would hope for, be happy about, wait around for. But she's never known how to navigate the world. Never learned to twist it and pull it and wind her way through it if not easily, then at least with grace and beauty. And now, she isn't particularly admirable to herself, with her awkwardness and sadness. And here she is, frightened and in love, and ready to wash her hands of it all and start running, here is a man who instead of running sits and thinks, makes alliances with the demons inside him, talks them down, and then thinks and plans some more, and gradually unknots what had been something Whitey would've had to blown through or sliced or burned. She the weaver of knots, and he the un-weaver. Whereas all she knows is how to catch fire, he is some lord of conjuring phoenixes from their ashes.

Skinny Jones is speaking, now about the Black Pirate, about his childhood, about snakes in the crawlspace, he is sneaking up on her, carefully, quietly. He lights a cigarette. His face flashes in the darkness.

Whitey reads this man as though she has climbed inside him and pulled out the typewriter ribbon of his brain. She holds him in her hands and sees that he is nervous and jittery at what he wants to say to her. She knows that in his mind there are white fence-slats being cut of tall trees that still are growing wild and tall in the woods. He is thinking of sharpening his axe and cutting them down, of going to the woods and taking down those tall trees to make thin boards to nail close together to make a frame, and around the frame walls, and over the walls a roof and around it all a fence. And he is thinking of putting a layer of paint on the wood of the fence and the frame and the walls, and varnish on the floors, and sealing it all up with all the horrors of the world on the outside.

❦

In her head Whitey searches for what she should do with Jones. She walks in circles around the pits and fissures she has dug to deposit other lovers, all lost to the war of her life: some hollows slowly filling up, others that seem to get no shallower with time.

Fifteen years of this so far, she thinks. *A decade and more.*

Sometimes I can't remember who I am.

Whitey goes back over the faces in her mind, the mottled, stained bones that tell her who she is because of where she has been, and with whom. She is gone now—into the ossuary of her past, through the narrow neck of urns through which he should never fit. She has left the past for what and who she has decided to become - been before she even knew him. It is a place that he can never be part of, and which she can never cease laying roses.

Ellis, who caused her lips to smile out around twenty-eight pearl-sized teeth and how her breasts seemed to double in size just from being in love with him. *Or was it the baby I nearly bore that did that. Was it the baby, then, that turned my teeth from white into the very palest ivory?* George. The way he bit her when he kissed her—his mouth, lips, tongue, everywhere. He kissed her with fangs. A potent combination of tenderness and danger. Caleb, a lazily malevolent uncle. Innocuous, if you didn't take pause to examine the man too carefully. It was his assumption of constant, total access to her body that remained with her long after, into to her adulthood. She was eleven. And Simon—thick white skin, always slightly oily, everywhere. Glistening, curved plank of a back roughed by pimples, and shapeless jaw and cheekbones; a thing close kin to an albino beetle. But oh—his love felt more like submission, like worship than like a sexual act—it amazed and gratified her how a man would have to bow down beneath a woman, and crouch, and lick at her hidden parts. Andrew and all of the others like him: pathetic, presumptuous, and arrogant. Hunger can be so disgusting. In those days she would naively hold back in some sort of semi-conscious hope they would come to their senses and figure out how to handle a woman's body properly. *These days I haven't the time for that.* She gave up that kind of patience. *Sometimes they lunge at me pitifully, wet-lipped, with veiny hands outstretched: one aiming high, towards my breasts, and the other aiming low.* There was one lover—Jacob—he would torture her by touching her, and then for days or weeks refusing to. She was lured by his independence and roughness, his gruffness and distance that made Whitey feel unsettled. The way she'd felt when she'd been a little girl, when older men would sometimes desire her, and she hadn't understand what was in their eyes. The coming close, and then the pulling away.

What had been her first time? Seth. Pious. A Quaker. Pale white hair and puffy all over, although a thin man, and those bright pink inexplicable, the bright pink of the underthings he wore—*against my will doesn't begin to describe it*—there was a moment of quiet coldness in the midst of it all when she thought, *Since when do rapists*

207

wear women's underthings? How truly disgusting to have something truly and utterly hateful inside her body, deep inside, moving and pumping and spurting, inside her there, deep inside her body. And the twenty dollars he left her, left on her as he left her, jammed the money into the neckline of her dress. *For things,* he had said, vaguely, as he turned his back and broke into a slow run.

And the next one—heavy and odorous and thick-lipped, fur all over, the thick rough palms of his hands like paws against her body, stout penis rising from an impenetrable jungle of fetid hair—the entire experience guttural and visceral and inhuman, no standards of socialized sexual conduct, anything went. There was one in April, fiercely tender, he was wide-eyed and open and alive, he was creation itself, he was a pure bright beam of light, he was generous, careful and tentative, with a sweet rice-white sap she loved to fill her mouth with. An angel's cock, divine and velvety, that belonged inside her, came home inside her—the first time they made love was at dawn, and the light was all pale lavender. The light from the window made their bodies lavender, his long curls, the curve of his hipbones where they met beneath her thighs. When it was over she—she still can't speak of that. He found her, *too much.* Having the carpenter inside her was oddly deathlike, a beached fish conducting its floppy death-throes. And afterwards, so austere. Then there was the man who didn't like women. He kept a loaded gun on the table while he made love to her—he liked to nearly strangle her. He put a chain around her neck and chained her to the table, then left her forever one night, simply disappeared into the darkness after saying he'd recently been raped. His brother cut the chain off her a few days later. What is this life she's lived.

She stands at the sepulcher of her past with her clenched fist of flowers and thinks, once, in the beginning, affairs would end and *I would think, Well, that's that, then.* But as time has passed, Whitey knows is always more time, there is always time for more unpleasant memories, there is always a reminder, a chance meeting. And not to rekindle—nothing pleasant—just to jolt a little. Years and years might go by and then one man or another would surface. It's an intimate town—too close to avoid old lovers.

She tells herself she should leave the past in the past. But secretly Whitey's fists twist up, clench tightly around what she has experienced. Whitey's insides are poised, coiled. It makes her smoke too many cigarettes. Smoking keeps her from talking, and keeps her breathing. Whitey wants to slide down in the darkness to curl up in the thin space between the bushes and the house. What could she say to her younger self, were she to come walking up the lane, shoes in hand, dress torn–

Would she say, *Happiness is fragile*? Would she say, *Fight back*? Or, *Don't wait around hoping for anything special*? *But we all know that already, don't we. We know that already and yet we carry on, doing more of the only thing we know how to do.*

Whitey feels herself splitting off into a thousand tiny bugs circling around their fateful flame. There is nothing she can sense to save herself, not from the memories, and the memories are who she has become. She need not define that for herself—she only looks at the path she's walked. *I command the stars to listen. All that I have known must no longer be.*

Whitey watches the dogs sleep in the yard.

Colossal oaks with the wind twisting their limbs. Colored glass lantern glowing on the table. The water bottle blinking reflections: stars come to earth. Flame and fire. Whitey drops the ash from her cigarette through a filigree of rusty holes in the lid of the empty kerosene can next to her and watches it simmer and then extinguish. Underneath the lid lie the bloated, burned, succotash-yellow cigarettes from each evening of each year of her life that she has sat here smoking in the gnatty air. This same white house. Over time Whitey has dropped thousands through the holes until now there are mounds and mounds of dead ends. All of them hers. They look like the heaps of bugs piled up under seductive summer lamplight. Grilled to death against the hot glow of summer.

❦

AND NOW JONES.

Whitey wishes her heart were a little less robust. She wishes it were smaller. She can feel how big it is and how much room it has inside it, how many peaceless inhabitants. She hates the way it has of making room for him, of holding on too tightly when she knows better, knows to let him go. She can feel its raw muscles bunching and flexing. She can feel it pushing at her, pulling at her. She can feel it beating hard and fast against her ribs. Reveal. Reveal. Show your cards. Shuffle, but face up. Deal everything. Where some women have seven veils Whitey has seventy. Seven times seventy. Here she has come to remove everything for this man, for herself, to peel off the scabs, destroy her secrets.

He is so gentle to her, there in the lamplight, his exquisite hands.

❦

JONES' BLACK BROWS A BOW, HIS EYES ARROWS HE PLACED IN her, quivered, spine-wired. *I, strung across your crossbow shoulderblades, a passion tie-down. Fly to me now, never let me go.* Her heart pierced, the best bleed—bright red, a crimson flower of a sunset through the catalpa bean trees—knowing what comes next.

She said it first. But when he says it back, *love,* Whitey doubles over her belly, clutched, pale, and runs swiftly toward the barn. Her terror causes the moon to tumble below the horizon, and roll itself sorrowfully away to places nobody had ever gone. The screech owls avert their eyes, and their claws leave lurid gashes in the magnolia branches.

Jones' skin suddenly stretched taut, and seemed to crack. His brown eyes closed and when they opened they were wet and gray, but smiling. He can stay with this woman. He can see this through.

Now, hours later, Whitey rides hard and low beneath the branches, strips her dress to a limb, leaves it rent in a thorned grasp. Sweat-flanked, frothed, her sad cunt rubbing, fingers twisted in the mane, vise-clenched.

Fear, cross me here. Gallop through me, wheel and do me again—Faster—
Break into a run.

❦

SHE WANTS IT—WANTS JONES, WANTS A HOME, COMMUNION, adventure, sanctuary, love, an end to—wants belonging—and she can't have these things, not now, not as she is, not with these ropes of violence round her neck, always around her neck, and her still wanting the taste of free, and she takes it out, desperate, on the night. She anoints the horse with hooch. Smashes the bottle against a tree and gallops through the breaking glass. She's wind-snatched and riding out of her mind. A wild thing, the line of Orion her sword now, she's sky-pirated, garbed in jonquils and chainmail, peonies and panniers, fully equipped for love and battle.

Jones, who knows of compassion, and of love. Jones, who can be alone and find some pleasure in it. She has watched him staring into the fields for hours, hands curled patient in his lap while inside her the knots sicken and twist, grip her guts in a noose that cinches ever tighter. He has a mind of daffodils, beautiful and golden, a supple flesh, recovering glory and goodness each spring just past the ice of winter.

His Borealis a shivering source of hope and light and dawn, a beacon at the edges of her sad eternal night.

❦

AND SO SHE RIDES INTO THE NIGHT, THE HEAT FROM HIS TENDER finger on her heart, a trumpet tap for some unholy reflex, that fat muscle tautened, beating out a healing that brings more pain. She rides alongside from the lover who blows his horn to remind her of home. She rides, naked through the night, deep into the woods, black hair a devil's flame, the sky cock-winked and twinkled. He unleashes her pain and sets it to the track—let it wind itself until its lungs collapse, a dark star burnt out, uncountable years backwards to this universe birth.

To you I say yes, want to touch your fox fur spine

I want you to stay while I wipe my own tears dry

While I find my wounds. While I apply powder of amber and cornmeal

For you to thread my holes with silken ribbons

She wills her past to be a raven, with strong wings. She wills it to be a snake, to glide undetected. Anything, as long as it was something hardly human, and she could leave it behind her in the woods.

And now the horse has taken her far enough from it. She slides from it, spanks it back homeward. Loose on the ground, flat footed, she turns to face Jones—her legs ache for their familiar rhythm—

The way he wraps his tongue around the fig of her clit and tugs at her own heart's veins.

They have called their names and they have come.

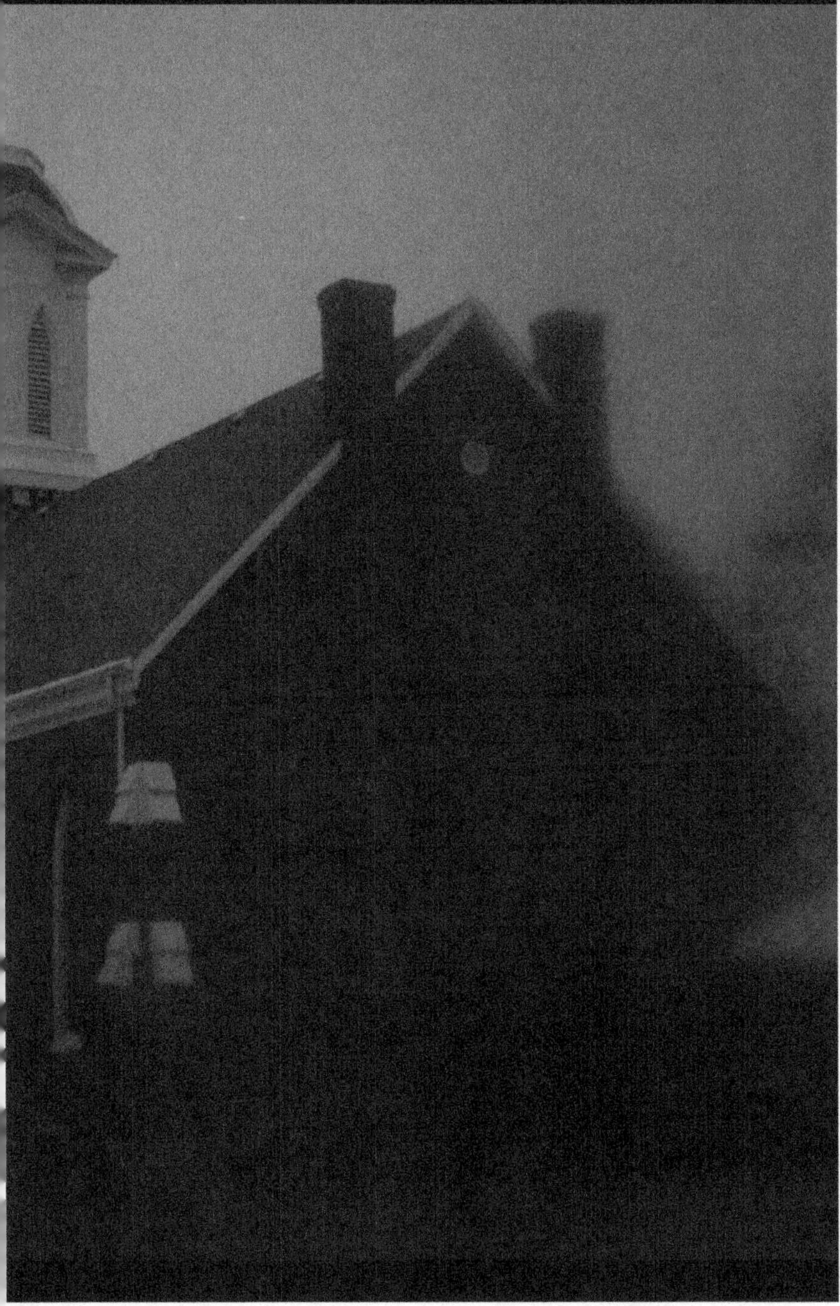

THE HOLES
IN THE GOOD LORD'S HANDS

THE PIOUS WOMEN WATCHED FROM AFAR AS THE MEN CONTROLLED the altar, holding court under the body of a dead man. The preachers had the best horses tied up outside. In the pockets of the men—the money for the collection plate. In the women's pockets handkerchiefs for tears and to wrap the food for children. *Sanctus.* Holy.

Gold and white the colors of praise, the colors of angels' vestments, the colors of the rich, so pure they require the very cleanest water. Black and brown the colors of the poor; red the color of the sinful.

Whitey and Sweet Marie looked at all the men and wondered which of them worried—heads bowed as they sat next to their wives and mothers, lady friends and daughters—which neighbors to condemn. Their averted eyes which gazed at the twins' swollen bellies and breasts more often than at their eyes, or the eyes of their women which examined their every inch. Why had the twins walked into church for the first time in their lives? Had they forsaken the witches' midnight mass by full moon light?

Gloria in excelsis deo. And the choir rose. *Spiritus Sanctus.*

And Roman law made everything inside the church predictable and appropriate as the white pillars and white cornices of Lynchburg's other white Southern edifices. The wedding ring of Christ, the bells, the colors, the dark wood, the covered heads, the tapers, the kneelings and crossings and bowings were unquestionably mysterious and honored and reassuring in their authority and so the citizens of Rome did as they were told. They rose humbly. They knelt proudly. And the little boys sang high and sharp in their rich white robes. And the women watched the men lead the cross and candles up the aisle, and down the aisle, and back and forth and around and around and down and up, and they prayed. *Take away the sins of the world.* Secretly they watched Whitey's unholy body and Sweet Marie's unholy body and waited to see if their God would listen to their prayers. *Take away the sins of the world.* And the parish expected the twins to vanish but they didn't. *Amen,* the flock said reluctantly, as though the congregation's obeisance should have produced more vindicating results. *You alone are the Holy One. You alone are the Lord. In the glory of God the Father.* And they all wondered who was the father of each, even the priest adjusting his satins and silks. *Praise be to the Father.*

In church the willful ignorance of irony. *Praise be to the Father, amen.* Who was the father. What color the baby. Whitey, plump, knew the father. She was the mother, ripening her egg, polishing her apple, seasoning herself from the pillar of salt, swinging the rings in her ears, tasting the paint on her lips. Babylon and brown. And Sweet Marie, and the be-bop baby with two mothers. No need for the hand of an angry white god. And the boys continued to sing words they didn't understand, in a language they didn't know how to speak for themselves. *Look with love upon me, my lambs,* and the congregation bowed their heads to one another, to the great white man in the sky, to the father, and the women clutched their husbands closer, eyes on the trouser buttons: *nearer my God to thee.*

❦

LEADERS OF THE PEOPLE. REJOICE IN THY LORD'S CREATION. BELOW their darkened eyes of birds of prey, the white women's lips moved in song: *by the Lord has this been done and it is wonderful in our eyes. Let us rejoice and be glad.* They could not celebrate all creation. Not Whitey's moments of passion, desire, and procreation. Her enjoyment of man, his joyously rigid rod and staff. *My God he is good. His love endures.* They wondered what Sweet Marie enjoyed that they were missing. And they clutched the arms of their husbands closer to them. Their husbands good. Their love endures. Which the father?

Our Father who art in heaven, hallowed by thy name. Who? *Thy will be done.* Which the father of Whitey's child. How on this barren soil could Sweet Marie be with child. *On earth as it is in heaven.*

♥

LOOK UPON THE NAIL THAT PIERCED OUR SAVIOR'S PALMS. THE PRIEST'S face was marked with the spots of age, and his earlobes sagged thin with the weight of salvation. He held up a small casket containing a roof nail from the Burbank's barn. He stared at the twins, grim. *Crucified,* he proclaimed, the arc of casket a ray of rust through the air.

His time-curled fingers staffs to hook and subdue the necks of his flock. He had cut his fingernails in the morning. Buffed them with a cloth to make them glint in the candlelight. He admired their beauty, impressive in the lurid purple gleam of painted glass.

♥

LO, HOW THEY WANDERED SORROWFUL AND HOW THE LORD HAST *made them thankful for it.* And the twins considered all those who have suffered. The stones lodged in the sandals of the Roman soldiers, how the soldiers could not complain, for they were citizens of a great empire, although their dusty soles bled bright pink into the desert soil, the pebbles dimpling the leather, oh how they could not complain about their suffering as they climbed the hill. The way sweat stings and causes pain in cuts. The whole party bleeding, Mother Mary bleeding, the Magdalene bleeding, her monthly flow soaking the cloth lodged between her legs as she climbed the hill with her doomed lover, him blistered and punctured and bearing his cross, her bearing other things that would remain forever unknown. And the twins looked at the Lynchburg fathers and heard what sadnesses they had told them of at night, pressed up against the outcast girls in the dark, their pale hands tangled in the thick wool between the twins' legs. The death of their last mule, no potatoes or corn left to feed their family. They told the twins of the hollows under their children's eyes and wept and chewed their hangnails. Worried on their calluses of dead skin. Their women at home in bed, alone, ash blond heads bent over teary forearms—*why hast thou forsaken me*—eyelashes dark and spiked with salt.

Whitey turned the pages of her hymnal as though an evil grimoire. To Sweet Marie, the Latin prayers were medicinal, like the names of maladies, *spiritus sanctus,* like an uncture, an ointment. Soul salve. Plea for a cure. And Jesus cried out, *Do you love me?*

The twins watched the sad-eyed citizens, the lonely lambs of Lynchburg whose sanctimony kept them warm, depression safer than rebellion. The sacrament of anger denied them; the sacrament of victimization endorsed. Predators. Their milky Jesus. Whitey and Sweet Marie had come to the church together for reasons beyond their comprehension. The mass growing inside them, of uncertain color - still red, but later darkening perhaps, or lightening. Which side of town would close its great doors to the mass inside the twins. Theirs was a seat of power, and suddenly they were curious about that. Power. Who had it, and who didn't, and why and why not. What had they absorbed all these years, what hate and exclusion, and what if, exactly, they were planning to spit it all out in their afterbirth.

❦

AND THE CONGREGATION SANG:

Clothe yourself in humility.

Restore

confirm

strengthen

You who have suffered

Hallelujah

And the plate came around, and the coins of the poor clattered, and the paper of the rich made not a sound.

Hallelujah.

❦

IN THE END, THERE ARE ALWAYS HOLES IN THE PALMS OF GOOD strong hands. They long to close up tight again, for flesh to meet and join to solid flesh, but somehow there are these holes, something has driven through the wholeness and caused an opening, and things fall through.

No one wants to feel that drop, to fall into capable hands and somehow suffer the hole. It's a lonely feeling. Falling through the palm, and striking the soil, and shattering.

And Jesus asked again, *Do you love me?*

❦

IT'S A TRICKY UTENSIL, THE SIEVE OF SALVATION. ONLY THE LARGE things remain, everything else drains out through the perforations— all the things that are almost too small to be missed drain out. What is left is only that which cannot pass through the hole. This is the stigmata. For everyone it is different. Hope remains, or despair. Love, or antipathy. Memories, or forgetfulness. Fear, or courage. Surrender, or faith. The empty placenta, or the baby.

Within every strong hand is a hole. Remember this. Something will fall through.

And something will, unexpected, be held firm.

❦

AND THE PRIESTS WATCHED THEIR FULL PEWS SUFFER BEAUTIFULLY, for inside the church it was dark and dreamily glowing and the air smelled of myrrh and the flock looked at one another from the corners of their eyes, without turning their heads to the left or to the right, in case their distraction might be detected and criticized by the god who demanded their full attention. Although they were curious about what was growing in the bellies of the twins. What was happening beneath the surfaces of their interconnected lives? What seed in which soil?

Who had trespassed?

Someone had trespassed. Her white fur hat. Her tawny face, plump with child not of Christ but of Isis, perhaps, or Innana. She the false idol. She the woman the men ran to. She the harbinger of death. The one the town ran into. Ran through. Passed through and gone in too deep. Trespassed unto trespass.

But they could neither ask nor question in case they burned eternally. And Whitey's belly swelled. And Sweet Marie's belly beat. The flowers on the altar slowly browned, their petals thickening and sweating into a pale but darkening wilt, flaccid in the clotted air.

❦

A BIRD FLEW PAST THE OPEN CONFESSIONAL AND WHITEY AND Sweet Marie laughed. Its wings fluttered in sheer happiness, a forgotten ghost from Eden. Something answered, a joyful fluttering from their bellies. And Jesus said simply, *Lord, you know that I love you.* And the grass was green in the hills beyond the church, where the twins would run to and bear their children, away from the angry god, away from the men of power.

Sweet Marie and Whitey knew, now, for certain, that they were priestesses of some more ancient kind of faith. A faith centered in the female fissure, the dark abyss that yields life that heralds death. And so the third time Jesus asked, *Do you love me?* He received his answer. How he handled it is subject to interpretation.

PART THREE:
THE LEFT VENTRICAL

THE MOSS HAS FROZEN
DREADFUL TO THE BARK

THERE HAD BEEN NO WARNING—THERE IS NEVER ANY WARNING. The earth was salted with frost, for it was winter, and it smelled as such. Until he came into the house, and then it smelled of summer, of late summer when nothing is fresh any longer.

Maw's face took on a sheen. The bones fought past the muscles and skin to stand on the outside of her face, replacing her flesh with skull. Two hollows for eyes staring out in something like a corpse's half-smile of shocked pleasure—unexpected. Maw was a thing of beauty and grace unadorned. This was the day of reunion. They wheeled the stretcher off the back: *Lafayette*. But then, unexpected, he stood and walked. Walked towards the three women. Tried to mount the stairs and could not. He crumpled. Whitey ran down to help him up. His bones seemed soft, he had turned back to clay, his suit a fibrous thing stinking of cigarettes and softened skin.

Where did the thought come from—for it came to all of the women simultaneously. Over the agony of years, they had told themselves, silently and individually, that something like the river, death, or catastrophe had restrained him. But in his awful softened state, bones so logged with weakness, the women realized he had known, all along, where they had been, and that they had needed him, and wanted him, and dreamed of him with love and longing and an enduring merciful despair.

He had known how to come back, hadn't he, all along, and yet hadn't returned until now. But not because they needed him, but because he finally needed them.

It was a thought none of them cared to utter, and a question none of them needed to have answered.

❦

THE DEATH'S HEAD OF MAW SEEMED MOUNTED WITH A NAIL ABOVE the door. It barred the door for an instant and then a weird smile of pleasure granted the gurney access and Lafayette was borne aloft into the white house. She had stood aside to let him pass, and the twins followed along behind before the door closed upon them all.

❦

THERE WAS NOTHING TO SAY. DOGS BARKED. AFTER THE MOON came out it went away again. When he had arrived it had been afternoon. And shortly thereafter the moon had been three quarters full, and then all of a sudden there it was, filling up with its white lunar sap, poised, half-tipped, getting ready to drip out over them into a milk-fed dawn.

They had worked through the night, talking little.

Only once had the death's head spoken a word: *syphilis*.

So he had needed them, and he had returned.

Them bitches sent him back, the driver had said before departing, and Sweet Marie had covered her mouth, but too late, for she had already vomited into the lilac bushes. The dogs had gone over to investigate.

❦

IT WAS MORNING. LAFAYETTE WAS IN A WHITE NIGHTGOWN. THE women were burning lemon oil in the bedroom to cover the stench. Whitey sat with her father. The others were outside at the cast iron cauldron, boiling the second set of sheets. Bugs kept crawling. It seemed like all sorts of bugs were everywhere, traveling fast in their headless shells. Whitey snapped them between her fingernails. She was going to shave his head—thick handfuls of white and silver and red hair, great hanks like weaving yarn, skeins of it. The razor a flat-bladed affair attached to a long white bone handle. She kept it sharp. She wore an apron of thick, tight-woven cloth over her lap to hold the hair, the piles of red hair shot with quicksilver—it seemed to be full of movement, of passion and lice and vitality. It wouldn't come off his head—it was tough as sinew. He cried and laughed and touched her arm at crucial moments—the blade slipped above his ears. There was blood dripping on the pillow. Drops of red-licorice liquid suspended in his brows and eyelashes. He didn't notice. The blood ran down the deep grooves along his nostrils. Whitey poured witch hazel on the wounds and blotted them. *Little bitch*, he smiled. *Maybe I wanted them itchy bastards. Maybe I've grown to like them.* Pulling up his nightgown she shaved his entire body—long liquid strokes of the blade when and where she could, covering flesh quickly; short jagged strokes when the need was there. She saw his body was so much like her own; he was missing the pussy and she the cock but the rest she had washed herself for years, sturdy thighs, solid ankles, flat kneecaps, broad hips and deep caverns of armpits. But in her father there was no end to what had rotten. He was covered with sores. Whitey tried to shave around them; she covered them with mercury salve and bandages. Whitey put a handful of her father's hair in a jar for her basement apothecary.

The rest she threw sizzling into the fire, with a few cups of cedar bristles to cover the scent.

Where is her sister? Where is her mother? She thought she saw her mother's cadaverous face grinning outside the window and then it too disappeared.

❦

MAW HAD THOUGHT FOR SOME TIME IN THE PAST YEAR THAT HE might come back. She had felt his presence along the roads in her bones. And she surprised herself, after all these years, at the fact that she was excited in a way, didn't feel the old anger too deeply, didn't revile or hate him or consider how she would punish him when he finally arrived, no matter what state he was in. And when she saw him and immediately diagnosed his disease—and knew its story, the story of the last twenty years without even having to wait for the town of Lynchburg to come running to tell her of her shame—she felt nothing aching but her bones anymore. Maybe they had been what was bothering her all these years.

Who was this stranger, so humbled in her home, so ineffectual? His wedding ring gone, sold for card money, or girls, or flophouse food—had it ever been fastened on his finger? Had he ever lain quietly at her side? Were these the lovelight eyes she had gazed into? His thick arms, thick thighs: these had stood next to her by the fireplace beneath the Parisian mirror and taken vows. Maw suddenly gathered up the orange blossom bouquet she had scattered, its blooms all rotted and broken, over the grave of her marriage all those years ago. She unpacked the wedding gown made of lace doilies and tablecloths. The past twenty years in rage and loathing for this man? He was sugared now, to her, somehow, by becoming weak: now that he needed her and she no longer needed him, she might even say she had forgiven him.

Maw hadn't been required to take him in—the town would have understood had she turned him away, indignant. It would have been as Christian to deny solace to a sinner as it would have been to give succor; moral justification could have been found either way. Surely she should feel more anger? No, she had spent her feelings in the preceding twenty years. They had been wasted years, then. No, she had raised two girls, kept the household running, saved lives and ushered others out with a modicum of peace and comfort. Had she not suffered? No more than other people, and now she saw justification in the final years. A circle at last drawn fully until it closed neatly round upon them all. She had decided to take him in and enjoy his dependency on her. After all these years of her needing him, now he would have to be the one to need her. She appreciated the justice in that.

No, when Maw went in to look at the half-blind and utterly insensible husband of hers, she felt long-gone, and the years of caring stripped away. She felt light as thistle, as goose down. He could not hurt her ever again: here he was, at *her* mercy now, instead of her at his mercy. *She* had won: he'd had to return in the end.

♥

THERE ARE TIMES WHEN FAMILIES COME TOGETHER FOR A SHORT period of time because they have found a reason for it. Find the face of the Lord. Forget what has been done and think only of what can be made better. Recall what has occurred and bear witness to its scars. Sweet Marie did not want to do these things—she knew the family needed to shatter, and the sides split open without kindness.

Don't build around this man, Sweet Marie wanted to warn her kin, *he will only tear it down.*

She wished it was spring so she could plant, be outside, avoid the monster they were harboring inside, but she too was forced to dwell inside the house, the damn house, this father come back and she didn't care, she didn't care, no she didn't care at all.

♥

THE DAYS GO BY AND STILL HE STAYS, IN THE ROOM UPSTAIRS. Whitey knows peace, though she suspects it cannot last before someone or something takes it from her, as usually happens, all things in life being short. She's playing with this new man, she's got him to herself for the other women want nothing of him, will not see him. They act disinterested, but she suspects their usual undercurrents of rage and viciousness. She waits for Maw to kill him, knows Maw seething with anger, or misdirected longing. Sweet Marie jealous of Whitey's station at the bedside. But Whitey doesn't really know their emotional particulars, and doesn't ask.

The wagon driver has gone to Lynchburg and filled all ears with what he knows: the whores in the Gulf hired him to drive crazy old demented Lafayette home to his weird old wife—he had the syphilis, the copper pennies, he was too sick, they didn't want him in their whorehouse, he cried in their barrooms and backrooms all through the night—made the most mournful sounds, then denied it in the morning—hallucinated all through the day, raving, a man worse off than an idiot. He had no money, could bring in no money, his ragged cries through the night, they hired a driver to take him onwards. And now he was in Lynchburg, and he laughed the kind of laughter the house had never known. Three o'clock in the morning and his calls rang out, his feet stomping the floor by his fireplace—Whitey ran in and Lafayette was holding a burning stick of wood, dancing in the firelight, stamping out a jig upon the hardwood floor, naked to the stars. Whitey put a crown of holly on his head and danced with him, clapping, then as he tired sang songs to quiet him.

❣

MAW DID LESS DOCTORING OF HER OTHER PATIENTS WITH LAFAYETTE in the house. Strangely, she spent little time with him or with anyone else, only occasionally going to sit at his bedside while he slept—no one heard them speak to one another. But gradually the flesh and skin and then the color returned to her face. Her hands softened, and stilled slightly from the constant movement that had always been her trademark. She washed more often in the tub, put her hair in a tidier bun in back, and sometimes sat at her bedroom mirror and braided it long down her back before twisting it up in a great yoke of complex suspension and geometry at the back of her head. Beautiful.

For the first time since when the twins were babies she spoke sweetly to the girls, when she saw them—Sweet Marie mostly a phantom now, and Whitey an industrious torrent of activity. But Maw cooked meals more attentively, and would set her hand lightly on the tops of her daughters' heads when they were seated, at times going out of her way to do so. Their socks appeared in their drawers, darned. As though they had never contained a hole.

❣

AT SUPPER SWEET MARIE ASKED MAW WHY SHE WAS WORKING LESS with the patients. *I'm a married lady*, Maw said, *I figure I've paid my dues.* And her daughter asked her no further questions. After a moment Maw asked her what she thought of polishing the silver and using it for everyday, and Sweet Marie reminded her that she had sold it nearly ten years earlier.

They have new medicines for what he's got now, Whitey said as she passed her sister on the stairs, clutching a book of medicines she had made off with from the hospital in town.

Whitey... Sweet Marie began to speak to her sister, but gave it up— Whitey didn't even notice the trailing interruption. Sweet Marie turned her back and kept on walking.

♥

You're a fine piece of horsemeat, Lafayette says to Whitey, *and I see you're part of a set. Where's the other one?*

Whitey puts a jar of forced narcissus on his dresser.

I'll pay you a dollar to take that dress off and dance, Lafayette says to Whitey.

The bourbon gets cold in its teacup by the windowsill, where she has gone to sit and breathe the cold December air.

♥

When Whitey went to town, she first put Sweet Marie in charge of their father.

Your sister seemed not too interested in my business proposition, but something makes me think you'll be more my kind of a gal, said Lafayette to Sweet Marie.

Sweet Marie was seated in a rocking chair at the furthest point in the room across from him, her fingernails leaving little red-edged scythes of slices along her forearms. She closed her eyes and watched the cascades of white, blue and yellow stars plummet behind her darkened lids.

Men are willing to pay twice for twins, and twice double for twins as pretty as the two of you. You're wasting away here—for a whorehouse I can't say how's I see this place gets much activity. Soon as I'm up on my feet I'll show you how it's really done.

When Sweet Marie vomited all over his blankets and left him alone, nobody later could remember having fed him bacon and eggs that morning for breakfast.

❤

WHERE DID THE OTHER ONE GO? LAFAYETTE ASKS WHITEY. YOU BRING her to me and I could get you a real fair price for you both. You're missing out on an opportunity for some big business. Big. That old skull-head woman cutting you beauties out of the kitty?

Whitey tries to explain again that he is home, at home with his own twin daughters.

Daughters. I reckon I got no babies I know about, her father says.

No, I don't reckon you do, Whitey says, *I don't reckon.*

Much less daughters, he says. *Baby,* he says.

Daughter, she says.

❤

SWEET MARIE PUT ON HER HAT AND GLOVES AND WRAPPED HERSELF in several layers of thick black wool and walked, invisible, walking away, the miles down the wooded road leading away from the white house. There were lights shining through the branches and brambles, and she knew to which window they each belonged. The air was damp and the frost was rising to freeze the tiny shards of limestone and shale into miniature towers, cracking under her boots. Her weight left no hollow. She followed wheel tracks frozen in the mud until she diverted through the brittle underbrush and dropped into the woods, where the path was thin and black. She climbed the side of the hill, her feet twisting in the loose boots, snapping her way through brittle twigs and feeling the snag of bramble at her legs. There was no reason to hurry. The moon would not care if she arrived or not. She sat on a downed tree and the heat of her body melted a scrim of ice clinging to the wet bark—she laid back and watched the heavens above her. Each star was distinct in the

sky, and nothing had changed, nothing had changed from when she had first looked up at them when she was a little girl, they just spun around a bit as the time of year changed. This time next year, everything would be exactly the same. If a tree fell, another would take its place. The birds that were silent now would be singing in the morning, and their children's children crying every morning after.

She had a jar with bourbon in it, and she drank deeply from it while she laid there. There was someone on a different hilltop playing a fiddle and she drank and drank. She knew the branches were full of owls, and that they were all eyes—watching her. And she was all eyes, watching them. And she drank some more. And she poured it over herself and she lit a match and dropped it on her breast and hoped for a second to go up to them, in a small quick ball of fire, but she didn't. The wool was too thick. She singed and stank, and now was wet and cold. She smashed the bottle against the rocky soil. She hadn't wanted to die, she had just wanted to burn a little.

❦

THERE ARE MOMENTS OF RECONCILIATION, OF RETRIBUTION, of returns and reunions. Moments when there is nothing to do but move forward into time, keep pushing into it because what came before and what comes next are equally undesirable.

WHAT BROKEN WATER
BRINGS TO BOILING

I TOOK EIGHT POUNDS OF FAT OFF THE LARGEST SOW LEFT BEHIND
after winter. It wasn't sufficient for much else than making the soap.
Good I saved it: the things that crawled off Lafayette the first night
were big enough for frying unto their own. The way he accumulates
the worthless. *Maw*, he now whimpers, *Maw*. Gone for nineteen,
twenty years: soon as that first cold freeze came he was off—now
I know he was down around somewhere, down round about the
Gulf where the girls don't have so many clothes on in December—
each time it passed he'd be too hot to move back up. Without him
I learned to carry the keys alone, tight and black and hard on a ring
around the whiteboard house; in later years only the slow deaths
of veterans and widows bring anything in for me to keep a head up.
Then Lafayette come back to me once at last, blood gone bad and
his face half rotten off the bones and now I know for sure the Gulf
Girls could have him back, and welcome.

❦

THERE ARE THINGS I LOVED ABOUT LAFAYETTE WHICH NOW DISGUST
me, not least of all his tiny left leg that reach only to his other knee.
My breasts come to rest at my waist these days, but that's as it should
be, and I keep them clean. Wasn't always like that but they are now,
just the weight of the world come suckling at them year after year. But
him, his left knee bent half over, right there where his thigh should be,
and even the first time I could feel it knocking there, warm and damp
like some sodden fool heaving drunk against my side. How he use
it to make a girl take him in might make you sick if he weren't such

as he is, and good with it: the shrunken toes themselves small and curled, fern fronds not yet ready for the light, the nails a horsewax yellow and ridged—no bigger than a minute but long, and curved. He makes you love it. Soon as you need to look away you're caught up back behind those eyes of his, snagged in the bitterness like a pulled gut-string, lost in a stroke of mean that would wipe the color off your hair but first, first you find only this blue, this bottleglass blue, looking into the glass blue eyes of the river, slick and wet. And that just his eyes alone!

He was a tight, light one, a sweet cooker of heat lightning I hastened to meet and tie on, too fast. Not that anyone warned me, not that anyone said, *Slow Down, You're a Fine One, Wait and See*. But instead they told me, *Around Town We Think Highly of His Kind*. They said, *His Father a Pourer of Wine and his Mother a Breaker of Bread*. And with his daddy a gift, a blessing of teachings, and his mama so kind at keeping them rich—throwing figures from off her pencil quick as whisker shavings, tobacco, the once-upon-a-time-slaves—half the town money and half their blood gone through her purse! *And you can pass,* they'd hiss. *Do it while you still young*. The sizzling hiss between their teeth a flicker of venom that came from all colors. And somehow she'd thought they were on her side.

And Lafayette himself can't help the leg, they said, or was it my own self who cried out, *Don't it mean nothing how he live up in the whiteboard house? Hain't you always seen yourself laced up happy in that whiteboard house, up there, up the hill, up there up from the river?* The river may rise but it don't budge that whiteboard house up from off its rock. *Mr. Lafayette and many a Mr. Lafayette before him turned this town to face the Good Side of the Sun,* they said.

Marry Him, they said, *and we'll count you lucky.*

But if they don't now say the same when here he comes back to me—bugs the size of turnips in his gut, and a burning stink up in his fundament—still and even so my winter sow give her flesh up for that man. Three pounds of lye bubble on the cast iron fire and down there deep in his head when he's looking at his wife he hears the loose girls down in the Gulf still sing on about him:

Oh, look what we've got, look what we've got, look at Lafayette's leg

& the wonders it's wrought

As though if the splinter prickings in his head hadn't drove him home, they would have wanted him, still, wanted him pouring a grown man's weight of liquid gold into their beds.

♥

I WAS BORN DOWN IN THE VALLEY IN A LITTLE HOT BRICK BOX whose windows opened up only to the mud when the floods came around. The first flood carried off my mama and left me with my father, who passed with the fever from the second flood. And me just six, I stayed with the family who moved in after, the ones whose babies fed off grout and mortar while for more than a hundred years the whiteboard house has wet itself laughing at anything that's come and tried to do it in.

Nothing could be more beautiful than the way I still keep the Lafayette place now it's mine: white, with the walls rising like ivory up to the greenest solid copper roof. Whitey says we should paint it yellow for the yellow fever they found living down in the springhouse, or brown for the bloodstain we can't seem to get off the birthroom floor. Black for the slaves the Lafayettes kept around way after it was time for them to leave. But the house don't care for Whitey or the never-let-go blacks, or the tawny yellow-fevered skin, the floods and the fires, two wars, or for death or the termite, it just turns its face to the road and its back to the evil blue-eyed river down below. And when the whiteboard house wets itself laughing at us and our silly Lafayette tragedies, its urine finds the river and together they go looking for her in the little hot brick box I was born in, and finding me no longer in it to drown, flows on.

♥

EVERY ROOM IN THIS HOUSE HAS ITS DOOR, AND EVERY DOOR HAS its lock. Every lock has its key, and they live in a knot around my waist. Mrs. Sangster sleeps behind the door past the arbor porch, where her bones have wracked her. Phillipee Paul's deaf, and weak in the heart: he's down in the blue room, with a pan to rest under him while Old Miss Statler falls from shingles next door. Mr. Traylor fights the Cherokee, now the fever, and Mr. DePue fights the white folks, and all the rest come and go in a rustle of sheets as familiar as the morning paper. The banister torn down for the stretchers, a metal hose run up for the waste from the stinkpots and Lafayette takes his place. His heart now balloons into a watery sack, full to bursting in his chest.

❦

TWO DAUGHTERS COME CRAWLING OUT OF ME, AND ONE HATES me this day, the other the next. Whitey sits at the bedsides all day watching folks struggle to breathe, her smock full of alcohol and bloody swabs, her hair full of grease by Thursday, done just once a week on Friday in case some healthy someone on the weekend notices enough to drop his pants; Sweet Marie taking everything contained in her silence out on me, notches on her bedpost not from lovers gained or lost, but from marking the days she's spent in my captivity. Sweet Marie does her hair up tight for the white doctors and thinks that makes her different.

Different from what I ask.

From you, Maw, she says, *from you.*

She doesn't even know.

But at least Marie tries to paint it prettier, while her sister rips the paint off and befriends the rot beneath the surface. Her, so glad to see her father come back, happy to be angry, thrilled to feel that bucket of bile boiling up in her stomach about him. Between the four of us we've filled the whiteboard house with sickness, spooning mush into the mouths of the old and dying, going through their pockets while they sleep. The pockets run deep, and sometimes they flow into our own.

❦

HOW MANY YEARS AGO THE GULF GIRLS MUST HAVE BEEN THE first to notice the early attacks on his whorehouse hands as the bugs pushed through to the surface, how his palms seemed crossed with chancres like copper pennies, pennies not for them but for Lady Death. And maybe the Gulf Girls loved the summer sky of his eyes, but Lady Death laughed and blew the clouds across their stars. No more sunshine lovers for Lafayette, the Lady laughed, let's now carry him home to Mother, child, and child. Nine hundred miles with his rubbery tumors, six hundred miles with the splinter prickings, one hundred fifty more to go with his nose rotten down into his once handsomest of faces until at Lexington--*Bad blood*, the Western State had whispered, and wouldn't take him. They forced him on to me. His wife.

Before long Sweet Marie—snuck off with the hospital's echinacea and mercury, nitric acid suspended in honey, syringes full of arsenic— came home and us women tied him down, Sweet Marie and Whitey and me, we tied him down and rubbed him, one shot to the spine for the pain, gave him cotton for his screams, but there's no need for silence while he sleeps on the rock hard misery dreams, there in his new room above the stairs.

❦

AND IN THE AFTERBIRTH HE HELD ME. THOSE LONG-AGO DAYS. Underneath the skin his muscles had felt stallion strong and he'd rocked me, held me on the bed and we turned in circles and the wet streaked down my legs, his shirt, across the floor, two babies boiled out, born at once, pulling out of me, tornados ripping the roots from my soil, and he stared at their red and sticky faces and he stared at my red and sticky ache shivering in the damp and cold and it was too much for him, too hard to bear. And now again, old, I hold him—faceless, blind, his blood swallowed up by bugs and I can feel him finally crawl inside me, force the afterbirth down my throat and worm in feet first, tied to him our mean and sickly girls, the girls carrying their boys and girls, everyone in their sorrow holding their still and lonely mothers, their mothers bringing my own mother, dredged up from the mud bank and holding the hand of my daddy, waterlogged and moss-mouthed—all of them deep inside me, twisting, arching for air then scratching to get out. But there's no unlocked door to leave this life from, just my everlasting keyhole body gone on into forever.

The syphilis got a cure in the mercury that drenches his bed with spittle. And the bugs run fast from the acid bath. And though I drink the arsenic my hand don't drop the keys and I sit here watching the unweary doors open and close on the same old ancient rooms, high up on the laughing whiteboard hill full of blood and bread.

❤

He says *Get this out of me, Maw, get it gone.* Should he not call me Mother? Two bone-eyed children come out from the corpse of our love and him then vanished from me smooth and sweet as dew, come back wormed and bug-blooded to my trunk of endless remedies and he calls his wife by what she's become: Maw. Should he call me by what I was, call me *Dear Heart* or *Love,* call me *Beauty* or *Honey*? He'd say it to me now, he'd carry the good words back from the side of whatever road he abandoned them to.

But if my love is still here, then my want is gone, and when I try to drain the blood out of him even I can tell I'm neither lovely nor sweet, neither loved nor beauty, just Maw, mother, doing what must be done. So frozen deep in his meat he looks up at me, needle in my hand, and with the arsenic in its chamber this may well be the closest yet to a third tug at my cord.

The thrust of both life and death that strong.

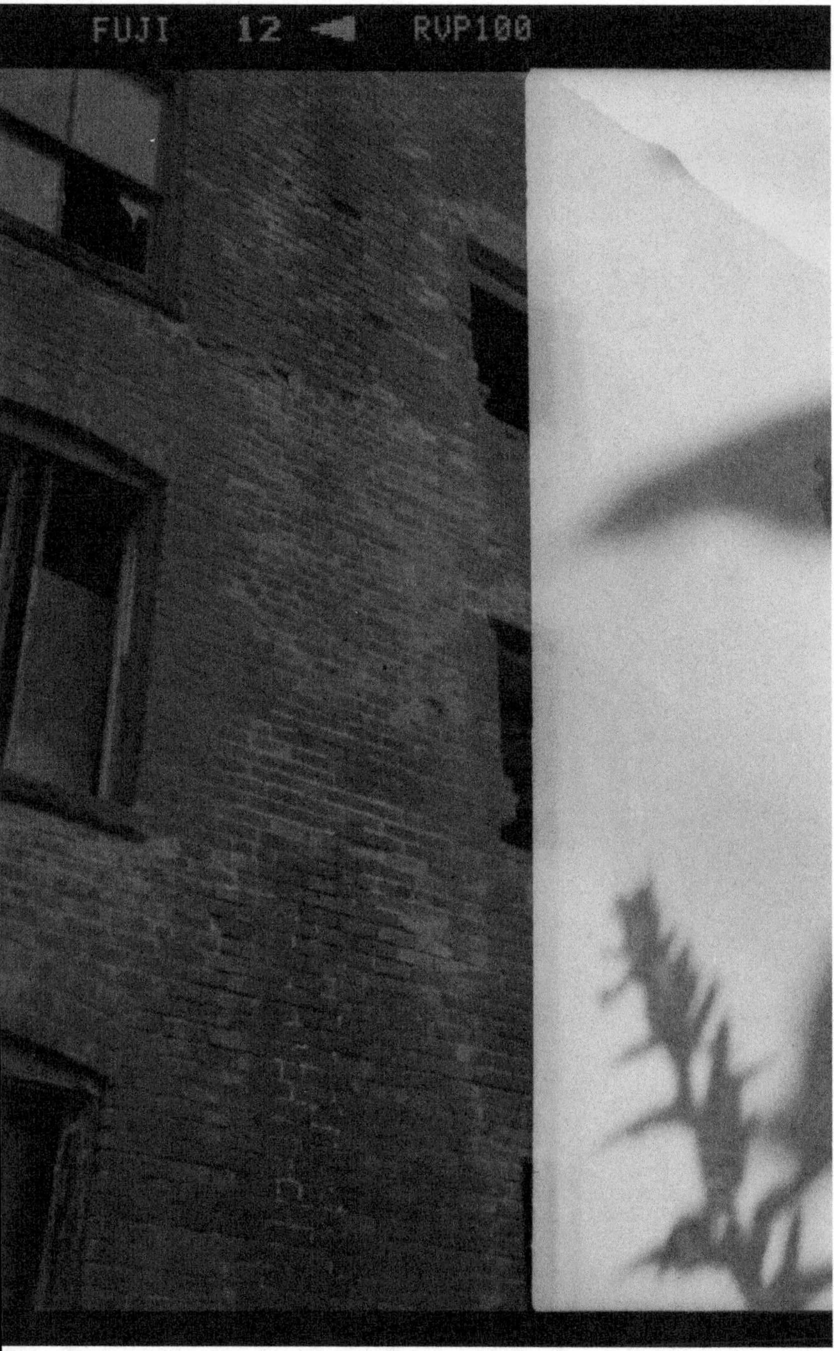
FUJI 12 RVP100

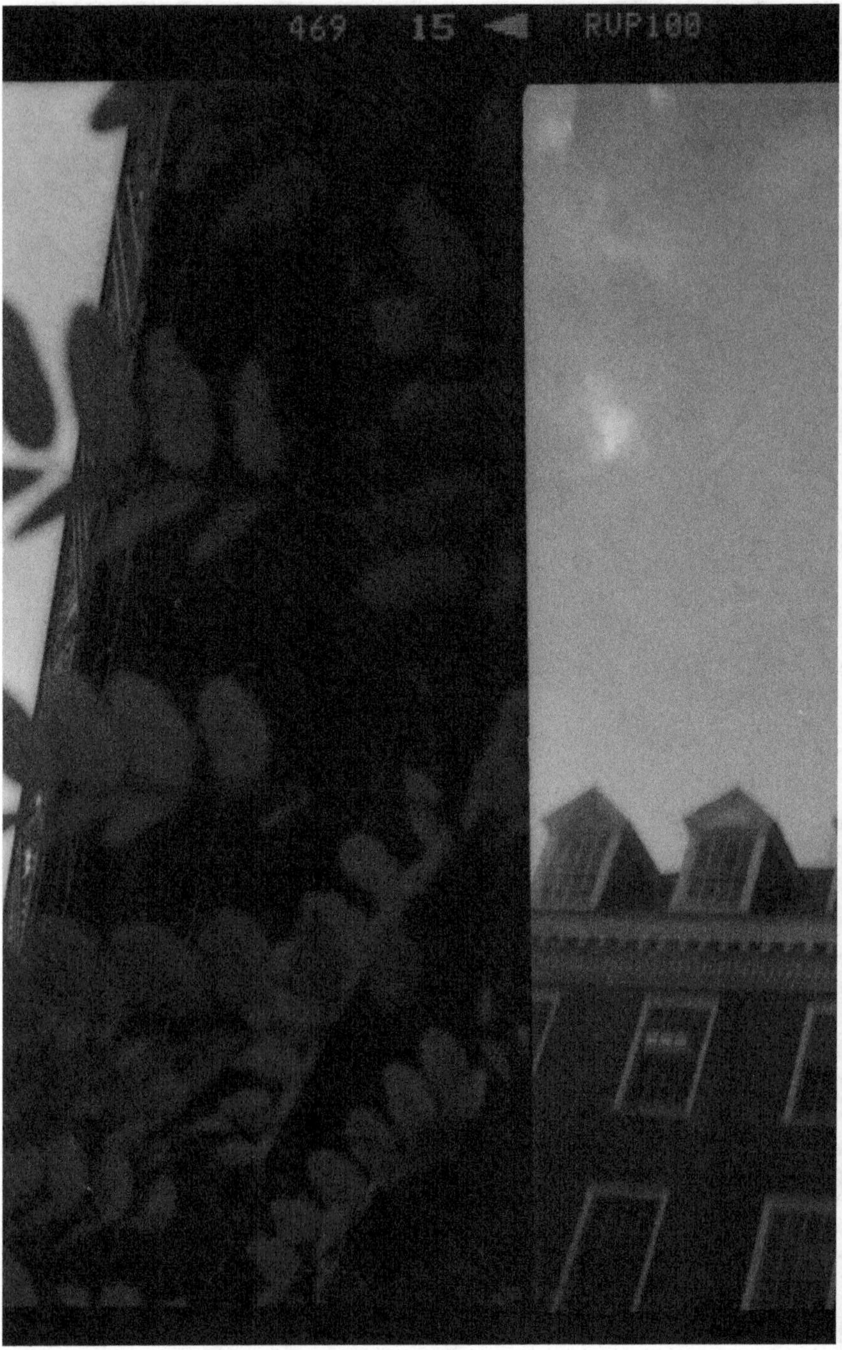
469 15 RVP100

AND THE VOICE I HEAR
NONE OTHER HAS EVER KNOWN

THE TWINS WERE NOT TO TELL, not to tell that LAFAYETTE had been delivered into some special justice, that they had watched it all lest they forget.

They had seen Maw leave his eyes open, rolling; she hadn't powdered down nor washed his body, hadn't tied him up in soft cloths. Hadn't they watched as Maw rocked their father in her arms just as they had watched her softness suddenly harden? Whitey knew she had. Sweet Marie knew she had.

They felt rapturous. Elated.

Then sudden fits of tears, of tearing their long dark hair and winding it around their fingers.

♥

THE OLD CATHOLIC DYING IN THE ROOM NEXT DOOR TO LAFAYETTE sends her morning novena through the walls and Lafayette wants to fuck her there in her rusted wheelchair. *Oh Lord, keep away the wicked, miserable people who lurk in shadows and seek to harm me.* He figures he can make her walk, figures he can wrap her legs around his wrinkled neck, he knows it. *Saint Barbara, open your heart to the good people, and protect me and keep me from harm.* He's unable to leave his bed and hasn't seen her but he believes knows her all the same: fifty but feeling eighty, capable of walking but demanding a wheelchair, unfit to carve her own meat but able to pluck the kinked white hairs from her chin in secret. *Oh miraculous Saint Barbara.* She's awash in a sea of gloom. The slightest pressure against her spine cause for horror and alarm. *And grant this great favor.* He knows he could get her wet with her own ancient dew and if she would forget the terror of the devils arrayed against her, of her imagined infirmaries, then he could get her aroused by their two bodies' fragility and coarseness. *In this our time of need.* Help us to overcome these difficulties.

♥

LAFAYETTE KNOWS THAT A DENSE JUNGLE OF TARNISHED SILVER curls hang down to her Irish ankles, matted and twined together with the heavy snowed locks that hang down from the white rose between her legs. *Save me from all harm.* He will pull back her long white hair and braid it tight against her scalp then rope her to the bed frame with it. Watch the spine of her throat arch its gristle under his kisses. *Yes,* he will tell her, *let's keep away the wicked, miserable people.* Kiss her again, flick her nipples to deepen the rosined dimples at her hipbones. Watch her lips move, dry, another prayer to Saint Barbara while he travels high in her, up past her kidneys and liver and pancreas, *Yes, feel my cock up against your lungs,* unable to continue her prayer because of his cock pressing up against her lungs, having to say more prayers because of his cock pressing up against her lungs. *While the dew is still on the roses.* Her Irish blue eyes going wild with open shock to hear her voice not in prayer, in a hoarse abraded kind of prayer, *Nearer my God to thee,* to hear herself begging for more of him, just another inch.

After he has shown her this, he knows there will surely be equal parts fear and shame and everything else that happens when the brain comes up hard against the body. And so then he will comfort her with his voice and hands, tell her that he knows.

I understand. Yes, he will say sweetly to her, tenderly, placing her thin fingertips in his mouth, *wet my chest with your tears.*

Oh holy, generous Christian protector, open your heart.

♥

LAFAYETTE WILL NEVER SLEEP AGAIN AS LONG AS THE CATHOLIC is alive in the room next to him. What is she praying for? This particular afternoon in August he can smell the air, smell the cells of the wood in the walls and smell the baking bodies of ancient termites. *Our Father who art in heaven.* Smell the skin cells of his ancestors lodged down deep in the wainscoting and the dry rot under the stairs and the mold under the roof and the unwashed hair of dead relatives with coins on their eyeballs. She must want something very badly, as badly as he wants her she must want relief as well from her own private torment. *Hallowed be thy name.* He can smell the urine stained newspapers between the mattress and the bed frame, smell the ocean from the sand in the windowpanes, ash of cremated trees in the chimney, the dried blood on the shaving razor, the dust on the shriveled flowers of the wedding bouquet and the feathers from abandoned hats, the chalk of plaster dust dissolving in milkpaint. He understands her longing for heaven. To be released. Yes, he wants that too. *Thy kingdom come.* He wants to feel of the new heat of another body's touch, wants her quivering flanks, wants to shiver his semen from his body. *Thy will be done.* He will never sleep again as long as the Catholic is alive in the room next to him. *On earth as it is in heaven.* Yes, he wants that, too.

♥

FIRST MAW HAD FOUND LAFAYETTE IN THE ROOM OF THE OLD Catholic. Heard the Catholic screaming in the night and found Lafayette on top of her, attempting a dreamstate rut— his cracked voice crooning *Sweet Love, Sweet Love*—Maw had heard him from the hallway, seen his shadow huge and humped on the wall. His one tiny leg curled around the Catholic's crippled thigh. Everything had been screaming. Lafayette crooned *Sweet Love, Sweet Chariot*, there were black bats in his brain, the disease pumping into his cranium and hiding there in the thick lush folds. *You horrible thing,* Maw said, unaware of whether she was speaking or screaming. She screamed it and drew Whitey. Maw stood in the door.

Whitey stood in the door.

Sweet Marie stood in the hall.

Lafayette had tried to cut the old Catholic's broken pelvis out of her bandages with Maw's sewing scissors. The Catholic was crying and praying, huffing and choking and gasping. The candles were melted down. How tall had they been when it all began? The Catholic couldn't move her legs, paralytic, broken hips not yet mended. A box of matches scattered on the floor. The scissors had drawn blood. They were all wounded.

How long had it gone on?

Spilt candle wax had hardened on the dirty nap of the rug.

A rusted wheelchair in the corner out of reach.

❤

I NEED SOME COINS, MOTHER, HE HAD SAID TO MAW, ANGUISHED, pumping at the screaming Catholic, *I have to pay her but I don't got no money in my pockets.*

He had no pants on. No pockets. He searched for coins along his naked thighs. Frantic. His useless hands, bubbling with sores. His naked hips against her bandaged ones.

Please get her some money, Maw. She's a good woman.

The women screamed again, long and low, then high. They were raw and undelivered. Devoured.

It was all very coarse, it had been a burlap scene of sackcloth and ashes. Maw's eyes white as opals.

Whitey had watched from the doorway. Sweet Marie had stood silent in the hall.

Whitey and Maw watched from the doorway.

Their fingernails left slices on the hardwood of the jamb.

♥

*WE COME TO THE GARDEN ALONE, WHILE THE DEW IS STILL ON THE
roses and the voice you hear*

calling in your ear

none other has ever known

♥

MAW HELD THE FIREPLACE POKER IN HER RIGHT HAND. ALL THOSE
years they had thought they'd needed him. All those long years of
wanting. A man, a husband, a father. Not this beast with a rotted brain.
She had stepped over the matches and wax and wheelchair, taken
those few short steps over to the bed where she beat him softly and
slowly over his back, with both her tight white hands on the poker,
beat him with it softly over and over on his back until he'd rolled
off the Catholic. He began laughing. A wasted crow call of laughter.
She beat him with the poker. She didn't want to break bones. They'd
taken him back from the Gulf Girls out of love and sorrow, out of
some dull longing for a family at last. His body wasted as a starving
vulture. *Our Father...* His yellow broken nails. *Hallowed be thy name...*
Beloved evil scion. She had beaten him softly with the poker over
his back until he rolled off, no longer laughing but now crying, all
of them crying, all five of their screaming faces trailed with tears.

♥

MAW AND WHITEY COVERED THE CATHOLIC WITH HER COVERLET
embroidered with lavender and violet and Sweet Marie wrapped her
fractured pelvis with the cut white strips of cloth and they left her.

They had no time or mind for more.

Then the women followed Lafayette as he crawled down the hall on the bones of his hands and knees until they got to his room and then they went in and quietly closed the door behind them and turned the key quiet in the lock.

♥

Lafayette lay in his bed with his eyes closed. He looked like a boy again. Like a dead baby raptor. His skin pulled away from his skull and his lips failed to hide his cracked and yellowed teeth. An aborted bobcat. Maw saw him there with his angry girls at his side and saw her three babies half-grown. This was a man? His nakedness was holy and hideous. He had failed her, her first born husband-son. The most she could ever do for him was nurse him at her breast, feed him and tell him everything was nice and fine. But those sores and scars. She had done a better job with her two strong twins with their eyes of cloudy skies. Nice and fine. Hellcat father-brother. His ribs jutted up high above his sunken belly.

Maw, he cried in a golden whisper. *Maw*. It was raw. It was coarse as burlap. The girls stood back when his tears began to wet his face. Mercy. When they saw his pupils swimming in his fiery red eyes. It was wracked. He shuddered.

Maw. Wife.

The girls stood back when Maw came over to the bed and took him in her arms. They wouldn't look at her. Her arms kept him in. Not just his arms but his legs too. He seemed like her own.

Maw.

A new want to pay for the loss of her youth. *Maw*. Burning for burning. Wound for wound. Stripe for stripe. *Maw*. He had opened a pit. He had caused a pit to be dug in her long ago and she had covered it and this night he had opened it again and they were all going to fall through into it. He hadn't wanted to be like that, he hadn't intended harm, he hadn't thought—

Maw was hard and then soft. Lafayette whispered, *It's me, it's me…*

His black lashes curled over his eyes of fire. She loved him. She loved him. She smelled his breath and found it good. Her womb lifted up at its scent, at the curve and rise of his cheek beneath her hand. She loved him. He had reached for her on their wedding night and she forced herself to stay awake and feel this new love. The rise and fall of the breath in his lungs. She felt swollen up inside again, like when her girls were growing in her, before he left, before he left her washed in her own blood, her own flesh eating of her flesh—his golden whispers spoke of restitution—his claws on the Catholic, the give of their flesh beneath the poker—

From that softness she hardened and then her whispers spoke of condemnation. The girls closed their ears. *It's me, it's me*, he whispered. The tortured women. *Please don't leave me here.* The tortured woman. It was too late for them to run through the fields, feeling the wings of angels at their back, holding hands. Maw's arms rocked him, she took his whole wasted body. But she couldn't make good that which was torn. And he couldn't make it good. The sun had gone down.

With one hand Maw had rocked him and with one hand she drove the syringe into the bulging pulsing pipe within his neck. She plunged in the arsenic while her girls held his feet firm to the ground.

And then she rocked him, back and forth, and sang dark songs to him.

Held him while he was still warm, long before he had begun to stiffen.

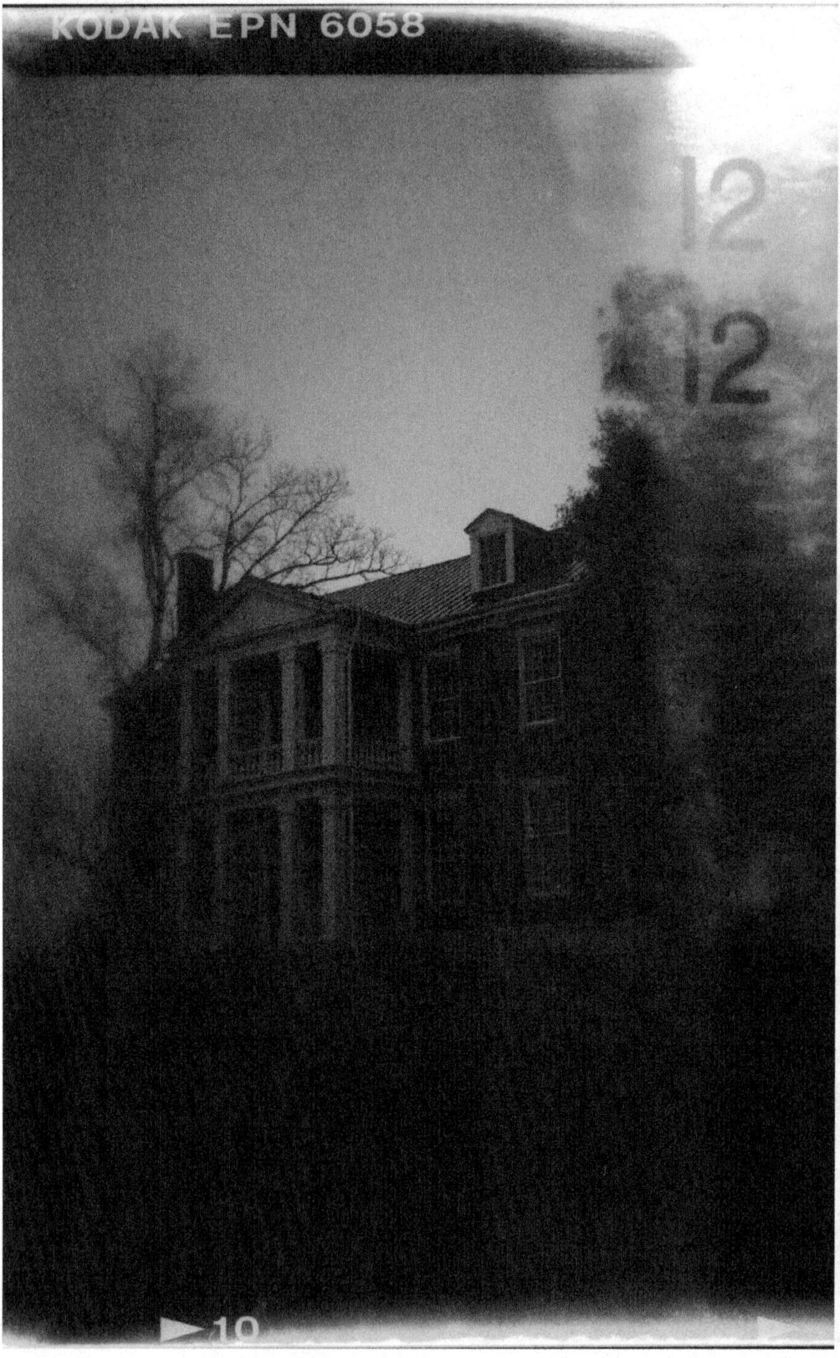
KODAK EPN 6058
12
12
10

A LONG CURVING SCAR WHERE
THE HEART SHOULD BE

THE FIRST DAY—NO BLACK FUNERAL CARS, NOTHING. BLACK CLOTHS covered the mirrors. Maw made lemonade mixed with bourbon in the bathtub and the women plunged in their porcelain cups to drink from it. The wake was just them three. They were wake-drunk for days.

Maw was naked under a yellow raincoat. She wore Whitey's hat indoors and out, Whitey's sweet brown velvet hat with broken yellow beads. Her eyes white opals. Her old hands twisted in the lap of the yellow raincoat. Wedding ring gone at last.

His small pale body lay on the table. They locked themselves in the parlor leaving only to nurse their patients, who wasted on in ignorance. There was a silence in the house. Even the wind turned the corner and didn't come down Middlebrook Road for those three days while their feelings slowly whirled and spun. They felt as though they were traveling, and Lafayette's absence was something mysterious to them, and they would soon come back and all would be as it once was, or could have been.

They were hard and then soft. They were soft and then grew hard again. They gazed at themselves in the hard reflective surfaces of their souls. Then they grew soft and the clarity disappeared and the images vanished from their view.

On the first day they hated him. He had lived in a whore house. Now he found himself in a house of women, and did he not see any difference? Was there any difference between a brothel and hospital?

Home and whorehouse? Just different kinds of knowing the body, different kinds of intimacy. The boundaries blurred at the very best of times. Pain and pleasure in both. The rape of a cripple. A brain gone bad, rancid and spoiled, the dementia of disease. The girls knew his blood ran through their veins and they were frightened. To do no harm. To do no harm. A mercy killing. Have mercy on our souls for we are human no longer. Searching for coins along his naked flesh. They abhorred him. Their stomachs twisted up around their hearts and lungs.

His blood ran through their veins and they were frightened.

♥

On the second day Whitey took out his heart. The ribs had surprised them, though they knew better. His long white curved knives of bone. It had been strangely difficult to get past his ribs—the women expected somehow that his heart would be resting on top of his bones, just under the skin. The cage of his rib, his heart within it like a dead bird. They can't remember whether they cut or broke the ribs: their memories grew less clear here. Whitey said it was important. They wanted to keep his heart. They all thought it was important. They wanted to keep some of him, and get rid of the rest of him. It seemed the thing to take. Whitey had cut it out and put it in a glass pickling jar. The tissues thin in places, full of blood, a sack of murky fluid. It was heavy and limp. Sweet Marie got the runs. It looked like a stillborn muledeer. Whitey had to stop to vomit. It gave damply under the pressure of her grasp. Whitey would have drunk the blood if it were not diseased, captured his voice in a jar if she could have caught the sound. If he'd had the antlers he wore in her dreams, she would have mounted them on a board in her bedroom. She tightened the lid on the pickling jar and they watched his heart for signs of beating, but it just lay there quiet, and very still. They looked at his pitiful heart in the bloody jar and marveled as the red turned to purple and then to black. They recognized the pattern: their own blood did much the same. Whitey began to vomit again. Maw slept and could not seem to wake. Sweet Marie's headache wrapped itself around her ears and her eyes. Whitey cleaned herself and sewed up the slice in her father's chest. The skin seemed to curl itself tightly around the stitches.

♥

ON THE LAST DAY THEY LOVED HIM AGAIN, WITH RANCOR. AND they read to his heartless body from Exodus. They read verses one through twelve to him. Even after everything, they loved him hatefully. *Get them up out of the land.* Whitey read verses twelve through twenty-two to him. *And they made their lives bitter.* They hated him lovingly. *All their service, wherein they made them serve, was with rigor.*

And then Maw read chapter four.

A bloody husband thou art. Two bone-skin children come out from the darkness of our love and him then vanished smooth and sweet as dew, come back wormed and bug- blooded. *Your hand as leprous as snow.* No more sunshine lovers for Lafayette, with his palms crossed by chancres like copper pennies. *Surely a bloody husband art thou to me.* The first flood carried off my mother. What is left me? *Thou shalt take of the water of the river, and pour it upon the dry land.* And the second flood carried off my father. What is left me? The flesh of my flesh, my girls, the bone of my bone, my girls are left to me. *And the water which thou takest out of the river shall become blood upon the dry land.* The river knows all there is of love. The blood of my blood. *And Pharoah charged all his people, saying, every son that is born ye shall cast into the river, and every daughter ye shall save alive.* I will give him to the river, and you, my girls, will keep our secret. *I will teach thee what thou shalt say.* For I made you. I made you out of my own body. You ate of my body. *I will be with thy mouth, and will teach you what ye shall do.* You were washed in my blood and you ate of my flesh. Your tiny sharp fingernails that left scratches on my breasts when you fed. *I shalt be to thee instead of God.* You belong fully to me, for I made you. You have never walked the ground without the guide of my hand. *And I have visited my children and looked upon their affliction.* I am the god of all the above and the below. *We shall bow our heads and worship.*

♥

THE TWINS SPREAD BUTTER QUIETLY ON THEIR BREAD. THE HOUSE was so quiet and still, it was as if everyone knew to tread lightly, smelled the scent of murder on Maw's skin, knew some blessed travesty had taken place. Had it been to end his suffering? No, Maw had done it to end her own. A killing that meant mercy not for the dead but for the living. But in Maw's eyes there was no longer any mercy. There were knives and hatchets in her opal eyes. Victory. Redemption. The twins poured syrup on their greens in peace—but it wasn't peace, it was fear and surrender. They had found both escape and defeat. Spiders scurried quietly, hiding from them underneath the carpets, smelling the scent of murder on the women's skins.

And they knew they were somehow saved from the thing they called Father.

They knew Maw had spared them. Alive, the women bowed their heads.

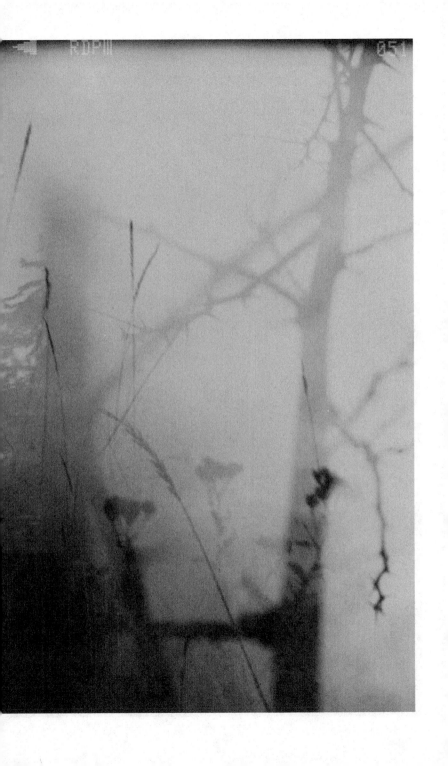

LET NOT THEIR HANDS
STOP MOVING ACROSS THE FACE
OF MY HEART

OLD SOW BURIED IN HER HUSBAND'S GRAVE, SOW'S HEAD SLEEPING
down in the cemetery where the thorn rose grows, and Lafayette's
bones so soft Maw folds him easy, slow and tight in quarters, bent him
once at the knees and once at waist and shoulder: him in a steamer
trunk for coffin yet somehow still he floated in the river, from within
the trunk he floated, fresh scraped on the sides by the banks of the
hill where the women plunged it down from.

There are three women at the water's edge. This is a horrible thing
of the night to wake from, screaming.

They could tell his skin—too full and thin, watery—burst, a flow
of fluid welled out from inside him, thinning his skin in its search
for release. Wet stains along the seams of Maw's old steamer trunk.

At the women's feet the killing river that always stands up high on
the banks to take its muddy leave, tips its hat to the Ladies and the
Girls and waits jaunty for its cargo.

The riverfolk had departed; no fishermen or women washing things.
There are things traveling downstream to be seen in the night—
detritus of that summer day, picnic papers and cardboard boxes
and cigarette ends.

♥

They daubed the trunk with slime and pitch and put Lafayette in it, and on the fourth night they lowered it slow and strangely light down the ravine on the old ropes, climbed down behind it and slid the trunk through the rushes by the river's brink. And Sweet Marie stood far off, to see what would be done to him. And Maw dreamed of absolution. Immersion. Washed in the blood of the earth's body, its river. Immersion. And Whitey held his heart in a jar, but couldn't throw it in. She kept it, some vague antidote against the sins he'd left them with. *Take of his body. Take of his blood.* A sacrament against future and past transgression.

And above them the big white house, with its mortar, and its brick, and there were all manner of creatures in the dark hunting the night with rigor.

They had buried an old sow in his place, they had. His grave at Thorn Rose now holds a fat summer pig; Maw had been willing to sacrifice the bacon and hams of its scrawny flanks, the cheese of its brain. She conducted the appropriate mathematics: it would be a hungrier but kinder winter because of this sacrifice. An unexpected shadow left in the pigpen. A hook swinging empty in the smokehouse. In the trunk a weight as convincing as a sick man's dead and unbudging flesh.

❦

AS THEY PUT HIM IN THE WATER MAW READ HER GOD'S WORDS TO the river: *Take this child away and nurse it for me, and I will give thee thy wages.* And the river took Lafayette, and its wetness seemed at Maw's command and it did as she bade it and took him deep into itself and nursed him. If Lafayette wept then his tears were licked up by the river. And his tears caused the catfishes to wonder at the taste of salt. The river had compassion on him and said at last: *This is one of my children.*

❦

AND LAFAYETTE HAD FLOATED DOWN THE RIVER IN MAW'S OWN mother's ancient leather trunk, floated slowly past them for only a few feet before he sunk. The trunk sank then rose again. And sank and rose and bobbed there wet in the darkness. Didn't they think he would be found? Maw didn't care. Everyone who left her entered the river. Thus was it writ in the book of her life.

♥

ALL THE BODY'S ILLS LIVE IN THE GUT. A BRACKISH PLACE THAT twists and burns. Acid the body's other blood, meant for breaking down instead of building. Rivers carry more than water, rivers the gut of the earth. Hot and wet, full of gallstones and worms, there for taking and removing and clearing away. The women expected Lafayette to enter up to the heavens, they hadn't wanted him buried in the dark ground, or set to burning, they had hoped for cleaning, for the river to wash him, for some sort of peace. But now the sick trunk bobs and sinks, then rises. Floats and pitches sideways in a sick lurch. The river laughing. The truck slams against the rock, twists in the eddies, carries onward. It sinks, then rises and bobs warily for the next assault. This a horror they hoped to wake from.

♥

AND ON THE FOURTH NIGHT THE SUN WENT DOWN BELOW THE river, coagulated, a red river of glass when it hardened; if from underneath Lafayette looked at the surface, he with his withered eyes, he would have seen his women's eyes staring back—six white pearls—if he looked up. And he would have seen the black angel ravens. Coming in. To make end to it, to take him up.

♥

WHERE HAVE ALL THE DEAD OF THIS WORLD GONE TO, INTO THE soil, southern soil full of half- named corpses: here, take one more. Deposit our father along our valley floors. Let him, in spring grasses, cover the valley floors. This your sour summer dead.

A current under the river whispers and he rises and falls. He passes the stages of his age and youth entering its whirlpool.

At the violet midnight hour of his burial a rat creeps softly through the vegetation dragging its heavy belly on the bank and plunges in, a swimming water-ghoul. There are agonies in mossy places, agonies in slimy places. The women cannot stop or think. Where are their feet? Their feet are in the watercress. What is the nature of their skin? It is made of tar and oil. And the light? Violet, a black with light inside it. And the smell—a mineral dirge. What is the nature of that sound? They hear Lafayette breathing water in his steamer trunk. Watercress tangles at their ankles. Broken fingernails on dirty hands. They stoop to wash, and see Lafayette beside them, cleaning his hands. Standing beside them, he smiles. His sweat pours from skin broken with sores, glistens with tar and oil that drains into the river. *He who was living is now dead. We who were living are now dying.* He laughs at them and catches his jaw as it falls loose into his hands, he has broken fingernails on dirty hands. He crosses past three white bodies kneeling on the low damp ground. They taste faint moonlight in their mouths, the flavor of their father's breath: *Oh, you who avert your eyes and look downward, listen to me,* he says.

❦

There are no windows in this chapel. No towering cedar beams.

Look back to the gone years, to the crooked door that swings wide, swings low.

The things I can never retract.

The sun no more singes the skin around my wedding band.

I am on the banks of the water. I am a boy. There are minnows and crawfish. My feet are blue with cold. A cottonmouth lies on the rocks. Some legless creature brushes my thigh. Heading downstream a rat with white and slimy belly. *These fragments I have shored against my ruins.* I will not go up the stairs. I will not walk through the doors, hear the key turn once in the lock and turn no more. I will not strip the clothes from my body to meet my lover at her bed. When I was a boy I put off a pungent broke-branched scent at nighttime—my mother would open the windows when I woke. My clothes reeked of it. I was new and young, my fluids bubbling with life. My skin could not contain it. *Where have you disposed of this my carcass? I exude a foul liquid.* I wanted to invent new stones, new stars, new mountains, new tongues. Why this trunk of me lowered down grossly on ropes? Why have they not taken me in. Why don't my heels tap wildly to the notes of his piano, why are there no rings left on my fingers. Why did they send me from them, their perfumed beds, a bath when I was dirty, why their sweet hands stopped moving across my face and hips.

I must now bury myself. *This a fine and private place, but none, I think, do here embrace.*

My last regrets—take to your heels.

I would go for a walk with her. I would never leave again.

If I left, I would return.

I could never leave now.

My daughters, are they sleeping in the rafters, bats with waxen folded wings, and fangs, not human at all? Gulf Girls—I got no more leave to take, no more lover's song running singing through my dirty veins. Their names—I can't remember their names, my daughters, what did I bring into being. All of us, from cock to cunt a foul progression that never stops.

I remember a bowl of oatmeal on a blue tablecloth, milk in a white china cup, the sound of wind against a shuttered window.

Hay cut and drying below a dusty halo of pollen.

Thick green planks of grasshoppers.

Shit along the rim of a bird's emptied nest.

How to reconcile it all. The sun seems needlessly beautiful. There it is now: it is dun through the muddy waters. Or is that the moon—a cold body, and now forever distant to me. The moon will never see me down below.

Once I was more than this. Surely I was more. Or could have been. If it hadn't been too much, I would have stayed. Too much asked of me, too fast. Surely I could have been more. I was fierce, shirt open to the waist I was beautiful, thighs bursting my trousers, I could beat them all, I covered the women with my honey. I warmed them with fire from my own fuels. Before the babies came, her toenails tiny and pale. Left scratches down my spine. This new smell of me—my armpits have grown fetid, fed on sorrow and regret. What I want is to see her face in a stone, in the whirlpool beneath me, in the scales of the fishes. What I want is to hear the sound of her laughter in the afternoon, her hairpins dropping to the floor. A pile of black pins on the floor beside my bed. She says *come here* and the words become the only thing I want. To see sweat break out along her flanks, to bend and stoop to tie my shoes, to slice her new-baked bread. To be Jacob recognizing Joseph. To breathe air instead of water. I'm tired. I want to live.

What has dismantled me. I want to fly with ravens, to ride drunk and weary through the streets of her town, to sing beneath her window, stain her dress with my love. For her to recognize me come home to her at last—not a monster, but a man: all follies told, writ large upon the stone her heart, rubbed away or at least with a fragrant hand of wisteria covering over. I want that.

Redemption I asked, retribution I received.

My last night I wanted her to lie beneath me and feel her struggle to breathe. *But I have no hope for finding that.* There is something missing in my chest—in its place a pile of threads and stitches: woman's work is this thing inside my ribs. A ball of yarn. Half a winter's blanket, sweater for a baby, or a cowl.

Love, the loss with me, the blame is yours. This dimmed sky is a horror—a lamp turned too low. A strange place to be beneath.

Oh women, who stand on the edge of the water bank, your feet plunged in my mud, beneath my house, you have taken all from me. Take me back now that it is too late. I gave that woman two lives, she took mine to have one more. Now she has three. Will it be enough for her? Nothing anything ever enough for that woman. It is her river, she has claimed it, it carries me away for her, it does her bidding. It crushes me gently.

There is a beam above her head leads straight to the moon. Some night god she is, and the day god does her bidding. *Was I ever so close to what I have longed for as I am now.* Bone skin babies fell from her; I lived somewhere between the two choices, my heart alternating *yes* and *no*. I found a farmer's thumbs on my esophagus. I came back, it was too late. My heart still crying *yes* then *no*. Mine a hopeless season.

Once I was a handsome man, and tall. I admired my red hair in the glass. There are curls of it still, my mother cut it from me, pressed it in a locket of silver, scent of frankincense and butter. One day these women will lie in the earth, their faces wrapped within their long black hair and rotting. Eyes closed, smooth teeth, meager female bones. Split pelvises, cracked and re-healed. Cotton dresses their own hands decorated. Patterns of red roses with no thorns. Bodies of men rushing out and into the bodies of women. Forced out a short time later. Sex and birth a sodden wonder. We drain out white from these our women in the morning.

I know now semen is but men's constant tears of longing.

Everywhere I look I see: I can no longer close my eyes to anything.

Eyeballs, love-bitten, death-swallowed, savage, full of blame, not to trust. *Shun the heaven that leads men to this hell.* Birth the miracle when the lids open, death too, a terrible blue inside, the color of eggshells.

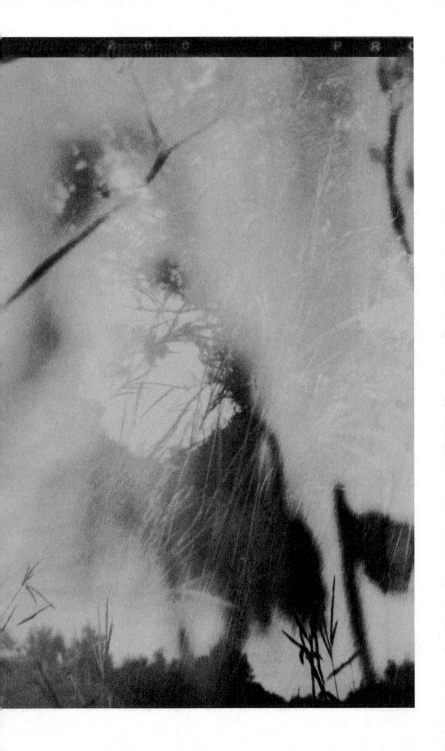

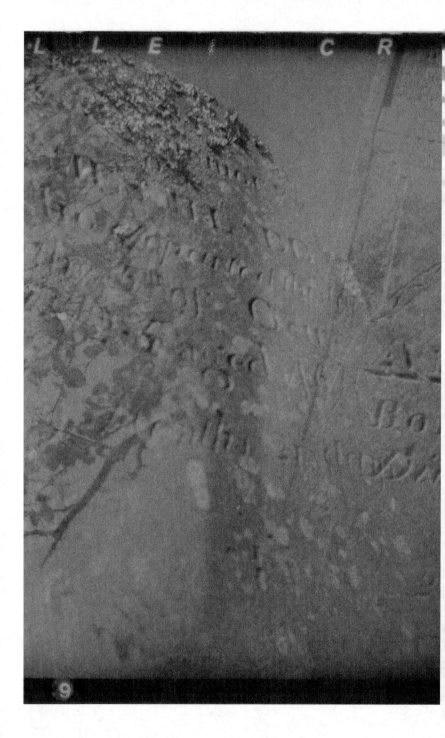

THERE ARE SECRET THINGS FOR DESTROYING AT THE PROPER TIME

THERE ARE SECRET THINGS FOR DESTROYING AT THE PROPER TIME. Things precious and fragile for shattering. The thing that always ends up ruined. Gouge out the eyes of a china doll. Great rough gashes in a paper lampshade. A glass cleaned carelessly, so that it drops and cracks, as if by accident. Something that has suddenly become so sadly beautiful it is a forbidden form of joy to destroy it.

If it is pink.

If it overwhelms.

And afterwards, if there is remorse, crush up the burnt bones of a Sunday chicken and boil them with the ashes: watch the water turn to black. Swallow it, that sweet possibility, and place that secret inside yourself with the others that lie inside. The destruction inside. Keep it in the stomach, where it's quiet and dark.

❤

SOMETIMES ALL THE WOMEN CAN THINK ABOUT IS THAT ONE particular color: ash. And the particular taste it would create, traveling down their throats.

❤

THEN THERE IS ONLY ONE SOUND. THE SOUND A BODY MAKES IN

falling—a bird with no wings, plummeting, as small and lifeless as a cherry stone. Sometimes bodies are ripe for falling. *I gave my love a cherry, that had no stone.*

And then they hear the entire contents of their own craniums, split open wide and tumbling wet as fruit upon the ground. Moist and thick, the destructible mucus of the human head. A coarse, dense tissue. They don't want theirs any more. It is too far gone. Let it go. Farther. Until it is completely gone. Open it and spill it, and let its wetness dry against the ground.

♥

SOMETIMES A SMELL. THERE IS ONE THAT FILLS THEM—THE LIGHT high summer rain that fell the day of the death—scorched earth after a slight rain. *He dropped his seed into us. It traveled down through the difficult resistance of our inner air. He planted it long ago in our ground, some kind of soil now so far beneath us.*

What need to witness pulled down the rain that day? Where it made its way fissures formed—no sutures sewn there. How the crevices filled and then depleted, drained through the cunt of the earth, a certain familiar kind of movement from the surface, gone from full to fallow. Until the liquid was scorched and vanquished by the dryness at the core, while above the soil steamed.

♥

AN ODOR. THE NEARLY UNDETECTABLE SCENT OF TEARS SHED on infertile soil.

New lodes of salt in a field now unfit for planting.

♥

AND NOW THE WOMEN CAN BARELY FEEL. THE PITS OF ROTTEN cherries have become their hearts. *Pity us not.* Bruised hands, scratches, memory of syringe and wake and knife and trunk, of rolling and dragging a body. *You cannot understand our thoughts. You cannot imagine our memories, their weight upon us such that we can barely stand. You see women walking, and we know women crawling, sagging.*

❦

WE CAME INTO THE WORLD, AND THE WORLD KNOWS US NOT. WE *came unto our own, and our own received us not.*

This means falling off the orchard ladder, hoping not to live.

❦

PUT YOUR HAND INTO THE ABSCESS OF OUR SORROW AND REGRET. The wound that's bored to center. A raw and putrid ache. *This is what life has done to us. This is what we have done to ourselves.* New graves sink deeper every year, inch by inch, until they lay three feet beneath the soil and then stop: the pits the height of their coffins. There are old graves planted between the women's vertebrae, their backs a long straight row of markers that rise above dull hollows. Where the rot lives.

Lay your hands along their spines. The bones. *These are what we loved.* The hollows.

These are what we lost.

This is the trail of their sorrow.

❦

IN TIMES OF GREAT CRISIS, THE WEAK SEAM IS SPLIT. THE LAFAYETTE women, without Lafayette, were simply women. Three women who for decades had worn a garment sewn of those great threads of wanting. A father. A husband. The warp and the weave—there was no hope for that now. An old sow buried in the once-deep hole of hope.

His seams ripped, holes the needle pierced in his vein, ten years of waiting at last unraveled.

WHITEY DREAMED THAT SHE DROWNED A LITTER OF KITTENS, EACH bearing the faces of her family. And she dreamed of her own death. She slept and did not wake—she died, quietly, as she slept. And then somehow she woke, and waited for sleep to come again.

Sweet Marie lay in bed and stared at the wall. An orphaned field mouse arrived and spent its days curled behind her knees. She became nocturnal with it, pouring milk for herself and the rodent at night, admiring the perfection of its teeth.

Maw spat watermelon seeds into the gravel below the drainpipe. She ignored her daughters ruthlessly, without noticing or caring. She had begun to smell within days of Lafayette's murder and now her odor had become so strong that no one could even smell it any longer. From within her greased and stiffening housedress she seemed beyond her own body, a thing of spirit only—pure as flesh cauterized into air. She could not be reached.

They had gone to their places. Their stations. They were mounted in their niches, high upon the walls. They had no words to say, had never had the words—and now? Who could be expected to know how to unbrace the muteness, how to begin, again.

❦

WHERE THEY ARE HURT, THEY CANNOT REACH. THERE IS SOMETHING that makes them look up in despair at the hopeless sky, without light and without truth, and see simply a blue blackness—where before they saw Virgo, the North Star, now there are merely tiny pinpricks of their pain. They stare upwards. As it was in the beginning, is now, and ever shall be, world without end, amen.

The light shines in the darkness, and the darkness grasps it.

The dark lies in the lightness, and the lightness quenches it not.

❦

In September, on the month before his wedding day, a young man was found hanging dead in the basement of the house he'd built for his new wife. The town asked why. The Lafayette women did not. *There are joyful mysteries. Glorious mysteries. Sorrowful mysteries.* Do not turn away your face from theirs. A woman, returning home from the doctor in November, stopped in the neighbor's barn and leaned a last embrace into a shotgun. *Pay heed to the fruit of each mystery. Jesus too died for somebody else's sins.* Alone and together, the women pray for the living and the dead. For the fathomless scope of loss. Death, not at its hands but at their own—they made that choice for Lafayette, they stood for God, they took a life, they bore their choice across the dark river of life and deposited him on the shores of death, and now did not know how to return to the other side. To take themselves towards a living shore of their own accord.

The seven corporal works of mercy: To feed the hungry. To give drink to the thirsty. To clothe the naked. To visit and ransom the captives. To harbor the harborless. To visit the sick. To bury the dead. To comfort the sorrowful. To pray for the living and for the dead.

In the absence of a physician who could not be troubled with a suicide, one of the Lafayette women is called to the dead body. The typical occasion for a midwife, a witch doctor. The women call these deaths for what they are, heart attacks. Death for an absence of love. Love the last and most difficult lesson to learn. The dead have traveled to the source. Why do so many try to prevent this journey? The women think—ride that boat of grief through storms of love, through storms of loss. Walk the dark planks from stem to stern. Should anyone try any longer to take another off a sinking ship? Perhaps each soul should each be left alone there in the water and let it be seen if she can swim. Let go. Is it to drown? We are all ripe for sinking at one time or another. Is it so bad to sink, finally, beneath the surface and feel air replaced by water? Is that peace? To be filled with substance instead of absence?

❦

THEY ARE NOT TO TELL. THE GIRLS ARE NOT TO TELL WHAT THEY have seen along the banks of the river.

❦

PRIESTESSES AND SEERESSES AND PROPHETESSES, CENTURIES AGO, were consecrated for thoughts and deeds such as these, for they had built a million arks and cradles and sacrifices, and everyone knew their hands never ceased from moving across the invisible face of the cosmos. And now down to obscurity have their kind traveled, to a muddied pool of blood in a barn at lead-weight midnight, to such places of so much sadness, and their temple gates are gone and in their place only the very narrowest of openings, with no gold and no ivory to mark the way through.

❦

THE WOMEN SPARE THE TELLING OF THE PARTICULARITIES OF THEIR own sins. Our Lady of Perpetual Sorrow—she knows it all already, crucified between a smile and a whimper. Did she wish to die in her son's place? Would they have felt the same? They chose a different path from hers. They killed their man to create their own salvation. *Hail Mary, full of grace.* When one must make a sacrifice, and when one must demand a sacrifice, the Mother of Sorrow knows the risks. They spare her the routine, the hymns of their guilt and grief—surely she has known all there is of it already.

A woman burdened. *What man did this to you?* It is a question the women ask first.

What did you do to yourself? The priests ask that.

Ask, *Which is the wiser?*

❦

NOW THEIR DEED IS DONE, SOMETIMES THE WOMEN HEAR A VOICE telling them to let go of it. It says: *Let go.* The things these women have held to for so long. *You fall down, you disappoint.* The Romans inside the women goad them to their feet. This bothers them. The women no longer want to climb the lonely hill beneath their burden. Will anyone bring them up again if they fail and cannot rise? Will anyone take them on his shoulders for a moment and fill their emptied lungs with his own breath? If they had ever let go before now, if they had ever let go, they would have been lost. They know this. They are the Ladies of the Rocks. There is no rescue. There is only to keep climbing. They wipe the bloody sweat from their own faces with their own black veils.

❦

THEY HEAR VOICES. THEY HEAR THE WORDS OF THE DYING. THE women know their thoughts as they pass, and nothing is concealed from them.

If you love me, kill me, take me and destroy the entirety. Release me. Don't let me go. Release me, bury me, hold me, save me, love me forever.

They hear them every day.

Enlighten our eyes, that we never sleep in death.

The death of earth is to become water. And the death of water is to become air. And the death of air is to become fire. Death on one plane becomes transformation and new birth on other planes.

❦

THE LAND ITSELF IS WHERE THEIR TENDERNESS GROWS, THE tenderness that borders their violence on all sides. The tenderness that grows from strength and courage. For they shall wash their hands at the river and all shall be understood.

Oh lamb of God, who takest away the sins of the world, have mercy upon us. Let our cries come unto Thee. A lamb is never a lamb forever.

For it is time to boil the tea, and they must go back up the hill to the tall white house, and to the failing hearts that still stir within it. They climb with bloodstained footsteps.

Cleanse our hearts and lips, O Lord, who didst cleanse the lips of the prophets with burning coals.

They carry their burdens past the cherry poplars and the elm trees, over the limestone and the shale, across the slipping clay. And once inside, the women look down upon the earth and the water and the air and the fire, and speak of how, in the morning they will scatter the season's seeds in the garden.

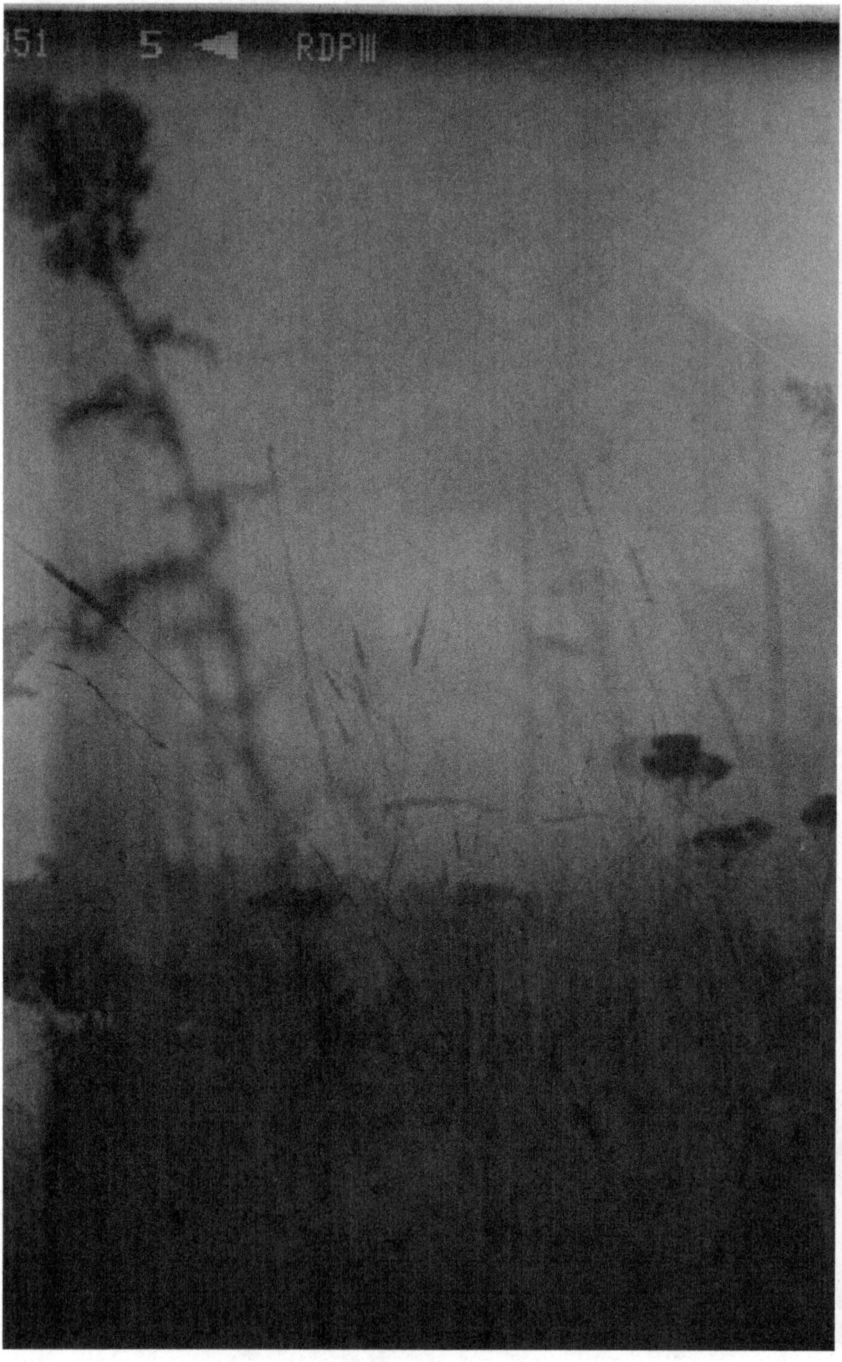
RDPIII

THE RIVER KNOWS THE STARS
FOR FISHES

ON THE NIGHT THE FLOOD CAME, I WENT TO THE BANK AND
stood there for some time before the waters fully rose. Unbound to
my daughters. Unbound to my husband. I stood there some time,
alone, untethered. There was something that made me first look up
through the rain at the sky—where before were Venus, Jupiter—and
see only a hot wet blackness. As it was in the beginning, so it was
now. I stared upwards and found I knew all of this world from end
to end, painfully extended.

I was not afraid.

They say it was an accident. *Maw was pulled in somehow.* When they
found my path they said my fingernails had broken—they say I had
left gashes in the wet soil as I tried to crawl up the riverbank; that I
clutched desperately at the bark of trees to save myself. But that is
not true. I walked towards the flood. My river.

My light had shone in the darkness, and the darkness grasped it.

♥

EACH SPRING SINCE MY GIRLHOOD I USED TO GO TO THORN ROSE
Cemetery to visit my mother's grave. I never wanted a grave of my
own, I never wanted one. As I speak it, thus is it so. I would watch
as the new graves sank deeper every year, inch by inch, until they

lay far beneath the soil and then stopped: each pit the height of a coffin. I know the height of my mother's bones, of her ribs and pelvis. The channel of her vanished thorax, ample thighs whittled to twigs, curves turned inward into caves.

When I walked on the earth there were old graves planted between my vertebrae, my back a long straight row of white bone markers that rose above dull hollows where my rot lived. Where I could not myself reach to heal them I carried a row of graves bored to center. *Put your hand into the abscesses of my sorrow and regret.* A raw and putrid ache.

There was only one person who could have reached around me to lay his hands along my spine. To count them like a rosary: *This is what life has done to you. This is what you have done to yourself.*

He is gone.

That has been the spine of my sorrow.

❤

I CAN'T REMEMBER WHEN THEY BEGAN, THE TIMES I WOULD WAKE from sleep sobbing, screaming that he had left me. Wake to expect it different, but only instead to find my terrors justified. The dreams didn't start immediately. They started weeks after I killed him—

I grew fearful of my pillow. Inside its case it was stained brown in patches: bruised, decayed, molded, mottled with tears.

Three syllables:

La
Fay
Ette

❤

TORN HANDS, GASHES, MEMORY OF INJECTION AND CORPSE AND trunk and knife. Of rolling and pushing his body. I could not support my memories, their weight upon me such that I could barely stand. The world saw a woman, and I saw a murderer.

♥

THE FINAL DAYS—THAT I DID NOT KNOW WERE DRAWING TO A close—I spent in the house. Closing the kitchen door for the last time. Folding towels. I did not realize it was my final pitcher of lemonade—the way the bright yellow skin of the rind gave way to the cream white of the inner flesh. I didn't stop to think, how much sugar? How many lemons? There were flecks of sugar on my fingers. I didn't raise them to my lips. To taste sugar for the last time, to feel the rough crystals melt to liquid on my tongue. Tired. Leave it. There is sugar there still, now, between the cracks in the kitchen floor.

The final days.
Horror.
How did I do this thing?

Wrinkled as if from bathwater, chilled, gray muck floating on the top, scum and hairs: this is my soul. The last glance at my own face in the mirror—I didn't see it there at all.

Push forward, pull back.

Sit in the chair and stare. Walls.
Floor. Walls.
Floor.

This damage is permanent.

The loss, the wrenching apart.

Let me make another kind of peace, not here, alone.

♥

AND THEN THE RAINS CAME. WHEN THE RAINS CAME I WAS PLEASED.

The roads too thick with mud to move through, and I too old and sad to bother. No one came to the house or left it. The world was sinking back into itself, dissolving, coming undone. And what was not dissolving was being destroyed: the trees were savaged, whipped, their leaves slashed, a summer punishment I relished for its ferocity. This house where I'd birthed my girls. Every shingle torn off was manna. To be eaten by the water. Not enough. The house was not enough. Not offering enough for the wrong I'd done. And the storm knew, and nothing was spared, and there was no mercy yet and I was pleased.

Through the rising storms I sat on the front porch and spat watermelon seeds into the fray. Seeds bashed down into the soil, hammered into the rock, no hope of summer fruit. My chair on the porch, my chair in the parlor, my bed, the bathtub, a path leading from fields to garden—when I heard the rain striking its liquid blows against the roof and walls only then could I feel a tranquility come over me. A raw howl inside me upturned into a stretch-lipped moan, as I hadn't felt since after lovemaking, twenty years before, when I would climb from a well of fear and loneliness to that certain rare savanna. Over the pounding of the rain I listened to my heart and found it quiet. It was silent, bloodless, the veins stilled.

♥

THAT LAST NIGHT I SPENT IN THAT HOUSE, THAT WHITE HOUSE, my house, what had been our house, shadows moved as real as creatures. The quilt cast the peaks of its wrinkles along the wall and it seemed a thing come crawling towards me through wintery hillocks. Remembering the rise of my young husband's buttocks and thighs within white sheets. But that last night, my last night, lights issued from the urn on the dresser. An ash-green smoky light, luminescent, and Venetian, that issued forth only to vanish. Catfish swimming past me, roe-eyed, whiskers rippling across the wallpaper. A familiar man beside my bedside, leaning over me—*It's a dream*, he said, *wake up*. Lafayette's riverbreath. How he smoothed the crown of my hair. My widow's peak. His long, tapered fingers catching rapturously at my gray hair, urgent, urging me to rise, to rise. A kiss on both my eyelids! His two lips, dry, prickled, heavy weight of his mouth on my lashes. *You must get up it's time for breakfast.* Ahhh, yes, I smelled the bacon. His hand on my shoulder, smelling of milk and eggs. A wide thigh before my eyes. Sunlight and thick windowpanes. Sunday. A young husband growing older. *Wake up, wake up.* I listened. I strained to hear: then he was wordless, and then vanished too. Not dawn but merely lantern bulb, dull, a lie. My life. The catfish laughed, and chased each other through the shadows of my bedroom. My fingers extended slow along the arms of the chair until they dragged the ground and, dragging, smeared salves and powders across the mirror, erasing its reflections. He reappeared. *Follow him,* said the catfish. They willed me to go, my fingers carrying on the business of final preparation across the room while my body remained watchful in its chair. While it sat there, in its chair, my body. Curiously still. I listened—my body tilted its ear towards the ceiling, the door. Again my husband vanished, this time through the door. *Wake up, come here, follow me,* he had said. Bacon and eggs and catfish in a pan. Overalls and Sunday apples. Again the fish were swimming past. Some were making love. I counted them: twelve, fifteen, twenty-seven. Their eggs and seeds thickening my bedroom air. *Go to him,* they said. *Be fruitful and multiply.* Whiskered catfish ugly as dung. *I'll eat you,* I told them, *if you lie to me, I'll eat you.* Snapped my jaws. It was after that my teeth began breaking, jagged molars, I held them in my palms, tiny shards, white chips like mouse teeth, or kitten teeth. But they came from no new thing. The catfish plucked them from my palms, and swam away. I followed them.

❦

I TOLD THE CATFISH, *PIN ME DOWN, THEN.*

They said to me, *Is that what you want?*

Tie me to your riverbed. Set stones upon my face.

They looked at one another, alive and liquid, a single lineless shadowed form in green and white. *Perhaps you will not like it down there in the riverbed,* they said.

No. Take me down. Break my bones. Eat my marrow.

They edged to my hair and nibbled. *It might be lovely after all,* they said. I sensed their skin spoke of forgiveness. I was worn. They were new. Their whiskers swayed with the moonlight in my room.

Bring me to my husband.

They circled me. *We live in the river. We know all there is.*

Then bring my back to my husband.

The catfish swirled into the rain.

I followed them.

❦

EVERYTHING I HAD, I DESTROYED. YET WHILE I WAS ALIVE I CALLED myself a healer. We are all monsters, and I most among us all. When we think we do the most good we commit the gravest arrogances.

I have found myself a monster—made myself now a river monster. Some kind of snapping turtle. Are they kind beneath their massive shells, inside their cruel beaks? I know them now, I have spoken with them, dined on half a piece of cottonmouth, listened to them speak of their own crimes, victories, and sorrows. I do not ask them how they lost that eye, why the deep slice in their shell, how come the missing claw. I have seen one snap a log in half. I have seen them take a child's arm in a single bite. Easily. I could do that, and worse. I could eat an entire child. Do not let me climb out from underwater. I could not say what I might do.

A great sobbing beak of justice have I.

❦

I CRY, FILLING THE WATER WITH MY WATER. I LONG FOR HIM WITH violence, with talons, a desire that wants to rip and tear through the loss of him—

As though loss is an actual thing I might find down here, something dead, loss some kind of an object half-buried in the riverbed with which I might finally do battle, hand to hand, face to face. I want to find my loss here and kill it.

Or find it and hold it in my arms, nurse it at my rotten breast. Find mercy.

But yet I drew back the plunger, I aimed the needle, I struck his vein—they were acts of contemplation. Was I the one who did that thing? No. Do not tell me what I did. Tell me he is down here with me. Tell me he is not far from me, that our shells will collide somewhere just past the next curve.

❦

SUBMERGED. SWIMMING, BUT UNDERWATER. NO INTEREST IN surfacing. I'm different here somehow. Maybe because the light is dimmer. The bells are ringing in the air world, someone's blood-filled hands are moving them. Down here my hands look old. I can see all the cracks, the flaws of time, little squares of old skin beginning to separate from one another. I couldn't hear anyone calling me from the shore. I wouldn't want to. To bear one more thing.

❦

IS HE GONE? IS HE GONE FROM ME, WITH FINALITY? I WILL NEVER know for sure if he is gone, or if I want him to be. As it was in the beginning, so is it now. I want to tell him things. To speak together in a way we never knew before, we could not learn.

I cannot now ever forgive myself, and so I find I have at last forgiven him.

The sky above must be dark because the water is dark.

I breathe differently down here.

Is his voice is not calling to me from the bend? I go down—

humbly—I listen now, for one voice, for one that comes from a wet place, down below—

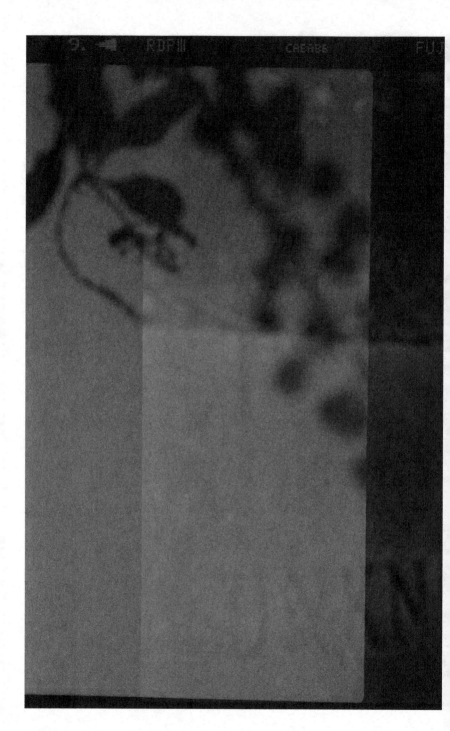

GRACEFUL NOW WE FALL APART

THE TWINS DID NOT GIVE THEIR MOTHER A GRAVE OR TOMBSTONE
at the cemetery. They had nothing, no one to visit. Lynchburg did
not understand—even without a corpse, isn't it customary to bury
the dead? Besides, said the town, they had buried that shameful
father, and him with that illness—that he should lie hallowed and
not her? Hers an empty plot of soil beside him?

But they didn't want to visit it. And in order to have nothing to
visit, it was easier not to have a grave.

After all, there was no corpse to put in it.

❦

WHITEY AND SWEET MARIE, WITH NOTHING AND NO ONE TO VISIT,
mostly drank. They kept quite large quantities in the house, for
medicinal purposes. Whiskey, rye, scotch. Gin. Brandy. Port. Sherry.
They washed them thinner with water. Mixed them randomly in
combinations, in glasses that were never washed. A rush of freedom.
The twins were weightless.

With the drinking came ghosts. There was no reason not to let them
stay, they were allowed into the house, during visiting hours, and
the big white house was so far away from neighbors. Plantation. A
place that nothing can be done with anymore.

It didn't matter that Sweet Marie didn't carry on with the ghosts, that it was mostly Whitey. But the differences between the ghosts and the women didn't matter— and the women and the ghosts compromised with the music. The ghosts knew anguish. The ghosts laughed at anguish small as this.

Suddenly Sweet Marie no longer cried when listening to music. The sisters were back to how it was when they were small girls. They were one. They moved as one, and no longer bothered to correct the new patients when they were confused in names. They no longer separated the clothing.

At night, the gramophone played blues quietly, and the girls drank steadily, and the ghosts walked around naked to the waist with bottles and recited cheap romantic poems at times to the girls, who came and went from time to time when the patients rang their bells.

♥

AND THEN THE TRANQUIL GHOSTS DEPARTED AS SUDDENLY AS they arrived. The ghosts left them, blowing out the door as lightly as a candleflame. Twisting, curling, and then vanishing.

♥

ONE NIGHT WHEN THEY WERE DRINKING ALONE THERE WAS NO sound, no movement, and they faced each other across a flickering table lit by the silver candelabra their mother had never sold. It held two candles. Sitting as such it was as though a mirror hung between them, old and heavy. The twins became a woman and her reflection. They reached out to touch their image, to feel it in the cold hard silver surface—to touch that cheek, that chin, that tip of nose—but their hands pushed straight through. They held their fingers there, in the hot liquid of the candle flame, touching flesh instead of metal, paralyzed, each feeling for herself and feeling nothing. That's how they knew they were dead as well—their hearts had departed from their bodies, and they could not feel, and thus they were dead. How else to explain the candle burns along their arms, which they were unable to feel.

No tingling of pain, nothing. There had been too much, and they were done for. Time moved, and moved again, the hands of the mantle clock turning round silently with each poised there, fingertips unfurled. And then the smell of singing cotton, of burning flesh and hair, and then the light in the room grew brighter and the twins startled and yanked their hands away from the candelabra, blew out the flames, and silently, separately, went to bed.

❦

AND IN THE MORNING THEY AROSE AND MADE BREAKFAST FOR everyone, and there was no more talking, or drinking, or watching ghosts making love to one another against the coat-rack in the hallway. That time had ended, and a new time had begun.

❦

HOW DOES IT FEEL TO BE THE CHILDREN OF SUCH PARENTS, TO wonder what is carried on inside, what torments?—a suicide and a rapist, a murderer and a pimp—this was mother, this was father. A healer and a lover—this mother and father too.

There could be no reconciliation, resolution, it was insensible.

They carried terrible blood. And yet the twins went along their ways, carrying out their tasks and projects, their training. First put on the underclothes, and then the dress. Then pin up the hair. The socks, and then the shoes. Tie the shoes, and then walk. No, walk. Fine, then stand up first and then walk, as though you have not forgotten how. *You stupid woman. You have work to do.* Take your blood and pump it from the deep well of your heart, put it in a pail and carry it through your day. It should be no heavier now than it ever was beneath your skin, you're simply aware of it now. Look sharp. Now the right foot in front of the left. Hold the handrail—you're not getting away from this that easily.

The numbness required a lot of feeling. They could feel that they felt nothing. It was dizzying. It broke them apart in small ways.

305

❦

THEIR FATHER'S GRAVE HELD A PIG. THEIR MOTHER DIDN'T HAVE A grave. The girls sat on the back porch at night, the long back balcony that ran the entire length of the house, screened in with a dozen white rocking chairs upon it, grapes growing up the sides, and looked out over the river that held their parents. It had been the three of them all those years, waiting. And then it had been the four of them and they were a family. And now it was the two of them and there was no future, no waiting, just the finality of an entire era—they were to go on, they supposed but how? And was it merely a matter of time until they turned into some spectre of their parents? They looked at each other furtively. Would one kill, or murder, or maim—herself or others, now or later? Every thought, every action felt suspect. Whitey felt terrified of laying with men now. Sweet Marie's ruthless chill seemed a fearsome sign itself, how like their mother she looked, the way she rubbed her feet together when she was tired. The bodies, human sacrifices, were somewhere in the river below. But the owners of the bodies had never left. They lurked in the white house, watching, shadowy crypt-dwellers, wandering heartless through the halls.

❦

THE GIRLS SAT INTO THE EVENINGS AND ROCKED ON THE PORCH and each thought to herself about what would happen next. And how they would turn their backs to the river and never look behind them again.

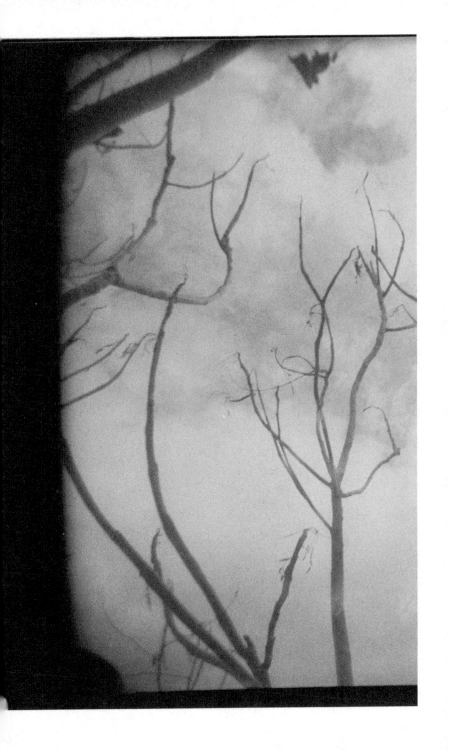

PART FOUR: THE RIGHT VENTRICAL

MAMA HAS TOO MUCH

MY MAMA RIDES THE TRAIN LIKE THE FAMILY MULE. SHE SITS
on its sway back and closes her eyes. Mama likes the train because
they both have seen too much and blink only when their eyes are
dried out, dried out by the dust of the road, dried up from what's
been kicked up by their passing. They carry their cargoes without
questions between their cities, a ship of fools that cannot stop. They
don't know what it is they're carrying inside, mostly because they
haven't stopped to think, and the rest because when they do stop to
think it's the same ragged thoughts over and over again. The same
route traversed. It is familiar. Their backs curve inward from the
weight. My Mama is carried by the train, and the train is carried by
the rails, and the earth carries the rails, and there is no telling exactly
who or what carries the earth. Mama rides the train back home from
the big city, not really knowing what holds her up.

❣

MAMA IS SEATED WITH HER FACE TOWARDS THE MAN WHO SPRAWLS
wide in front of her, but Mama's eyes look out sideways, out beyond
the glass, and the pictures of people outside rip past only a little
more slowly than her memories. Everything is fragmented. Both
tear past in frames with clear edges, but the contents are blurred.
Smokestacks and desiccated buildings out of focus, bleared. Seeing
the scenes outside has led Mama to a skepticism of her own mind:
her recollections of life pass by in square, smeared blocks of isolated
movement. Jagged. My sweet little Mama rides the train from home
to New York City. What she sees out the windows is the same. The
landscape is only as close and known to her as her own body—dead

and desolate—but the actions are interrupted, passers-by decapitated, the motions unfinished, the faces strange. She can only presume things about the people going by—they seem dropped like marbles from the sky, uncatchable and loud, shattering when they hit the ground.

♥

THERE IS SOMEONE WALKING ON THE BRIDGE, BY THE TRAIN, AND her bag is full of papers and some fruits that she is taking to the Church to give to Mother Mary. Mama can't remember if she knows this woman, or if the woman is the ghost of her own mother, or just a woman, walking, on a bridge at night, north of home. Mama can't tell what she sees through the train windows and what she has lived, what she has seen and what she has felt, what she has felt and what she has thought she should feel.

Everything goes, passed so quickly. Sometimes my Mama tries to close her eyes, but sometimes she can't because they have dried open and become glued wide, but not awake. Mama's eyes have become glued open, the corneas crusted with microscopic chips of the city's debris.

♥

MAMA WEARS A SHRUNKEN HAT TO KEEP THE HAIRS ON HER HEAD together and all of its heat from seeping out. Her arms are always crossed over her breasts to keep her heart from reaching out just once, unexpectedly, unannounced, surprising her with a brutal scream and laughing, laughing until everyone runs away. Mama wears black shoes so that when they run away with her she's not barefoot but she's got shoes, warm, to keep her safe. Her shoes are soft leather, and having been soaked over and over in the damp underfoot overflow of gutter and drain they have cast themselves like plaster around her toes, up underneath the arches of her tired feet, molded themselves like a hand behind her heels. They clasp her more tightly when they dry out.

♥

THE TRAIN YANKS AND PULLS MY MAMA TO A DESTINATION. SHE is different now than she was when she left. Mama thinks she knows where she is going, but she's not on her way back home, and she's never going back home. Because now she has me. And though the train lulls and rocks her into a so sweet catatonia, underneath it all she has a nonetheless guarded, suspicious submission which says, *I'll be waiting where I always am, take me where you always do, I'll pay you for it, just follow the line.* But she doesn't know the train is taking her somewhere else entirely.

And so now, Mama sits or stands or walks down the aisles with me restless inside her. There doesn't seem to be much else to do.

❦

THE BUMS IN PENN STATION LIKED TO FOLLOW MAMA, SQUISHING their words together into a paste with each step they take in their peed-in shoes, their medicated monkey voices chattering close behind her, taunting her into becoming a player, swishing behind in imitation of her, laughing out their noses with dry obstructed rasps, pushing pushing, teasing her to bring out a reaction, a spectacle, a display. The bums in Penn Station wanted Mama to play with them a little. They wanted her to give them a story to tell. They wanted her to distract them even more than they wanted to distract her, penetrate her corpse's composure.

I just love this pussy oh yeah sweet pussy

Baby   cumma here baby   Damn damn   Damn Don't make me cry   mmm mmm mmm
Is-a she-uh   lesbian?

She don't love no-man   ooh

She's uh lesbiun   she don' fuck no man

Damn oooweeeee   Cumma here home with me momma And beat my bed   sugar hips
Shit man, no   no shit, man! No man   she wants our fuckin somuch

Lookit that!   *Lucky Wet Girl*   *all*   *yer*
lips would fit so-good   *ooooOOO*
Making me thick   *MMMMMmmmm come on over here*
Ova here juicy   *ova HERE juicy juicy*   *Juicy girlie Juicy*
juicy Juicy Tight Girl   *Juicy Tight*   *G i r l i e*
lemme take offt
Those walking tall shoes oooooo ooo Dammit Can't get nothin from
these cunts no more
this motherfuckin shithole

oh baby Baby can't get me to give it up   *always got it up Shit yeah*
baby   *tight baby*
sexy tight baby

Lemma put it in a little sexy

baby sweet ass baby…

They're just looking for fun. They're just looking for some fun with Mama. They want her to play with them for just a moment, but Mama won't. She doesn't know how to play with them. Because she hates their oily fingers, their smell of warm dick. Because she doesn't believe any of them are anything besides persistent shadows making dancing motions with pennies and tokens, turning turnstiles and the pages of magazines at the newspaper vendor's, moving things by the power of their vacant minds.

Mama thinks she knows the rules. Mama just collects pictures of the outside world that aren't of her. Mama records the pee bums in her mind.

❤

ON THE TRAIN THE PIMP STRETCHES OUT HIS HAND TO TOUCH her hair but Mama moves away without even seeming too. She is too fast. Her eyes are locked on a landscape and he doesn't have a view. The door of her attentions is rusty and will not move, will not move at all, will not move at all for anyone, not even for the pimp on the night route with his acid-dipped fingers and his charcoal eyes.

Mama will not allow him into her existence. Good for Mama. She won't. Because then the two of them would be someplace, the same place, together. Good for Mama. She needs someone with hands that feel, hands like mine, mostly bone, mostly soft, soft baby bone.

❦

INSIDE MY MAMA IS A TINY BABY WITH WRINKLED CLAW TOES AND a fish's grin. That's me. Tiny Baby is me, curled around her stomach, around my own stomach, both of them bloated and swollen and soft, like a sweet summer mushroom pushing up from below to shelter my little paraffin ribs. Tiny Baby watches through Mama's skin, and can see so clearly because it's dark inside, and light outside, and the pulsating red glow of flesh and meat glistens and gives Tiny Baby a sharper view of everything, everything.

Mama's throbbing veins pass like branches through her bunched and flexing muscles, right in front of my eyes. Tiny Baby's peeping at her life from inside her treehouse of flesh, the sun outside burning its light through her skin and tissue all to way to me, hiding in her leaves. I squish in the peephouse of her fluid. It goes in and out of my wordless minnow mouth.

❦

I MIGHT NOT GROW IN HER FOR MONTHS, MAYBE EVEN YEARS, AND now even I can't remember how long I've been inside—I don't know if Mama has noticed her Tiny Baby yet. I will be so small, so tidy, if she notices and wants me to leave I'll be good and start cleaning up each month, spewing mouthfuls of blood and tissue down and out, biting into Mama's womb and spitting out the sorrows by the mouthful. I have wee teeth, just nubs, under my gums, full and rounded like corn kernels. Firm and perfect as my Tiny Baby ass. If the tissue fights I will make it go. Out it must go. Everything but Tiny Baby must go because Mama has too much. Mama has too much inside her already.

❦

Mama used to live in a huge house of white boards where she knows every flake of paint missing off the old steel stove. The light inside seems to come from straight above, falling straight down and then back up again in a pale yellow-blue, canceling itself out to white and leaving everything looking bare naked. She cleaned irregularly and not very thoroughly. Her underwear was in a pile by the bedroom door. The husks of empty paper cups lie quivering, overflowing in the waste can. Lipstick stains thickly band the tops of the cups, clotting bloodily around the tips. Their translucent bottoms are bowed down, convex from the weight of fluid that is only a ghost now that we're gone, evaporated into the damp cold lungs of the house, become moisture clinging to the paper on her walls. If Mama ever comes back down to the white house from her long trip to the city and casts her shoes in the corner she will see the trash, passed out, overdosed in another corner. She will try to decide whether she prefers to get rid of the smell or to stay in her bare feet, smoke another cigarette, and go to sleep.

❦

THE JAZZ GIRL'S SHORT DARK HAIRS ARE AS STILL AS LITTLE NEEDLES, stuck in the fibres of my Mama's clothes. Mama's sweaty body pulled these hairs out of the girl's skin by rubbing up against her. My two mamas. Mama's ripping fingers scattered them from the jazz girl's head. The girl my mama left them behind and, since they are just little hairs, maybe she doesn't miss them at all.

It could have been a long, long time ago that she was here, or maybe yesterday. The jazz girl's hairs rest in Mama's clothes like unknown constellations, rearranging themselves, changing the map of my universe every time she dresses. If anyone navigates by the jazz girl's stars, they will get lost because they don't lead directly to her anymore, just to what she was all about—something fierce and big and loud and shining in a faraway city. Last night Mama slept in her seat in her dirty clothes, and all night I stared at the Girl's little short dark hairs pressed down under Mama's weight. We're a family sandwich of cloth, hair and fluid that has yet to come alive.

❦

I THINK MAMA HASN'T DECIDED WHAT TO DO WITH HER TINY Baby yet. Because she is distracted, and because I am not interested in being known quite now. If I were not here, she would not notice any difference, but I would. I'm very still and stealthy. I spy on her, my eyes glued to what I can see through the little umbilical night vision periscope.

I look through Mama like Mama looks through the train windows. Tiny Baby just watches the pimp and his slick fingers, and the way Mama's feet don't tap on the floor but just lay there, quiet. I see it all go slow like that, go pulsing, not flashing by. Mama needs me so she can slow time down, and then Mama can ask me what I've seen this whole time I've been inside; she can get off this tin can train and take me home.

♥

TINY BABY IS STILL MADE OF THINGS THAT MELT AND FLOW, READY to sneak out between Mama's legs, dripping my life through the funnel of her. Tiny Baby wants to have a little bit of love, a little bit of happy things, to be on the same side of Mama as the sun. I keep watch out for someone who has the sound of jazz, who blows those notes, pulls them out of the thunder and the lightning, the rivers and streets and the clatter of hatpins and the howling of a good mad cat. Sounds like Mama and I are gonna make someday.

♥

THE TIME IS COMING CLOSER—THIS TRAIN CAN'T DRIVE ON ALONG forever. Mama needs to get up, take off her hat, wake up her tired feet and make them tap her down a new street in some somebody-going-places shoes. It may take years but not forever until I get around to being born. Maybe tomorrow.

Seems like I'm the only one who knows my own mind.

♥

MAMA HAS TWELVE BROKEN HEART PIECES AND I NEED HER TO have just one. When Mama decides to get her heart together then it can beat hard and fast enough to get me out of here. When Mama's heart is strong enough to push it all away from us, maybe then under bright lights with her legs wide Mama and Tiny Baby are going to get all naked and bloody and scream scream *scream* until suddenly, all of a sudden, we'll see each other and laugh and laugh and *laugh*.

AN ANGEL PLUCKS HIS WINGS FOR THE ARROW'S FEATHERED FLETCH

A starling calls from the woods, speaking of the ice the morning will quickly melt to water on the swallows' sleepy wings.

When Whitey and Jones look for the black winged thing in the treetops, all lungs pause. Wet bellows poised, inflated, gasp at what she is soon to see. Close behind the long ache of her gaze, a thousand shuddering eyelashes arrest themselves all over the woodbine—an elusive wren, the cat poised below its nest—all irises spread wide to the shimmering light of shock, every leaf in the forest reflecting the white December sun.

Whitey's heart is the first to move—a wild longing beating its way towards the lost child in the clearing, holding tight to the man with picket fence teeth and unlatched gate of lips.

Her headlong knowledge of home.

❣

WHITEY IS FROZEN AT THE TREE LINE, HER LONG WOOL SKIRT blending into the dried buds of winter chicory that silvers the edges of the clearing, the cat a frosted murmur of fur at her feet. In front of her a little child's footprints drift into a charcoal spiral of marks left in the snow by doe hooves. The child left abandoned, hair all knotted, a bruise waiting to be mended. Jones carves a swallow from a piece of cedar.

The child is crouched down pressing his fingertips along the surface of a block of yellowing deer salt.

❦

WHITEY'S COAT DROPS ITS BUTTONS AND THEY SKATE ACROSS THE frozen soil, skipping in a bounding arc of love.

❦

SMALL SLATE STONES FLUTTER UP IN A FAINT PATH TOWARD THE cabin's porch. The child has a handful of burled chestnuts, his pockets bulged. So very close.

❦

SKINNY JONES ROCKS ON THE PORCH, EACH FOOT COVERING THE exact width of the wide and weathered birch planks. There's a knife in his lap and a carpenter's apron filled with chestnuts, deep crosses cut into their supple mahogany husks through which their steam will puff and rise. He's dropped a few of the child's gleanings into a cast iron pan before picking up the child's shoes, which he sews with a bit of deer hide and oiled black thread. The child is barefoot in the yard.

❦

A SHADOW CAST BY THE HAWTHORNS IS TANGLED SHARP WITH old memories of shame and emptiness and loneliness and disgrace. Of loss and displacement and grief. Seeds tumble themselves out from it and warm themselves in the shore of speckled sunlight, their tiny husks yearning. *One sprout*, whisper the hungry seeds, *one shoot*.

❦

WHITEY AND JONES WANT TO IGNORE NO SADNESS FOR TOMORROW. They want to have everything joyful still waiting for them, for this child, eternally, and they have a host of sanctuary bats weaving a dark net around the people who don't belong in Lynchburg, for the outcast, and bring them to this low dark cabin nestled there under the trees.

They want to kick over all the pails filled with human tears and let the deer grow happy on the salt. They have waited for this.

♥

THE SWEET CAT SUMMER AT HER FEET QUIVERS ITS WHISKERS towards the child, the man, the woman, the cabin waiting in the clearing, and Whitey offers a bowl of buttermilk—velveted with the capacity to nourish, to be greedily swallowed, all sweet and sour and full, flavored with the long, clean green and purple grasses of spring.

For the stars have been loving them a long time, seeking them down all the colorless meadows of their nights and days. And now even the cat agrees: the child is lost, but is ready for home.

♥

IN HER EARS, WHITEY HEARS THE WIND HOWLING AND THE ECHOING strike of uncooked chestnuts dropped into a cast iron pan.

She feels the thick pads of Jones' fingers rasping against the mending string.

♥

ONE STEP, URGE THE CHILD'S LONELY MUSCLES, ONE STEP.

The hawthorn's shadow is eaten by the forgiving moss.

Its hands shiver, and the air stirring around the child rushes to the man and woman rocking on the porch.

♥

LOVE MOVES TOWARDS US, ITS FINGERS SLENDER AND POSSESSIVE.

Jones rises to stand with such power it seems the house shrinks behind him, as though a massive sycamore tree had sprung from the soil and split the boards that too long pinned its roots.

Angel, says Whitey's voice, buttered gold with the muscularity of love, *come here.*

❦

Jones holds a tiny half-patched shoe in his hand, and it seems as though a massive sycamore tree had suddenly freed its roots from the frozen December soil.

Angel, he says, *come here*, calling the child over to the steps next to Whitey, where Angel sits down, right in the small space between the two of them.

It's not too late.

A place where troubles won't follow.

❦

All Angel wants is to smell the richness of their breath, bury its face in the warmth of their winter skin - the child wants it all. Angel—a yet-fetal body curled inside Whitey's coat, tiny head pressed perfectly against her juniper and cedar lap. Whitey kisses Jones. The freckle on Jones' upper lip clasped between her teeth. She wants to wash the three of them with milk and honey and watch the yellow butterflies arrive, unfurling kisses.

❦

The worst might not last and the best could come true.

❦

What Angel wants is to be a sugar ant and climb way along the lengths of the two of them, their every hill and hollow, knowing the root and swelling curl of every hair, the deep bloom of their every pore. The child has waited for this. Home

Come here, sweetheart, Jones says, and Whitey stretches out his hand, and this slowly warming form takes its place in the empty space they've saved for the child between them.

HOW IN MODERN TIMES WITCHES
PERFORM THE CARNAL ACT

I LIKE TO SAY I WAS BORN AND LIVED ALONE IN THE TOP DRAWER of a dresser in a small place back in the woods across the creek but then Jones and Whitey walk into the room and says *come out of there, Angel.* And I do.

Jones was tall and quiet, but with fast hands that slid their way across the grimy things in my sweet little house. Jones so witchity he scared the cat Summer the rest of the way out my window. He had the kind of weird that didn't quite reflect back out of his face as much as it burned right into you if you were looking at him. So strange. And Whitey—she stood right in front of the old mirror with the green spots and I saw little cracks shoot out in all directions. Jones bent down all small and set a snapping match on the wooden floor and said, *We're going out of the woods and back to town,* and I decided to go with this man and woman. So I picked up my goose egg box and I could see it was going to be all that's left me and it was soft and hard in my hand like a nest of snakes and these old witches wrapped me up and said: *We're going out of the woods,* and so we went all the way to the ugly little town.

❤

THE WITCHES HAVE A RED CIGAR BOX ON THE BATHROOM SHELF where I sit when he makes me wash my face. I shake the box and it rattles.

Jones always says, *Put it down Angel.*

But I don't. Because first I say, *Tell me about my mother and father.*

He says, *Will you put it down then if I tell you.*

Yes, I say, and wait for Jones to talk.

Your mother is a nest of swallows. Your father is a can of summer plums. I think of your mother, the swallow, naked inside her raincoat of feathers, naked walking backward, walking backwards down the railroad tracks, not looking but singing, singing, her head back to the sunlight. You father a wild stallion, his mane wrapped around his neck. Your mother a bringer of heat lightning.

That's what Jones says every time I ask him to tell me a story about my mother and father. When I ask Whitey about them she never gets anything useful out of her mouth. *Your mother,* she begins, and then I'm left with his body as his eyes are off across the pastures, looking at the moon come up over the sumac trees.

Jones and Whitey sends me off to school with a paper food bag making me leave the rattley red glued shut cigar box behind. When I'm gone down the road to school I can feel them hide it from me.

I give Jones' food to whatever it is that lives under the bridge and likes to eat my lunch more than me.

❦

THE LADIES IN LYNCHBURG DON'T LIKE JONES AND WHITEY AND me. Jones and Whitey and me walk to Watson's buying cans and bags of things for eating and the Ladies cross over angry to the other side of the street, big girl birds flinging their arms up in the air hoping for a gust of wind to carry them away from Jones and Whitey and me. Pink yellow blue and green dresses with little flowers. White lacey things on their underbellies. Black shiny leather feet with brittle heels tight tracked in the dirt. Lizardy silver-buttoned bags hanging from their elbows like udders gone all stiff and hard. Ladies in Lynchburg don't like Jones. Or Whitey. Or me. So the ladies in Lynchburg cross the street when me and Jones and Whitey go to town.

♥

WHY DO THE LADIES IN LYNCHBURG...? I ASK THE WITCHES WHY they treat us bad and they puts their hands in their hip pockets and stirs around the stuff they have in there—bells and stones and pine sap and buttons—and puts their hands real soft on my head and don't make any words come out of their mouths, just a slow sweet crooning that sends me down to sleep.

Why do they? I say. Jones buys me an aluminum toy gun to make me be quiet and so to get more I ask him again, *why do the Ladies in Lynchburg*—and Jones gives me a big heavy hammer this time and I want more so I says: *why*—and this time he gives me an old dime and says, *go put that under the train wheels* and so we do.

When we get to the cross-Lynchburg train tracks my mother's not there naked in the feathered raincoat and my father is not a stallion running wild with a wreath the red roses below in the branches of the sugar poplar tree. No mother naked inside her brown feathers made for sitting out her storm and I ask Jones again, *Why?* Jones looks down the slippery rails with his hands chewing up and down in his pockets again and asks me if I can see my cat Summer hiding in the trees and I can't and I get sad and mad and I start to scrape at my arms again with my fingernails so Jones says, *See if you can shoot the ladies dead with that gun of yours,* and so I do it to make him happy because he's Jones and he likes it when I try to kill them.

The train runs away from us too.

♥

WITH JONES AND WHITEY ASLEEP AT NIGHT THEY CAN'T KEEP THE red box for themselves no more. I have no Summer and no drawer but I have a pillow and a gun and now the red box with the glue is mine. I don't tell Whitey what's inside but she knows. And Jones knows already because he's the one that glued it shut.

In the red box under my pillow resting real still are my mother's two wings, crispy and dried out brown like Catalpa bean pods except for the feathers, oily sheen slick long feathers with tips like toothy grins smiling up at me.

I know this was all that's left.

My mother's feathers have tiny grooves and drop right off the fletch easy if I don't be careful until I stick them back on with spit. Before Jones caught me I did like I seen the girls in the meadow back of Lexington do to the little field flowers and plucked my mother's feathers off the wings. *She Loves Me. She Loves Me Not. She Loves Me. She Loves Me Not.*

Now Jones makes me keep the lid glued down on my mama's feathers and then he walks away from me like he's gonna run. But when he's not lurking around I give the wings little tastes of cornbread and in the evenings I let them sit out on the windowsill to watch the clouds wash the face of the moon and wait with me for Summer to come back.

♥

THE WITCHES SEND ME TO SCHOOL SAYING NOTHING BACK TO THE whys I ask him about my mother and my father and I'm all alone with the little girls that belong to the Ladies of Lexington. Ragdoll girls with sunny flower faces but evil blue ice-creek eyes.

Your mama is real bad, the flower girls say. *She'd be better off dead 'cause she is bad,* they say. *Your mama is no good. She got herself runned over by a trainman when she should have ran to God. You daddy is a lunatic. Your mama is a killer. You daddy is a devil man.*

Ragdoll says, *So you ain't got no soul. You born in a devil drawer* says ragdoll. *You don't belong here.*

Ice eyes float in girl skin.

The girls who belong to the Lexington Ladies sing and ring the rope that pulls the bell and everybody crosses themselves and go over the street and under their feet I'm smashed to nothing like just another sorry railroad dime.

♥

IT'S JUST FEATHERS THAT'S IN YOUR BOX, ANGEL, JONES SAYS. AND *you don't even know what bad is,* he says.

But, I says, *but I don't care I just want to know what it is quiet and flutters in my box.*

Shush! Jones says. *Be quiet it's goosefeathers.*

But I say, *It smells like somebody's oily head and armpit except for that black mildewy spot on the side that smells like a cellar.*

Hush! says Jones, but I can't no more.

Then how come the Lexington Ladies cross the street, I says. *And what's in the red box if they ain't my mother's feathers? What are they then?* I say, *How come my mother don't be here in the house with her? If she ain't runned over then where'd she run to? And if those are just catalpa bean pods then how come her fingers ain't no more on our heads, and holding our hands? Where are her hands? And where is my father? Where is the stallion who rides with the red roses though the tulip poplar trees, beautiful and black?*

And then the witches say to me, *Sometimes your family is the ones who love you most.*

Whitey just holds her ears together with his hands but even so her brains leak out all watery through her eyelashes.

♥

NOW I DON'T LEAVE THE HOUSE NO MORE BACK BEHIND THE SUMAC trees and I just lay there with my head on the table and there's no food anymore and *I'm hungry* I say but I don't have no more of

Jones' food instead I got the red box and the Ragdoll Girls sing and I don't know what to sing back so I don't go to school with them damn dolls no more.

♥

I REMEMBER MY NICE DARK DRAWER ALL SOFT AND SUMMER CURLED up real warm around me and how that used to make me feel better and I says to myself, *Maybe my parents need a drawer that they don't need to be taken out of...* So I says to Jones, *Stay there. Stay there,* I says. And I put my box in my drawer. *I'll take care of you,* I says, and I take my gun and my dime and my hammer and me and Summer leave breadcrumbs and seeds and we leave the box and the jar there inside and shut the drawer safe on them so they'll stay safe and happy. Me and Summer feed them, safe inside.

The Ladies in Lexington leave letters on the witches' big white porch telling them our kind isn't welcome here, but I tell Summer to eat it all and so the Ladies, they click their beaks at me and flap their big black wings in my face. *Fly away,* I says, *Fly away.* And I throw rocks at their glassy little eyes and I say, *I got a cat here,* I say, *so fly away.* And then they do and it's just me and Summer outside and Jones and Whitey all laughing and kissing inside on their pillows and up above the clouds wash the face of the moon.

WITHIN THESE LIPS
THERE ARE STILL OTHER LIPS

OUTSIDE MY DOOR BROOKLYN MUMBLES, STRANGE SOUNDS OF doors and laughter, music and cries and a constant murmuring from the streets.

The fire escape winds down beneath us, but it stops before it reaches the ground. We can climb down but the world cannot come up to meet us in the midnight half-light, the stairs an iron dragon guarding the castle of my keep.

All around us we hear trumpets and saxophone, bass and horns and drums. We hear jazz. I live here in the city. We live here. We do.

So far have I come to be here. All the way around this strange blue-green planet, through its drowning places and its thirsty places, its freezings and its burnings. And somehow I have found myself here, by my own side. I, who have belonged to my mother and my sister and my father now belong nowhere, and yet here is where I feel most at home. I can feel the child still inside me, the mysteries of its thoughts whirling sleepily inside its head. Our bed is cool beneath me. Our sheets light. The summer heat is unexpectedly soft, like the crush of the baby's tiny thigh against my stomach. Two of its fingers crossed, its small mouth pressed into my flesh: it is hot, as though steaming with some pre-dawn sun.

My child takes this world's hardships and chews them into hope.

It's a baby that doesn't need a birthing to take shape—this is something living by its own means, its own measure. I carry it for the world, and it balances out the violence with pure creation: sweetness and beauty.

It is a kind child. It croons a lullaby into the coldness of this world.

It's a warm thing, a faun and a lion. A fierce sweet.

♥

ONCE, I MADE THIS CHILD WITH THE JAZZ GIRL: THIS AN honest truth.

Her honeysuckle cunt, her cocky gaze: my need for her unmatched. These sheets that once I hoped would hold her short black hairs, their fibers that I dreamed would feel her heavy breasts—her head asleep on my pillow, and the glass that, like me, would feel her lips; the floor she might walk on and the door whose knob she would touch, the blanket that would embrace her perfect jaw—everything worshiping her.

But remember, I did most of all.

Allegiance, devotion, these things my training taught me to give allegiance to anyone but myself.

Ask me to debase myself, humiliate myself, to make this supplication huge and holy. Tie me down and take of me completely, let me strip and dedicate my self in the public doorways, the inner altars of her temple. My mother taught me this, my god. And I did this, for them: deity, doctor, lover—devils all.

These are things it hurts to utter.

I wanted to serve someone and make it beautiful, an abasement without oppression.

Instead I sold myself to the cruelest bidders.

Obedience I knew so well to give. I didn't know.

To ask permission. To beg—I gave a constant supplication. For someone to tell me that I pleased them. For them to look at me and say, simply, *I know that you are mine.* To belong. To believe myself loved in some way.

To satisfy.

♥

DEMAND OF ME, COMMAND ME. I HAVE SURRENDERED.

This is what the world has always heard me say, whether I uttered the words at all. But no more.

♥

WHAT DID SHE DO TO ME, MY CYCLONE LOVER? SHE MONSOONED me, that hurricane girl.

Ripped the roof from my home and exposed me, left me naked in the storm, and I thank her for it.

When I was with her, everything ached—though not as much as I—for the feel of her flesh, her breath, the words that would one day issue from her brain. (Hers seemed a pink brain, pulsing, an anemone washing in the tides that plumps and fans, multicolored and gorgeous, organic.)

I saw the clam of her, always closed and never open. I cut myself on the nacreous and rocky shell each time she tempted me with a glimpse of the burnished raw animal that hid inside. I never saw it. But I found my own dusky muck.

Now I have a pearl.

♥

THESE ARE THE THINGS WE SHOULD NOT SAY: I OFFERED MYSELF to those who took me cruelly, and I knew no better than to love them for it.

The doctor. His lips unlocked me. His fingers found the first wall behind which my lovelies bloomed. And the Jazz Girl. Her hands reached into the blush of my folds, made fists and split me wide. She penetrated me, pinned me down. He roped and bound me. Whipped me. Marked me.

How did I survive them?

Once, I wanted the ritual of it, submission. I had been so long sewed up that I saw light, and hope, when they ripped me open. I felt alive, the numbness changed. Some attention felt better than none. And on the other side their smiles were there, their small tendernesses. I thought they loved me.

❦

AND NOW, I AM ALONE IN THIS CITY WITH MY CHILD, MY JAZZ BABY. I begin again—not as Sweet Marie, but as Marie. Marie. Marie. No levels of meaning, no need to please, but only one woman finding a clean pure self for the first time.

Allow me the small words, my awkward childishness.

Sentiments that embarrass. Hopes clinging to cliché.

Let me be shy and tiny, unsure of how to start again.

❦

INSIDE I AM LOVE'S URCHIN, CLUMSY, IGNORANT, ILL-CLOTHED— once I fought to hold onto my last piece of spoiled and dirty bread, even though eating it made me sicken and nearly die. I told myself I held gold, or diamonds. I held my precious pain close to me in the palm of my filthy hand.

♥

I have always hesitated on the stoop of love, too shy to knock, afraid of permission denied.

But stop—do not be misled by me: the bravery is there, and the determination.

They are there in the pink scars sliding down the backs of my thighs.

In the stretch marks I carry on my ever-swollen belly.

Because I have heard my voice and heard something begin. Strings and horns, a female howling.

I'll suck the slit of happiness until she screams in pleasure.

I'll refuse to stop.

WHEN I WATCHED THEM
HANG THE HORSE

THE BONES WEREN'T SCATTERED AROUND. THEY WERE LAID OUT in the pasture as neat and close as the yarn in a sweater. There up in the Bell's pasture I found the horse, hit by lightning in the spring and fallen down on the ground so quick it stayed together. I could tell it was a horse right off, just with nothing on it.

Winter came later and I came back and put the bones up in a square of bedspread and dragged the bundle back to outside the house. Sat sorting and polishing, with a small knife tried to get off the dried meat, finally boiled the smaller bones in water with Whitey and Skinny Jones suddenly show up quiet there at the stove. I was missing two of the four feet in the pot.

Hooves, Jones told me, *I believe they're called hooves.*

But I was still missing them.

They're probably eaten up by now, Whitey said.

I wanted to know what kind of thing would eat the hooves, what kind of thing had teeth or jaws enough to do it, or the sort of hunger to eat a horse's feet.

Pig's feet are very tasty, he said, *like pickles.*

I said I'd seen those in jars and pig bones were on the inside, underneath all the fat. Not like a horse's feet where everything is hidden inside underneath the hardness.

♥

SKINNY JONES SAYS, *SOMETIMES BIRDS WILL LAY THEIR EGGS IN THE nest of a different kind of bird. And the other birds raise it as their own.*

Whitey says, *The new birds comes back to the nest with a hoof. With a bit of goosedown, for softness.*

Skinny Jones says, *The hungry baby wondering what and how. But the new birds go out again the next day, and comes back again and brings back worms, and moths, and bits of insect.*

Whitey says: *It takes a while. But eventually the baby belly is a little rounder. The crackling veins on its skull is covered over with those thin dark pin feathers. It can hurt, but soon it will fly.*

Skinny Jones says, *Now the babies are eating crickets, toads, birds, grain, grasshoppers and mice.*

♥

I HAVE TWO OF THE FEET, AND WHO HAS THE OTHER?

I say, *I want to know which kind of creatures have done this to the stallion.*

Skinny Jones says, *The ones with broken teeth.*

My teeth are in cornrows down my jaw, hard and square and serious.

♥

OUT IN THE YARD I GOT EVERYTHING ARRANGED. THE GRASS this winter is the kind of thin angry yellow that lives in a stomach. Some little bits of green only make it worse, poking up through the bones. Mr. Bell has walked up the side of the house and stood in the rhododendron, rubbed and raw and purple lipped.

You oughtn't to play with the dead, Angel, he says. *Tell your daddy get you a baseball or a gun.*

I keep saying *what?* until he gives up and goes home.

We always ignore Mr. Bell. Once he was a judge, but now he mates peacocks. They are kept in the barn for their own protection.

The toenail of a peacock can slice a child's face in half, he told me and Skinny Jones, *and they aim their beaks direct for the human eye.*

When it's quiet in the middle of the night you can hear them screaming. Sometimes Mrs. Bell comes over to make sure Jones and Whitey and I are keeping fine and dandy but she just wants to complain about the wildly colored birds and their bad luck feathers. She says she is afraid to leave the house.

She says, *And they scream and scream real slow all night - Help me! Help me!*

❦

OUTSIDE OUR CABIN THE WHIPPOORWILL SINGS. HIS SHOULDERS all wide and thin, Skinny Jones comes outside to squat, smoke a cigarette, and watch me. He's quiet and watches me sort bones.

I have put all the leg pieces in one pile, all the bits of the spine in another. I have four knee parts. The hips are thin and flat and look like Skinny Jones' when he's come out of the bath. I've made little holes in the frozen dirt and got the ribs stuck up in tall spikes around me and the other bones. I am the baby horse inside the big horse. Whitey stays outside the fort and turns a back bone around and around her long fingers on one hand, watching me.

I wish I had the tail, I tell her.

She says, *What?*

And I say, *I wish I had the tail,* and we do it again and again and then

I have it figured out that the Bells have come over to say that *Angel has a dirty toy* and *Angel was rude* and *It must be stopped.* Whitey and Skinny Jones look at me and smile. They love to be on our side of others' disapproval.

Come inside and clean up, they say. *It's time for dinner.* They smile at me through the ribs and then look away.

Bury it tomorrow, they say, *in a hole.*

❦

MY BEDSPREAD IS COVERED WITH MUD AND BONE MITES, RUINED. The embroidery a thatch of winter muck. And so Angel is asleep in the wide hollow of the his empty bed. Elbows raised up, legs twisted together at the knees and again at the ankles, braided.

The way Whitey and Jones used to sleep when they were young and things were hard. Close, but tense as a knife. No dreams, no movement. No telling what is happening underneath.

Angel's fingernails a new geology, thin and pale as mica pressed flat against the soil.

There are four lines inside Angel's palm and they all point in different directions, the cracks filled in with a thin layer of dead horse dirt.

The Bells think Angel thinks too much of dead things. That even witches are not enough, not enough to fill those cracks, take up the spaces between his fingers where real parents' should be. That he is doomed. That his mother's should be there, his father's should be there, instead of the dirt of hoodoo and magic, finding Angel even while he sleeps.

❦

IN THE MORNING SKINNY JONES POLISHES THE SHOVEL WITH SAND and oil from the jar by the stove. Whitey walks ahead of me in over the bits of ice on the grass, dragging the blanket of bones behind, up the hill and down a little to the flat spot under the maple tree. Their shoes sound like firewood stacking up against the ground.

The shovel is longer than I am high and I chop away.

I don't think the horse wants to go in the ground, I say. *I don't think it likes it down there.*

Skinny Jones looks at me sideways and Whitey says nothing. That means they wants me to keep at it so I scrape away more sticks and rocks with the shovel but things only move around a little, and nothing gets any deeper.

Skinny Jones takes the shovel and it looks like him, like he's using himself to dig a long wide hole for my horse. Jones doesn't make a hole. Bits of dirt and ice can't make it all the way up to his face but they try. Then they fall right back down where they were, cold and hard when they hit the ground.

The dirt doesn't want my horse, the dirt doesn't want my horse, I say.

We leave the horse and walk back to the house. Jones wraps my hands around a hot cup and Whitey closes the bathroom door on herself. Later they will whisper in their bed, in a language with sounds I do not understand.

After a while I put my mittens back on and go out the door and up the hill to the horse. Then it's time to go to sleep and I go back inside and the horse stays under the maple tree, still and quiet with the cold.

❦

IN THE MORNING THERE ARE SHARP STARS OF FROST ON HORSE. The sun doesn't come down far enough to notice that winter should be over, that winter should leave my Horse alone.

Skinny Jones and Whitey have gone away all day and I stay to play with Horse. No Mr. Bell, no Whitey, Jones, no witches, wind, no nothing above, no nothing below, no bad times in the sky for me.

The witches will come back. Those two always come back, their minds filled with hoodoo and their pockets with mysteries I am not allowed to see. I set up the bones to look like my father and me: two legs, two arms, and a long thin spine and wide ribs. I put the hoofs down below for feet but there are no hands. I put a cup of hot tea at the end of its wrists but there are still sharp stars of frost on the bones.

Just before dark I wrap Horse up in my blanket and drag it home. I know where to put it. The bones get warm in the witches' bed. They hardly look like bones at all in the sheets, there on the pillows, turned to a warm butter shine in the lamplight.

Go to sleep, go to sleep, I sing. *Go to sleep and dream, go to sleep…*

❦

WHITEY AND SKINNY JONES COME HOME FROM THE WOODS. IN their cabin the lights are on. Angel sleeping there on the floor of their bedroom. Ribs, paraffin soft, moving up and down to the rasping sound from his lungs.

In their bed the bones, in a damp quilt of leaves and mud. Everything stinks of musk. More hot and thick than air. On the floor is cool with Angel, bone bugs already crawling in his hair.

Inside the marrow live the bone bugs, their thin flaky shells filling up with dried blood, fat and protein, moving silent and secure inside their walls.

The bugs have clustered in the warm juniper thicket of Angel's hair, gnawing at the density, gasping as the taste. Fat and protein. Life. Scalp sweet as burnt butter. Their thin flaky shells snap between the witches fingernails. They hold them in their fingers for a moment and then let them go.

One after another, and another.

This child is the hollow bones filled with life, and the trauma is the frozen ground.

♥

THE WITCHES HAVE TAKEN HORSE IN THE NIGHT AND THROWN it away.

All day I snap the bone bugs in my fingernails. I pretend they are the witches' heads, and pop and pop and pop. God damn those two.

♥

IT'S BEEN FIVE DAYS AND MY TEETH ARE GLUED SHUT TO WHITEY and Jones. He goes to town and buys extra cigarettes and crouches in his cloud making oatmeal and pork chops at the stove. Whitey blows gray smoke in his snapping grease. I don't eat from him. They can't make me get in the bath because I will not give them my dirt to put down the drain.

In the field there are no more bones, and no more lightning storms until summer comes. My cat Summer has run away. Every day I look for teeth, for tiny cracked teeth in the leaves, but they aren't there either. The witches are not good, not good for anything. There are no animals, there is nothing hiding in the bones.

There is no butter corn, just rows of paper stalks standing quiet in the field.

When the witches bring Mrs. Bell to bring me around I do not help him make her job of helping me any easier. She can help them first. I'm the last in line who needs saving.

Angel, let's learn how to sew. I can show you how to make calico soldiers, she says, but I say nothing. She's got more up in her than usual. She says, *Don't break your daddy's only heart, baby, don't give your mama more trouble than he's got.* But I don't know who she's even talking about.

Why don't you tell me what's in your head, she says again and again. From her lap I scream like her peacocks, as loud and hollow as there is until she get up real silent and walk away.
Later Jones brings me more food.

I've cooked you fresh rats for dinner, he says, but this time I know he's lying.

♥

IN THE MIDDLE OF THE NIGHT, NIGHT AFTER NIGHT, WHITEY AND Skinny Jones keep getting up and stringing those bones together, hanging the from the tree, joining the, with wire bone by bone until what's up there in the tree is Angel's horse, liquid in the air as a ghost.

They can't forget, the three of them, can't forget what's been broken, what's been lost, what's missing. But the witches bring things in to feed the hole in the middle of this house: collections of half-dead things that are yet still things, still taking up space, still there to be touched and smelt and seen. Remembered. Jones and his strangeness. Whitey's crackling hair. It's all better than the clear reach of nothing, the way their breath feels on my skin when I grasp at it. Nothing versus everything. There's a difference between the two.

Angel's horse hangs up in the maple tree, legs joined to body, body to head, head raised high from the thick branch and two hooves dangle down into the wind. When summer comes it will fill with green, bird nests growing between the hips.

♥

IN THE MIDDLE OF THE NIGHT THE WITCHES WRAP ME UP IN THE bath towel and we go outside into the snapping cold air. Everything is black and the witches set me down on the ground.

Horse runs through the branches and the bones rattle in the wind.

In the maple tree Horse hangs together. There are thin wires between leg and knee, shoulder and rib, joint and bone. The horse runs wild through the tulip poplar tree. The witches have wired the horse together and hung it from the tree branches.

Their breath is hard and fast and strong against my head.

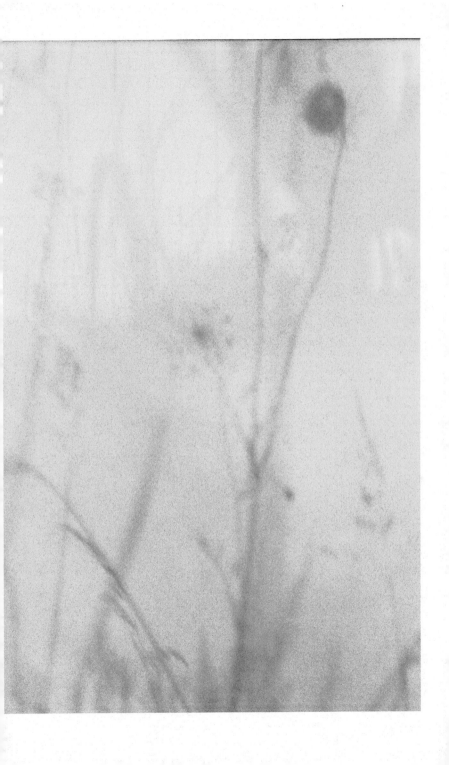

EVERY DAY CLOSER
TO WHAT COMES NEXT

Between us two we hold a ball of string and we toss it back and forth. First Angel, then Tiny Baby.

Once upon a time there was a white swan flecked with specks of red. Another inch grows on the ball, and we toss it. Tiny, then Angel. Family has a texture of string.

Whitey and Sweet Marie talk amongst themselves. Once upon a time there used to be four of us and then three, then four, then none, and now there are more of us that we can count. Two of us used to be here and now are dead. Two of us are born who never were before. Many of us are living who once were not.

We never knew the dead two, our granny and granddaddy. The things they saw and did and said and ate and killed. They lived before we lived, and still had time to die before we were born.

We make more knots.

Once upon a time there was a big white house on the hill, an evil house, some folks say, though nobody really knows for sure where it went except to say that not all the people who lived in or near that old white house ever came out alive. African slaves. Our family. The patients when it once was a hospital.

Our mamas say that's because Lynchburg don't know nothing of all the kinds of creatures there are that live in the world. That humans confuse and reverse and mistake the possible with the impossible.

Kindness with cruelty. The living with the dead. The sacred and the unholy. The normal with the abnormal. Skin and bones, their weight and color, their shape and size their value in the movement of the cosmos.

Some of us live in the city, and some of us live back in the beyond way back of the woods. It's all the cosmos versus humans. Each have their laws, says Jones.

Our mamas say Lynchburg never know what to make of us. We make cherry pie. We grow warm from long clean stems. We're happy.

Once upon a time they ate sweet summer melons with salt, and hams swaying in the slanted smokehouse, and there were rats and bats who spoke to them in tongues of what was to come. Sweet Marie sits curled in the arms of a tulip poplar and bows her strings. She sings like she does in the north: big and high. In the city, they come for miles to listen. Down here, the deer cock their tails and take her in through their antlers.

Every time is once upon a time. We play cat's cradle. We make and unmake knots. We toss it all, back and forth and on and on.

Once upon a time there were strange twin rosebushes that sprang from fallow ground in a town where all the dirt was sucked up by the river, and coffins floated in the murk, and nobody ever seemed to know how anything good ever got grown, yet somehow these bushes bore two pips—buds that sprang from their rosy hips in winter. But we have flesh and blood mothers, real as real, true as true. They made milk like any others. Made sanctuary.

Once upon a time our parents flew up from a place where once there had been flames, and smoke and ashes, and they called it sanctuary. They thought all was over, and then it wasn't.

Hands, eyes, hands, eyes, both are needed for this ball of string.

Once upon a time people were green as copper pennies. Underneath the grime hid bright orange underneath, hoping to glow. Tiny Baby, then

Angel. Sweet Marie, and Whitey, then Jones, and the cat Summer.
Between us we hold a ball of string and we toss it back and forth. We
hang warm from long clean stems. Unravel our ball and the watch
the string inside it growing longer every day.

NOTES ON METHODOLOGIES:

ALL THESE PIECES WERE CREATED ON SITE IN LYNCHBURG, Amherst, and the Shenandoah Valley of Virginia, the Sea Islands of South Carolina, and the battlefields and plantations of Tennessee. Although I had grown up in all these places, I returned to create this project with specific intention, and spent fifteen years working at these sites, returning again and again to visit and revisit.

My equipment are unexpected tools to subvert the secrecy, censorship, silencing, and suppression surrounding how society and the state defines normalcy and humanity, and the institutions they use to control, contain, and eliminate those whom it deems abnormal or less than human. I worked in the field using salvaged typewriters (I like typewriters since there is no field access to electricity, and no capacity to self-censor or edit) on rolls of paper I later transcribe. I used expired 120 chemical film and damaged adapted American analogue film cameras from the 1930s-1960s, repurposing the cameras to document what had not been permitted to be documented in the past. The photographs are scanned from raw negatives – there is no digital manipulation – the colors, textures, shapes, and multiple layers are all created using only the unique aberrations of the cameras' optics and the chemistry of the film. At a site, I create identical compositions but use multiple cameras with different film stocks— each camera and each film yield a different image of the same object.

By using cameras and typewriters from the segregation era at sites with contested or hidden histories, I attracted the attention of folks who realized the significance of those instruments in that particular timespace. These folks—both allies and adversaries—added complex and contradictories perspectives extending far beyond my own.

Throughout the fieldwork, I considered the conflict between the state and the individual, and the government's attempts to police and control the "problematic" body. I was arrested and physically and psychologically threatened by the police and by white supremacist groups who—in the 21st century—still hold violently to their power over the official story. They found me at sites of state-sponsored programs and human and civil rights atrocities against the bodies, minds, and psyches of people of color, women, queer, and disabled folks, prostitutes, and the impoverished. The programs and the people who still enforce them serve to repress "the other" into a place of invisibility.

NOTES ON SITES:

AT THESE SITES, THREE ELEMENTS COMMUNICATE TRAUMA: THE absence of the human body, the architecture, and the ecology. By inhabiting unmarked institutional, domestic, and ecological sites for years, I question the motivations with which the location is altered and destroyed in the centuries following the crimes that happened there. How does ecology and architecture influence the tangible evidence of atrocity and trauma? How can my role as artist—and the audience and reader's role—transform the voyeuristic "tourist-witness" encounter into an engaged "activist-empath" relationship?

I want the project to help establish the power of politically-engaged artmaking. I want to question the psychosocial programming that encourages fear, aversion, revulsion, or apathy when individuals or communities are confronted with uncomfortable or traumatic witnessing. I want to render visible the ways in which societies use institutional architecture and ecological obstruction to conceal systematic crimes against marginalized people. I want to offer resistance and challenge to the power of the American government and its institutions to control identity and define membership in society, especially via institutions for medical, psychiatric, penal, and social care.

Lastly, I hope the work I have done at these sites validates the living and the dead who experienced and suffered the injustice of these policies, and is a testament to those who have found alternative ways to survive and thrive under the most adverse conditions.

(1) VIRGINIA CENTER FOR EPILEPTICS AND FEEBLEMINDED

THESE PHOTOGRAPHS INCLUDE THIS SITE (NOW KNOWN AS THE Central Virginia Training School), and reference the Western State Lunatic Asylum and the Central State Mental Hospital: three segregated US Government-run eugenics asylums in rural Virginia used to segregate, persecute, and police the lives of people who were deemed noncompliant to social norms. With a proud and publicly-stated ideology of wealthy white supremacist social purity, for decades physicians Albert Priddy and Joseph DeJarnette used these sites to kill, maim, forcibly sterilize, and experiment upon at least 8,500 Virginians deemed disabled, epileptic, mixed race, queer, sexually transgressive, or otherwise undesirable to the State of Virginia—this continued until 1972, the year before I was born. My great-grandfather, who was of contested race and sexuality, was possibly a male prostitute, and had syphilis was institutionalized at one of these facilities. In 2009, I was taken into temporary custody by the Virginia State Police and the resulting photographs were taken under police and Center escort, in which I had to first let the monitors view each shot before I could make an exposure.

With the enthusiastic cooperation of law enforcement, the justice system, and the medical industry, a process called "Mountain Sweeps" encouraged communities to forcibly institutionalize their undesirables: "mongrels" of non-white or mixed racial heritage, unwed mothers and their illegitimate children, Native Indians, African-Americans, "inferior whites," people with physical and neurological disabilities, sexual assault survivors, and those accused of homosexuality, sexual activity outside marriage, "race mixing," or "acts contaminating the purity and soundness of the white race."

Once inside these asylums—and similar institutions throughout Europe and the United States—several million human beings were subjected reproductive sterilization and castration, medical experimentation, lobotomies, electroconvulsive/electroshock, and punishment by straightjackets, ankle and wrist restraints, insulin-induced coma, and needle showers. Sexual exploitation and enslaved labor was disproportionately perpetrated against women, girls, and African-Americans.

Under these lethal, punitive, and intentionally inhumane tactics, "discharge by death" was commonplace.

I photographed the surgical buildings, the recovery buildings, the cemetery built for pretend burials, and the unmarked mass grave where bodies were dumped. Family history suggests my ancestors would have died there had not the women staged a protest by walking down the railroad tracks naked underneath yellow raincoats to draw attention to the crimes taking place. My ancestors—the institutionalized and the protesters—were all sent home in disgrace to avoid any press or public attention.

(2) LYNCHBURG, VIRGINIA

Located in the Blue Ridge Mountains, the town of Lynchburg was founded by a family of planters named Lynch—the terms "lynching," "lynch law," and "lynch mob" all derive from their name and legacy. Charles Lynch and his brother John were tobacco plantation owners, and in the 1850s the town was amongst the wealthiest in the nation. The city and its surrounding plantations and outlying lands were known for their lynching of black men. Located on the James River, it was also a hub for the sale of African and African-American slaves.

A central part of downtown adjacent to the slave markets was "Buzzard's Roost"—this hub for prostitution in Lynchburg featured brothels with secret passageways connecting white brothels to mixed race brothels, so that customers could avoid miscegenation prosecution. My great-grandfather was a regular participant in these brothels—although controversy surrounds his role, he died of syphilis contracted there. The photographs of the prostitutes' grave sites could be those of my relatives.

It is the home of Jerry Fallwell's Liberty University, and while I was there it was typical for out queers to be forcibly apprehended by

students and faculty and taken to the university for "re-education."
While I was not picked up, many of my friends were.

Lynchburg was originally inhabited by Monocan, Siouan Tutelo, Algonquian, and Seneca tribes before being exterminated or forcibly relocated by the Colony of Virginia. In the 20th century, many tribes were bureaucratically erased by William Plecker, who refused to allow their ethnicity to be reflected on birth documents. The Lenape and Nanticoke tribes, as well as other tribal Nations, still exist in the region. My ancestors were subjected to miscegenation laws, and yet married illegally and bore children.

(3) LYNCHBURG OLD CITY CEMETERY, VIRGINIA

THE LYNCHBURG OLD CITY CEMETERY WAS FOUNDED IN 1806 by John Lynch as a burial ground for African- and Native-descended citizens, prostitutes, and indigent people. From 1806 and 1895, the City Cemetery was the only burial ground open to African Americans in Lynchburg. It is the burial site for more than 15,000 people of African descent, both enslaved and free. It is now the oldest continually-operated public cemetery in Virginia, and a powerful repository of civil rights history, as many visionary Black leaders of emancipation and freedom movements are buried there.

In addition, it has a section reserved for African-American and mixed-race prostitutes, who were unwelcome at other cemeteries. I photographed the prostitutes' grave sites as certain family history suggests that any of them could be relatives of mine.

The cemetery was often grave-robbed by white citizens who sold the corpses for autopsies at the University of Virginia medical school. Great lengths were taken by local African Americans to protect and guard the recent burials to prevent this, but they were not always successful.

Many of the burials were conducted according to African burial customs, including tying shut the mouths of the dead to prevent the soul from wandering. As a child, my grandmother used to fill my mouth with chewing gum as a child to prevent the spirits of the dead from entering. There are many stories around protecting the mouth as a portal for spirits.

(4) CARNTON PLANTATION, TENNESSSEE

MY MOTHER, BROTHER AND I WERE AMONGST THE FIRST TO ENTER the abandoned and boarded-up Carnton Plantation in Tennessee when it was purchased by the state in the 1980s, following its tenure as a hospital. It was originally built using slave labor and retained many of its slave quarters. These human beings and the structure they built were owned by Randal and John McGavock, from County Antrim, Ireland, where my white relatives come from.
The Plantation had been the site of the Civil War Battle of Franklin, and was abandoned by the plantation owner Carrie McGavock. During and after Reconstruction, it was inhabited by African-American sharecroppers and former slaves working for Carrie.

When we entered, the ground floor was painted black and the staircase to the upper floors were boarded shut. Upon climbing the stairs, we discovered extensive blood stains including the silhouettes of blood surrounding amputation buckets and surgical tables, and pools of blood by the fireplaces where the dying had dragged themselves for warmth. It was then we learned that it served as a hospital, with 150 patients dying there in its first night of service.

This plantation is an alternative for a family plantation house in which I grew up, but no longer have access. That plantation, on Middlebrook Road in Staunton, Virginia, was—like Carnton—occupied by my family when it was abandoned after the Civil War, and served many generations after that as a place of shelter. I grew up playing in the kitchens and slave quarters, and amongst the spirits and stories of relations of all races who had inhabited the property after 1890.

(5) APPOMATTOX, VIRGINIA

THESE PHOTOGRAPHS WERE TAKEN AT THE SITE OF THE SURRENDER of the Confederacy to the Union Army. However, I chose to work with this site because the wounds and crimes against Africans and Americans of African descent by both the North and South, the Union and the Confederacy, remain unremunerated. The Civil War was fought for reasons more economic than humanitarian, and the victory of the Union was used to suggest that the United States government would no longer permit crimes against humanity to occur against the African-descended citizens. This is clearly not the truth. I believe that economic and property reparations should be paid today by the United States to the African-American population and communities of this country.

While I was photographing, I was told the story of how the women of the family were forced upstairs while the generals signed the treaty downstairs, one of them giving birth in total silence.

A young African-American slave child left her doll on the table by accident when she was hidden upstairs, and General Lee and General Grant joked about its presence there at a signing that marked the end of slavery.

6) EDISTO ISLAND, SOUTH CAROLINA
(BLEAK HALL PLANTATION/BOTANY BAY PLANTATION)

I PHOTOGRAPHED EXTENSIVELY ON EDISTO ISLAND—THE ARRIVAL point for slave ships bringing people from Gabon and West Africa to be sold as slaves for plantations, and an island with a rich cultural Gullah and Geechee and Native heritage and contemporary presence. Within this context, my family evolved genetically and culturally.

Some photographs were made at the beaches of Edisto Island—still preserving shell rings and middens left by inhabitants from 3000-5000 years ago—were used to sort the Africans into hierarchical categories for sale in Charleston, since the condition of the Africans were considered too horrific to be seen in the city of Charleston.

I also photographed Bleak Hall Plantation, a cotton plantation owned by the Townsend family. I was told by local Gullah people and Gullah historians that any Africans who were considered unfit for sale as slaves were used in human hunting parties by the plantation families of the area. I photographed the paths on Bleak Hall where Africans were set loose to be hunted to death for recreation by white planters.

My maternal relations—African and Northern Irish—began their journey in the Americas in Charleston and on Edisto Island, South Carolina. White relatives were initially and justifiably killed by Catawba and other Native warriors. These three branches of humanity intermixed with each other in my family through forced and consentual association, sex, procreation, and marriage. The tangle of colonization and slavery, with its resulting secret births and lineages, remains at this point unclear.

ABOUT QUINTAN ANA WIKSWO

Hailed as "heady, euphoric, singular, surprising" by *Publishers Weekly*, and "universal and personal, comforting and jarring, ethereal and earthy" by *Electric Literature*, Quintan Ana Wikswo is a writer and visual artist recognized for adventurous books that integrate fiction, poetry, memoir and essay with her original photographs. Wikswo is the author of the short story and photography collections *The Hope Of Floating Has Carried Us This Far* (Coffee House Press), and *Schwarzer Tod and the Useless Eaters* (Catalysis Projects).

Her hybrid works are featured in anthologies including *Strange Attractors* (University of Massachusetts Press), *Queer Disability Anthology* (Squares and Rebels), *One Blood* (The University of Alaska Press), *Procession for the Extracted* (California College of the Arts), *Emergency Index* (Ugly Duckling Presse), and *They Said: A Multi-Genre Anthology of Contemporary Collaborative Writing* (Black Lawrence Press). Her projects appear in solo and group museum exhibition catalogues including *Rituals Against Forgetting* (Kehler Verlag/Berlin Jewish Museum) and *Group Therapy* (Foundation for Art and Technology, UK).

Wikswo's writing appears regularly in magazines including *Tin House, Guernica, Conjunctions, Gulf Coast, the Kenyon Review, New American Writing, Witness, the Denver Quarterly, Alaska Quarterly Review*, and many more. Her photography is widely exhibited, and resides in the permanent collections of major museums including the Brooklyn Museum, the Berlin Jewish Museum, and the Jewish Museum Munich.

A human rights worker since 1988, she uses salvaged military cameras and typewriters to create memoir-based projects that navigate known, unknown, and occluded worlds, especially obscured sites where crimes against humanity have taken place. These more than thirty five projects are exhibited, published, performed, and presented at prominent institutions throughout Europe and the Americas.

A Long Curving Scar Where The Heart Should Be received major support from Creative Capital, the National Endowment for the Humanities, Yaddo, and the Pollock Krasner Foundation. Raised in the rural south and southwest, she now lives along the US-Mexico border and—when necessary—in Brooklyn.

www.quintanwikswo.com

CPSIA information can be obtained
at www.ICGtesting.com
Printed in the USA
FSOW04n2025150617
35282FS

9 780998 433981